TRANSFORMED

SUZANNE FALTER & JACK HARVEY

TRANSFORMED
QUIRKY TRANSGENDER SPY NOVELS

San Francisco

NEW HEIGHTS PUBLISHING

NEW HEIGHTS PUBLISHING

Book design by Maureen Cutajar
www.gopublished.com

ISBN: 978-0-9969981-0-9

*To all brave souls
who go searching for love.*

C harley ran as fast as he possibly could. He raced the mile and a half up the course toward the top of Hayes Street Hill as crowds of groggy early-morning partiers gathered to watch the race. People milled around dressed in all manner of regalia, from nude to fully costumed.

Some stopped to watch him, an unexpected runner in street clothes far ahead of the front runners. In fact, the race hadn't even started yet.

Charley glanced at his watch. Two minutes clicked by, and then three. Did he still have a five-minute mile in him?

Now spectators began to scream for Charley as he tore along the race course, giving it everything he had. For a moment, it reminded him of his quarterback days back with the Blue Jays when they were high school divisional champs.

Somewhere behind him, he could hear sirens. Charley hastened his pace. No police car was going to break through this logjam of humanity. He hoped they had their bikes.

The apartment building was just ahead. Hayes Street Hill was widely known as the best place to see the full breadth of the moving cocktail party that was the Bay to Breakers foot race. As usual, the sidewalk was packed.

Little did they know that every last one of them could be dead in just a matter of moments. That is, unless Charley made it to the rooftop first.

Charley reached the buzzers of the building and began pressing every button without stopping to catch his breath. Within seconds, two apartments had buzzed him in.

That's how it is on a party weekend in the city, he thought happily as he tore inside.

Chaos made everything easy.

CHAPTER

1

The news would not be good.

Pamela Delacroix knew that before her fingers even closed around today's *Chronicle*. She stared at the newspaper that had just been tossed on her walkway. She considered ripping off the plastic shroud that covered it like an ill-fitting condom and racing directly to the offending article. She considered shredding the damn thing into a million pieces, marching straight across town, and tossing it all into the bay. She considered legal action—no, a personal attack—against the executive editor, that smug SOB she dated a million years ago.

Instead, she did nothing but walk back into the house. This called for coffee. Strong coffee.

An hour later, a perfectly coiffed Pamela stood in line at the Blue Bottle kiosk. The offending newspaper, still in its condom, was tucked into her Prada tote. There weren't enough yoga classes in the world to take down her ire at this point; she knew that. Jock lay down at her feet and yawned as she leaned toward the java boy.

"An espresso," she hissed. "Make it a double." The dog would help her get through this.

Ten minutes later, Pamela was seated on a bench at Patricia's Green, a heart-healthy walk from her house on Alamo Square. She took a slug of espresso and steeled herself. Then she opened the paper and began to read.

"The Society Dom Lands in SF in Strategic Career Move" trumpeted the headline. Pamela felt a flame of white-hot anger surge through her body. Those fuckers. When she had refused an interview, she had no idea just how far they would take this. She read on.

Pamela Delacroix—the socialite-turned-dominatrix known as the 'Society Dom'—recently arrived in San Francisco to rebuild a new life after her widely publicized divorce from New York philanthropist Linton J. Delacroix. Friends say she is hoping to return to a simple life, which explains the purchase of a 1.6-million-dollar house in Hayes Valley, as opposed to the much bigger manse she might have purchased in Pac Heights had she won in court.

But, alas, winning is hard to do when you're caught in bed with the husbands of your friends. Especially when you're serving as their amateur dominatrix. So it is with open arms that San Franciscans have welcomed the Society Dom, who declined to be interviewed for this piece . . .

Pamela slammed the paper shut and stuffed the offending newspaper into a nearby trashcan. She would be forever tarnished for the rest of her life for one, well, okay, six indiscretions. A young man passing by looked at her and smiled. *Does he know me?* she wondered. *Has he heard of the Society Dom?*

She didn't have to answer that question for herself. Everybody had.

———◆———

Pamela cradled her cell phone, staring intently at it. She would try one more time. Obviously. Why wouldn't she? Mothers loved their daughters. Mothers needed their daughters. She needed Peyton even if Peyton didn't appear to need her.

It was a phase, of course. Twenty-somethings always moved to their own rhythm, didn't they? Some were slower than others to embrace their parents. Like Peyton (who was actually pushing thirty, but who was counting?). Wasn't it plausible she was having a late-in-life teenage rebellion?

Pamela pushed her daughter's number on speed dial and waited, smartphone shoved up tight to her ear. It rang, rang, and then rang again. Peyton's carefully modulated voice came on as usual. "It's Peyton. Can't talk now. Call you later?" Pamela hung up without leaving a message.

She had called her daughter nearly every day for eighteen months . . . ever since the crisis began. And always there was no answer. Perhaps there never would be.

She shoved the thought out of her mind.

Instead, Pamela thought about the night before she left Manhattan, when she went to Peyton's apartment and rang the buzzer. A Food Emporium delivery guy had let her slip in right behind him. Her heart pounded wildly as the elevator ascended. She walked to her daughter's door and pressed the buzzer. She could hear Peyton talking on the phone behind the door. "Hold on a second, someone's here." Footsteps approached, the doorknob turned, and there was her daughter.

She looked at her mother in shock.

"Peyton—honey . . ." Pamela began the carefully rehearsed speech. She hadn't seen her daughter since the night her father threw Pamela out. "I just want you to know that I love—"

The door slammed shut. "Peyton! Peyton . . . Please. Just listen to me. For one moment. Please . . . Please . . . honey . . . shit." Pamela stopped pounding on her daughter's apartment door.

Now she understood; there was nothing more she could say. Sliding down the wall beside her, Pamela crumpled into a small ball on the floor and wept, a broken doll, a crushed moth. A star descending. She really didn't remember how she got home, or to California for that matter.

I will call my daughter again tomorrow, Pamela thought. One day Peyton was going to answer, because she had to.

Didn't she?

———◆———

Pamela contemplated the billowy white dress bag from Nordstrom with that old sinking feeling—the one that said, *you don't belong here and you never, ever will.*

Pamela had no idea why, and she didn't care. She only knew that she couldn't put on the dress again; in fact, she wouldn't. She would pass on tonight's benefit for Guillain-Barre research . . . or was it Lou Gehrig's disease? Whatever. It was yet another plunge into a world in which she seriously no longer belonged. Yet if she never went to another benefit . . . where would she go?

Where would she ever find any friends?

Fuck, Pamela thought miserably. She pulled the offending dress bag off its hook, wadded it up, and stuffed it into the back of her closet. *Screw the whole damn thing*, she thought. Then, yanking open her bureau drawer, she pulled out her black leather corset, her leather garter belt, and a handful of sheer black hosiery. She retrieved her six-inch high stiletto boots. Immediately she felt better.

Moments later, Pamela inhaled sharply, gave a final yank to the corset, and knotted it expertly behind her. An explosion of warmth surged through her body, settling into a small pulse in her groin. She inspected herself in the mirror, gave a little turn, and smiled. She still had it, whatever "it" was, didn't she? Even at fifty-two, she still looked good.

All those hours and hours of working out and starving herself during her in-corset training had paid off. And then there were the stilettos, nothing less than boot camp for the feet. If the whole thing, painful as it was, hadn't given her a gut-deep satisfaction, she would never have tried it. Pamela regretted nothing. Instead, she stood admiring herself. She gave her black riding crop a little slap against her hand.

The "Society Dom," indeed, she thought. Then she pulled the rejected dress out of the trashcan. Who said you couldn't wear black leather under Halston . . . along with six-inch stilettos? Chuckling to herself, she slipped the dress on over her leatherwear. Maybe she'd even bring her riding crop along.

Electra *is in the house*, she thought with satisfaction.

2

C harley MacElroy heard the door shut with an empty
click. *There goes another one,* he thought wearily.
At such a moment, another man might have reached
down beneath the sheets and held his offended cock. He
might have comforted himself with an orgasm, or at least
patted his member reassuringly. But Charley didn't have such
options. Instead he avoided his genitals altogether, given that
they were the source of the problem.

This time he'd had such high hopes. Allegra was pretty—
beautiful, really—in that patrician way he loved. She was
funny, too, which was also a turn on. She spoke fluent
Russian and kicked ass in court. She'd even soloed half the
Pacific Crest Trail. His mind scanned the vacations they'd
made, the wine country getaways, the intimate dinners for
two, the hikes at Yosemite. And he'd met her parents. Didn't
that count for something?

But Allegra was never really onboard; he could feel it that
first night in bed. Charley was her first transman, and while
there was sort of a fun, funky curiosity to it, ultimately

Allegra wasn't signing up for a penis-free marriage. She wanted kids. She wanted "real sex," as she'd told him only moments before she walked out. Now Allegra's words ricocheted around his mind like a bullet gone awry.

Who in the hell would *want me*, he thought blearily. Charley rolled over with a sigh, sick to death of feeling like the only transgendered pansexual on the planet. Couldn't he just be normal for a while?

All those years ago when Grandfather began the blockers, nobody really thought this part through. Yes, the hormone shots worked so well he got to be a football star. Yes, Honey Island even accepted him, which wasn't surprising given that his family was the island's only employer. And yes, he was happy to be a boy, and then a man. Or as a character on TV put it, "a guy with a vadge."

Quite happy, in fact.

But the question of bottom surgery was back. As he crawled toward thirty-five, it just seemed to be more and more inevitable. Tears began in his throat and welled up and up, filling his whole body with grief. He wept silently as loneliness overtook him, and soon his whole body was shaking with quiet sobs. Did he even *want* a penis?

How in God's name was he ever going to resolve this? There was no way out but through, that much he knew. Get it or be done with it forever. Post-surgical photographs he'd seen flashed through his brain, the forearm with fat and nerves removed, skin tight to skeletal bones. An upper back, neatly sectioned like a turkey breast. "Tissue harvesting," they called it. Revulsion pushed through him. He wouldn't. He just couldn't.

Grandfather's chiding talk about waiting until the surgery was perfected resurfaced: "Someday somebody's going to figure this out, but you'd better wait until then, son." Oh, for God's sake! And when would that be? He'd been waiting for twenty years already.

Maybe he should pray?

————•—•————

Charley pumped his bike hard up the crest of the Marina and then, going into a tuck, sailed down the other side. A dark blue bay spread out before him. He aimed for Alcatraz, which was appropriate given the mood he was in. He wished he'd caved and gone to Bi-Rite for a pint of salted caramel instead. Call it a mental health day or an emergency. He couldn't handle people today, so all appointments were canceled.

Charley's ennui wasn't really about losing Allegra. His distress was about something deeper and far more disturbing, which her rejection of him simply named. He had no idea who he was anymore . . . or what he wanted. For the first time in his entire life, he felt like a stranger in his own body. He pedaled on, wondering if this was just a very early midlife crisis.

When he reached Crissy Field, Charley locked up his bike, set his watch, and began a measured run along the path. The Golden Gate, or the "GG'" as locals called it, was its usual reassuring self—the gate at the end of the rainbow. Just seeing it always made him feel better.

As Charley ran, he tried to imagine life with a surgically constructed penis, one which may or may not work. The entire idea of phalloplasty had a strange Frankensteinian quality that was just plain creepy. On the other hand, he'd finally be able to join the other men at the urinals, assuming his brand-new organ actually worked. Like transmen everywhere, he always felt self conscious in the men's room, imagining the inner dialogue of the other guys.

Why's that dude sitting down in a stall to pee?

With a penis he could also stop hiding in locker rooms and getting interrogated at airports. He could even go naked at Baker Beach. Maybe. He'd probably have to keep his shirt on to cover up the massive section taken out of his side or his back or his arm to make the damn thing in the first place. He sighed and pushed on.

Charley would never be able to have his own kids; it was adopt or nothing. He'd already accepted that fact. As for sex, well . . . if he got a penis, he might have another orgasm again in his lifetime. Or maybe he wouldn't. It could go either way. At least now with his clitoris and vagina in tact he knew he could count on that one small victory. It wasn't even clear a manufactured penis would work well enough to make his lovers happy.

For now, these lovers tended to be supportive women (and a few curious gay men) who liked the whole pansexual thing. But they all moved on eventually, one after another, backing away in a slow parade of remorse as if they just hadn't imagined how . . . different . . . this would be.

He understood. Most of the time it hadn't really bothered him. But somehow now, as he passed the thirty-five-year mark, it did more than bother him. For the first time in his life, Charley was afraid.

He broke into a sprint. He was afraid of being alone for the rest of his life, afraid of never having a settled feeling. Of never having the home he longed for, with teenagers tramping through the living room and spaghetti sauce bubbling on the stove. He was afraid of never finding the love who waited for him in their bed, night after night. His woman. The one who laughed easily and made love often.

Instead, here he was—the attractive, mysterious, unknowable Charley MacElroy, the eternal "plus one" at dinner parties. Sweat poured down his neck and shoulders and his heart began to pound as he pressed on. He sped past dog-walking retirees, tourists pedaling heavy bikes with maps, and marina moms pushing strollers. He took the steps of the Coastal Trail hill two at a time, mumbling, "On your left," to two clueless lovers, hands entwined.

To his right, two kiteboarders took off across the bay, their sails brilliant slashes against the Golden Gate and the Marin Headlands. As he pounded up the path to the bridge, he could see them weaving in and out of the small waves just below, keeping pace with him. He passed beneath the enormous rust-colored girders of the bridge. The drone of the cars overhead was deafening.

Coming out into the sunlight on the other side, the whole Pacific opened up to him, and he smiled. Just to his right he caught sight of first one kiteboarder, and then the other. They, too, had passed through the Gate and were heading for the open sea. A winding dirt path rose up and down the hills ahead of him against the brilliant, sunswept ocean. Charley picked up his pace, inspired, and ran even faster.

There was no wrong here, only right. Charley felt that intuitively. He'd be okay. In fact, he would be better than just okay—he'd be great.

At the end of the day, Charley always was.

3

"I have the Secretary of State on six, Mr. Willeker." Hazel's nasal voice buzzed through the intercom, and R.J. wheeled in his chair.

Seriously? He picked up quickly. "Mr. Secretary!" he began.

The secretary got right to the point. "Nice work on the Marseille report, R.J. . . . Not the usual mealy crap."

"I'm so pleased you are satisfied, Mr. Secretary."

"Not only am I satisfied, I want more from this guy. Beautiful detail about Gagné's favorite liquor . . . and how did he get this stuff about his impotence? Did he grill his lover or plant himself in the locker room? Or . . . was it a female agent?"

"No, no, sir. That's Charley MacElroy. MacElroy Dark Rum is his family, so he knows booze. And he can get pretty much anything on anyone. A very gifted agent."

"Huh. Well, I want him on TerraCo. Does he speak German?"

"Yes, I believe he does."

"Zurich next?"

"I'll give him Zurich next for sure, Mr. Secretary."

The secretary clicked off. R.J. hung up and gave a happy sigh. As the former head of the Agency, the secretary knew when someone was exceptional—and when someone was screwing with him. Intimately. Sometimes, albeit rarely, R.J.'s job was just plain fun.

Hazel buzzed again. "Standridge in accounting is on five," she intoned.

R.J. picked up the phone more slowly this time. "Hello, Jim," he began warily. It was never good news when accounting called.

Ever.

———•◦•———

R.J. stood at the urinal and despaired as he thought about the call he just got from accounting.

"Willful failure to file a tax return is a misdemeanor pursuant to IRC 7203," droned the accountant.

Charley hadn't filed taxes the previous year and had blown off all the letters, the penalties, the works. He was now being charged with a misdemeanor. R.J. was going to have to call him and determine if, in fact, it was willful or he just somehow managed to forget. Either way he would have to be suspended.

Lawyers would be involved. Charley would be disgraced. R.J. was going to be the bad guy. Then there was the Secretary. R.J. was going to have to call the bloody Secretary of State and tell him his favorite new agent couldn't serve in Zurich because he hadn't filed his goddamn taxes.

Why did shit like this have to happen?

So who was going to do the Zurich job? Pensky was already maxed on two jobs in Europe. Mitchell was off on maternity leave—and she didn't have the German. And Zorik was . . . well . . . Zorik. R.J. stood looking out his window at the blanket of fog moving in on the city.

Why the hell didn't Charley pay his taxes, for Christ's sake? It's not rocket science. You take your shoebox of receipts to the accountant, sign some papers, and then you pay your bill. And as for the money—well, Charley certainly had money. He had to—he was booze royalty. And he was R.J.'s only agent who actually lived in San Francisco, in a brand new house he'd built on Nob Hill no less.

R.J. closed his eyes and leaned his head against the window. He knew why Charley hadn't paid his taxes. Charley was weak on the details. Money, paperwork, taxes—it was all one big grey fog to him, but who gave a shit? He was one of the most talented agents R.J. had ever had. He could get anything on anyone, at any place, any time.

Charley was the kind of guy who became a legend—and R.J. had enlisted him himself.

This was not only sad and frustrating, it was a genuine crisis. R.J. picked up the phone and dialed slowly. He would have to get Charley in here to tell him face to face. There was no other way.

CHAPTER

4

Pamela surveyed herself in the ladies room mirror. A tired attendant sat in the corner, fanning herself in what seemed to be an eternal hot flash. Outside, a hundred men in black tuxes and "colorful" cummerbunds whirled a hundred women in competing gowns around the dance floor to the same old thunk-a-thunk-a-thunk-a hits from the eighties.

The chicken had been served. The speeches had been made. There was nobody to talk to, not one bloody soul in this entire soulless town. Pamela missed New York, and she was bored out of her mind. But she couldn't bring herself to go home yet.

She'd had such high expectations when she moved to San Francisco. She'd imagined it to be a great sea of diversity. Here she was going to find her tribe, her people, her caste. Here she was going to reinvent and rise like a triumphant phoenix from the ashes. And so far . . . well, Pamela had been to three tepid benefits, certainly not as well produced as they had been in New York. San Francisco had become merely a lame rerun of her former life, without decent bagels.

19

A young woman in an iridescent taffeta cocktail dress stepped up to the sink beside her and inspected her hair. Giving it a little toss, she then drew a lipstick out of her tiny purse and applied it to her lips. She gave Pamela a quick glance, and then she did a double take. *Here it comes*, Pamela thought wearily. The young woman awkwardly snatched up the purse that lay between them and hurried back to the party, her lipstick half applied.

Pamela had been getting that treatment all night, and she didn't even bring her riding crop. *Blame it on the heels*, she thought. They did make her tower over most of the men. They all recognized her, of course, but so far only two people had said anything. One of them actually asked for a selfie.

Outside, the band ended with a flourish and announced a break. As they did, a pair of middle-aged women rolled into the ladies room, deep in conversation. Unnoticed, Pamela slipped into a stall, took a seat and listened.

"Would I know her?" one woman was saying.

"Oh, you can't miss her," said the other. "She's wearing black—Halston. And she's got to be well over six feet in those heels. She's wearing six-inch stiletto boots loaded with straps and . . . well, you know. They are the tackiest things."

"Why do we always get the kinky leftovers?" whined the first woman, letting herself into the stall next to Pamela's. The woman began to pee.

"As far as I'm concerned, Pamela Delacroix is a menace to us all," declared the other through the walls of the stall. "I want nothing to do with her."

"Agreed!" said the first woman. "Batten down the husbands!"

Both women laughed.

Pamela waited until the two were at the sink. Then, standing up, she drew herself up to her full height and swept out of her stall.

"Hello, ladies," she said with a little smile.

She began to wash her hands serenely as they looked at her in stunned silence.

"I really have to thank you," she continued, reaching for a hand towel. "I'd forgotten what a waste of time these benefits are." She paused for a moment, drying her hands. "Oh, and by the way, I go by Electra now," she mentioned congenially. "Not Pamela."

The women watched silently, their faces frozen halfway between shock and horror.

"Bye-bye," Pamela said as she headed out into the party once more. Now where the hell was her coat?

On the other side of the large ballroom, Charley MacElroy feigned interest in the endless rambling of a small, grey-haired women often described on the *Chronicle* as a "jet setter."

"Mrs. Dunroy," he began. Mrs. Dunroy continued to prattle on, oblivious. She was now warming up to the real meat of her topic: her years in India. "Mrs. Dunroy," he interrupted a little more fervently.

She stopped, confused. "Huh? What?"

Charley fixed her with his signature look. Blue eyes blazing, he loomed over her for a moment, and like most women, the aging Mrs. Dunroy began to melt a little. Charley used such silences to build connection, authority, and above all, trust. After all, Mrs. Dunroy knew a hell of a lot of people in the world.

"I'm so sorry," he began, drawling just a little for effect. "But I am simply exhausted." He took the elderly woman's hand conspiratorially, and he winked. "I'm not going to tell you what I've been up to lately, but trust me, it didn't involve a lot of sleep."

Mrs. Dunroy flushed and smiled. "You go right ahead, dear," she concurred. "But, Charley, I'm expecting you for tea . . . or a drink," she chimed after him. "You have to meet the dogs!"

"I'm going to do exactly that, Mrs. Dunroy!" he concurred jauntily over his shoulder, giving a little wave.

God Almighty, that was endless, he thought to himself. Heading for the opposite corner, he set about finding his coat. His work here was done.

Pamela's coat still had not been retrieved. She stood silently, waiting. *How hard could it be?* she thought with annoyance.

The attendant returned empty-handed. "I'm sorry. I just . . . I . . . can't find it," she stammered. "Are you sure this is your ticket?"

"You gave it to me," Pamela said pointedly. "It's a Burberry raincoat. It's one of those!" Behind the woman, a hundred or so lookalike raincoats hung on the racks. "Can't I just come in and look for it?" Pamela implored.

The young woman shook her head fervently. "Sorry, ma'am. I can't let you back here for security reasons," she said.

"Security reasons!" Pamela protested. "Oh, for God's sake! Really, it won't take a minute." Pamela reached across the small counter between them to let herself in.

"Hey!" the attendant interrupted, grabbing her wrist and pushing her back to the other side of the counter. "I said you can't come in here!"

The two women looked at each other, and the attendant dropped Pamela's wrist.

"Do you know who I am?" Pamela hissed. She opened her mouth to hurl another invective, but suddenly she stopped. Someone, a younger blond man roughly her height, was watching with an amused smile.

"Perhaps I can help," he suggested calmly. Then he stuck out his hand. "Charles MacElroy," he said. "They call me Charley."

"Oh . . . thank you," she said, feeling a small flush of embarrassment. *Fuck it,* she thought as the next sentence just came rolling out of her mouth. "Electra," she said. "Just . . . Electra."

What the hell is my last name? she thought.

Charley raised his eyebrows slightly. "Great name," he remarked.

Great eyes, thought Pamela.

Charley now dazzled a smile on the girl in the coat check. "What seems to be the problem, love? Caught between a rock and a hard place?" His voice was honeyed with the slightest trace of a southern accent as he leaned toward the young woman conspiratorially. It had an engaging rasp, Electra noticed.

The young attendant practically exploded. "Exactly!" she burst. "Her ticket doesn't match any coats—I just can't find it. I mean, I want to help the lady—I'm trying—but I can't let anyone in here. My boss is going to walk in and see her back here, and I'm going to lose my job and I really, really need it cause I just started community college!"

"Sounds painful," Charley commented. "Tell you what. I'll call your boss and tell him what a great job you're doing protecting the home front. Then we'll get him to let my friend in so she can find her coat. What do you think?"

The attendee grimaced. "He's Pakistani," she said, as if that explained everything. "He'll never go for it."

Charley pulled out his phone. "Let's just try, okay? Now you just give me his number, and we'll be all set."

The attendee shrugged and produced the number. Pamela watched curiously. *Who is this guy?*

Exactly four minutes later, they were walking away with Electra's coat in hand.

"How did you do that?" she murmured. "I still don't understand it."

"Simple. I just banked on the nearly always true possibility that the young lady was doing the best she could."

Electra shook her head. "If only life was so simple," she said.

"But it is," Charley remarked with a smile. He took her arm. "Can I buy you a drink?"

Moments later, they were seated at a small table at Farallon. Luminescent jellyfish swam overhead, trailing tendrils. A midnight blue ceiling above them was dotted with tiny star spotlights. The entire restaurant seemed to follow the billowing curves of underwater sea grass. It was a place that undulated.

Electra ordered a scotch on the rocks.

"Whiskey neat," Charley told the waiter, "and a dozen oysters. Will you join me?" he asked Electra.

"I'd be delighted," she said.

They'd barely spoken since they left the party. There seemed to be quite a lot to say, but still, they were oddly formal with each other on the walk down the hill into Union Square.

Once they were seated, she began. "So?" she asked. Did he recognize her? That much wasn't even clear.

Charley gave her a smile that traveled straight down to her groin. "I'm fortunate to be in the company of such a beautiful woman," he began.

"Let's not get off on the wrong foot, Charley," she retorted.

He gave a small chuckle. "Why not? I like wrong feet."

"Because I'm old enough to be your mother. Or are you someone who likes to sleep with celebrities?"

"You're a celebrity, too? Cool."

Electra sighed. "Maybe you don't read the *Chronicle*?"

"No, actually. Call me a Luddite, but I'm old fashioned that way. Should I know you?"

"It's not important, believe me," Electra countered.

"Sounds very important."

"Only if you enjoy the smutty side of life."

"I take a smut-neutral position," Charley said. "But it certainly has its uses."

Electra changed topics. "Tell me something about you."

"I grew up in Louisiana on an island inhabited by only 137 people. And I know every last one of them."

"How exotic."

"Actually, it was a strange place full of untraditional traditions, but it's home. My family has been making rum there for 150 years," he explained.

She looked at him curiously. What was it about this man that made him so appealing? "But you don't make rum because . . ."

"Because I ran away to become a travel writer more or less."

"Why more or less?"

"When I want to write more, I do, but sometimes I don't write at all."

The waiter delivered the drinks. Electra stirred hers for a moment. "Where can I find your books?"

"A good used bookstore most likely," he said. "They go out of print quickly."

Charley sat back and took a pull of his whiskey. "Now it's your turn, my dear."

"I am a refugee from Manhattan without a single friend in this town."

Charley smiled. "Well, consider me your first one. Did you just arrive?"

This guy really doesn't know who I am, Electra thought. She smiled, but then her smile faded. He would find out eventually, so she might as well tell him. Or . . . should she? How nice to be someone other than the Society Dom for a while.

"After twenty years in New York, I feel like a fish out of water here," she replied.

"Say more," he urged.

Electra looked at him. "Do you know the East Coast?"

"In that way that all visitors do. It's not the South, that's for damn sure."

A waiter arrived bearing oysters nestled in a tray of ice.

"Are you familiar with kusshis?" Charley asked. They contemplated the tiny oysters arrayed before them. He ladled a bit of mignonette sauce into some of the half shells and offered her the first one.

Electra picked up the oyster shell and sipped up its fruit; a sweet, briny explosion burst in her mouth. She closed her eyes in delight, savoring the flavor.

"They are raised to be tumbled over and over very aggressively in the ocean—so it breaks the thin outer edge. Makes them retreat more deeply and grow harder shells. So they're smaller than the other oysters and far more delicious." He paused, watching her reaction with delight. "Their name means 'precious,'" he said.

She looked at him with new respect. The oysters were exceptional.

"Have another," he suggested. Then he lifted his glass. "In praise of hard shells," he said as they clinked glasses.

"Here, here," she said. *He has to know*, she thought. Electra took a sip of her drink. She was enjoying herself. "I like you," she said.

He returned her gaze. "Good."

"I'm too old for you, you know."

"So be my friend," he suggested. She lifted her drink in agreement.

One by one, the kusshis had disappeared, and first one whiskey was drunk and then another until it was truly time to go home. Pamela leaned back in her seat and smiled at Charley.

"I needed this," she concluded.

"Yeah. Me, too," he agreed.

"You know, Charley, you asked earlier why people know me. It seems important to say—given that we've just met." Pamela drew in a deep breath and hesitated. "I mean, if we're truly going to be friends."

"I'd like to know," he said. "And I'm sure it won't matter one damn bit."

He really is a charmer, she thought.

"Some would say I'm a dominatrix, and I suppose I am in an amateur kind of way," she began. "I cheated on the man I was married to with some of the husbands of our friends. He left me. Then the details of our divorce hearings were on every major news channel and in every newspaper in this country for six months. I made a mistake, for which I'm known hither and yon."

Electra drained the last of her whisky and put down her glass. "They call me the Society Dom. And just about every person on the planet has heard of me except for you."

"Bravo," said Charley, smiling.

Bravo?

"I realize that sounds glib, but I actually mean it," he continued. "You clearly have more guts than most women."

"Thank you," Electra replied. She felt a wave of relief wash through her body. Maybe he really *didn't* know her. The thought was reassuring. "But the fallout has been harsh. I generally can't go anywhere without people requesting selfies. It's the modern day equivalent of an autograph, and it's something of a nightmare."

"But you do want to be a dominatrix, right?"

Electra swirled the ice cubes in her glass, unsure of what to say. She looked at the ceiling and then she looked at him. "Yes," she heard herself say. Again, her reply just came tumbling out of nowhere.

Who is this guy? And how is he getting me to say these things? He is so . . . intimate.

Immediately, Electra backpedaled. "Of course, it's a crazy thing to want to do—my family would never stand for it. After all, we are the Delacroixes," she explained.

"And . . . ?" asked Charley.

"'Dominatrix' is simply not done," she explained. They looked at each other and laughed out loud.

"So you're waiting for permission?" he mused gently.

Pamela was silent. It was true. She was a free agent after the divorce and its hefty losses. Only her daughter still tugged at her consciousness. It's just that being a dom seemed so untoward. Her mother would roll in her grave.

"I don't know, Charley." She shook her head. "I have a daughter, and she would never speak to me again." *Not that she did now.*

He raised his eyebrows. "Shouldn't we be exactly who we are, no matter how unconventional? It's our birthright. Even our children understand that."

Pamela sighed.

"And . . . Electra?" he continued.

"It's my dom name. My real name is Pamela."

"Electra's much better," Charley remarked. "You should use it all the time."

Just then, a young man approached the table. He was carrying an iPhone. "Are you Pamela Delacroix?" he began. "Any chance I can get a picture with you?"

Her jaw tightened, and she glared at the young man, who withered palpably under her stare. "Oh . . . uh . . ." he stammered. "I'm sorry . . ."

There was an uncomfortable pause.

"Why not, Electra?" Charley murmured to her. "This is your currency, isn't it? You'll make his night."

Was it her currency? Was she actually more Electra than Pamela . . . and she was just trying to avoid it?

"Okay," she said, shaking her head. "Okay. Whatever."

The young man handed his phone to Charley and hunkered in close to her as she gave a tight smile. He held up the phone and flashed a picture. The barkeeper looked up and said something to another patron at the bar. Electra could hear the low murmur of her name being repeated.

The young man darted happily back to his date waiting near the door. Electra turned to Charley. "I don't generally do that, you know."

"What's the harm? Your public is beckoning, Electra." He paused. "It *is* Electra, right?"

She paused. She looked down at her lap and then up at him. "Yes, it is Electra," she confirmed.

What a remarkable evening this had turned out to be.

———•◆•———

Three hours later, Charley let himself happily into his house, stepping over Buster, the basset hound who snored lightly on the entry rug. *Thank God I don't need a watchdog*, he thought to himself for the thousandth time.

Charley hummed as he fed the dog and wrote out a check for the housekeeper coming tomorrow. He continued humming as he double-checked the locks and turned off the lights. Puccini's aria *Un Bel di Vedremo* kept pushing through his head.

> *Chi sarà? chi sarà?*
> *E come sarà giunto*
> *che dirà? che dirà?*

Charley hummed as he untied his tie and hung up his suit. He hummed as he brushed his teeth.

> *Who is it? Who is it?*
> *And as he arrives*
> *What will he say?*
> *What will he say?*

He could not turn off the love track in his head. This was not to say that Charley was infatuated . . . only that something very interesting had happened tonight. Something so interesting, he pulled a Puccini aria out of nowhere.

Suddenly everything Charley knew to be true about his small, circumscribed life had been challenged. And by nothing more than a few drinks with a beautiful woman. Maybe even an extraordinary woman.

Perhaps this is the answer, he thought easily. Maybe finding peace wasn't about having the surgery or not having the surgery. Maybe finding peace was about finding the right person, an unusual person. A person with infinite capacity for variety—and just plain strangeness.

Already he felt closer to a solution.

Charley checked his voicemail. R.J. had called. *Odd*, he thought, listening to the message. R.J. sounded terse—annoyed even. Charley replayed the message one more time.

"Call me, MacElroy. I need you to come in. We've got to talk."

Suddenly, he felt unsettled. When had R.J. ever even called him by his last name? This was definitely not the R.J. who called with enthusiasm when he had a new, juicy assignment to drop in Charley's lap. And to come in—that meant a flight back East. Something was definitely happening.

Charley turned off his phone and, yawning, climbed into bed. Still, he felt good. Better than good, he felt hopeful for the first time in days.

5

R andy "Evangelical" Tytus compulsively folded and
refolded the red plastic straw that came in his ginger
ale as he looked down at the earth from 30,000 feet.
Brown circles hedged into green boxes spread across the
Midwestern landscape like well-organized checkers. *This is my
land and these are my people*, he thought.

Still . . . there were problems.

America, he thought with a sigh. Land of the free and home
of the binge drinker, the lying, cheating adulterer, and the
weed-smoking homo pervert. Thank God the good people of
the Midwest were so anchored, so solid, abiding by the kind
of values that built this country. He closed his eyes and tried
to summon up the Lord.

Instead, he got an image of his late, long-suffering mother, Marilyn. *Of course she would come to me at a time like this*, he
thought, *riding in on her cloud of glory to comfort me in my fear*.
Randy didn't like to fly, and it was so far so good on this
flight, but at any moment it could all go to hell. It usually
did.

If only San Francisco wasn't so far away. On the other hand, thank the Lord it wasn't closer. Randy didn't need any proximity to those people on a regular basis . . . and he'd done plenty of praying before he even stepped onto the plane. Taking out his well-worn King James Bible, he randomly opened to Leviticus 12:1-8 and began to read. This was how he knew what the Lord was thinking about him at any given moment.

And if she be not able to bring a lamb, then she shall bring two turtles, or two young pigeons; the one for the burnt offering, and the other for a sin offering: and the priest shall make an atonement for her, and she shall be clean.

Of course the Lord was thinking of his cleanliness. Why wouldn't He be? And how would Randy ever be clean after even one week in the City of Heathens? What kind of atonement could he possibly make, even if he *was* travelling there on the Lord's business? All he could do was pray, pray, and pray some more. If he had to make a sacrifice when he got home, he'd come up with something, a squirrel, perhaps, or a stray cat, or maybe Dumpling, the yappy Chihuahua that lived next door.

That had a certain poetic justice to it.

Still, Randy was pretty sure that making a scouting trip for his personal war on hedonism put him in a different category from the average wager of sin. After all, he was doing as he was told, as it was his sacred duty to warn others of God's anger. He was also memorializing his father, Rudy "Evangelical" Tytus, internationally known creator of the "Kill the Fags" campaign. Daddy would be so proud.

Suddenly, the plane hit a rapid string of bumps, and Randy felt his stomach drop. The gravely, ultra-calm voice of the pilot came on, assuring them that they had hit "a little turbulence." It was unexpected and should last for "only" a half hour or so. *Naturally,* thought Randy grimly. The pilot ended by invoking the crew to abandon the beverage service and take their seats.

Great, thought Randy. Closing his Bible, he took a long, shaking breath and closed his eyes as the plane bucked a few more times and then made a sudden, short drop. The woman behind him gave a stifled scream. Randy began reciting the Lord's Prayer under his breath.

"Nervous?" asked the man next to him. The bespectacled young man looked like a latter day John Denver. He leaned toward Randy conspiratorially. "I used to be really nervous on planes and shit, but one day I just said to myself, 'Fuck it, man. If I'm going down, I'm going down.' Then everything changed. Been fine ever since."

There was an awkward silence.

"Want me to teach you some yoga breathing? Nadhi Shuddhi, purification of the Nadhis. I'll show you if you want . . ." Randy didn't bother answering this yahoo in a Hawaiian shirt. Looking down, he noticed a rippling tattoo across his ultra-tanned forearm, just above the bracelet of wooden beads. It took the shape of a large lizard slithering toward the young man's elbow. Fine golden hairs dotted his skin.

"Got it in Maui." His affable neighbor grinned, seeing Randy eye his tattoo.

"Oh," said Randy, and then he closed his eyes again. There had to be a way to turn this idiot off.

"You ever get a tattoo? It's like serious hella pain—but hey, it's all good," continued the John Denver lookalike. "My lady likes it."

"I'm going to rest," asserted Randy, still not opening his eyes.

"Yeah, good idea . . . if you can sleep." The young man leaned back and drained the rest of his beer. He gave a snort of laughter. "You know, one time my buddy and me—"

"Shut up," blurted Randy, snapping his eyes open. "Just . . . be quiet."

The John Denver lookalike seemed slightly stunned. "Oh," he said slowly. "Yeah. Okay. Sorry, man."

Immediately Randy felt a pang of remorse. "I'm sorry—I just—"

"No, it's fine, man. You're nervous and shit."

"Yes," said Randy a little too tartly. "I'm nervous and . . . so forth."

"Okay, preacher," concluded the young man as the plane lurched to the right.

Randy didn't bother to correct him. Instead, he opened his Bible to the twenty-third Psalm.

Yea, though I walk through the valley of the shadow of Death, I will fear no evil; For thou art with me; Thy rod and thy staff they comfort me . . .

This, too, would pass.

Randy moved in fluorescent slow motion through SFO like the rest of the emerging passengers. People sitting still for too many hours now seemed like misplaced dolls, plunked down a few thousand miles from home. He took a deep breath as he rounded the security gates and walked into the arrivals area.

Children grabbed on to grandmothers. Squealing teenage girls jumped up and down. Lovers embraced and kissed. Still, he walked on. No one was meeting him. No one ever met him. Even when Daddy was alive, he just sent his driver. *That was enough*, he thought. It had to be.

You are the son of Rudy "Evangelical" Tytus. You are a class above, and so directed by the will of God and God alone. You have been charged with the abomination of the whoring of the world, and for this you have been sanctified. You have been chosen. Never forget that.

Grabbing his black roller bag, Randy neatly clicked open the handle and walked off to find the Super Shuttle. God's will would, indeed, be done.

Randy had been given a mighty charge by God: *kill the blasphemers of San Francisco*. Those were his instructions, delivered one night not long after his father's death after a short battle with cancer. Jesus appeared in a dream wearing his crown of thorns and told Randy, in no uncertain terms, to rid the world of these sinners. Before he left, Jesus added reassuringly, "Many are invited, but few are chosen, Randy."

For a while, Randy ignored the vision, overcome as he was by grief. Frankly, such a big task seemed . . . well, impractical. After all, there were a lot of sinners in San Francisco—what was Jesus thinking? And who was Randy to take on such a mighty task? But now, nearly six months later, Randy found himself ready to act.

What had happened was nothing less than a revelation. He began to pray fervently for guidance, and as he did, his tears of grief magically dried and a fire in his belly he had never known before appeared. Over time, Randy came to understand that he was now on Team Jesus, and that Jesus's atonement for the sin of his people was his atonement as well.

The attack he was planning would be a memorial tribute to his father, the one who had shown him the way like no other. His father, the man who had controlled, raised, loved, and cossetted him—especially after his mother's death. Whatever came to pass as Randy attempted to wipe out the street scum (not just faggots, of course, but the entire slew of wine-soaked, party-hardy potheads who populated this hellhole) was in the name of Christ, and his Daddy, of course.

It was the least he could do.

If Randy died in the process, so be it. After all, Jesus did. As was written in Matthew, *he gave his life as a ransom for many.* So hey, he reasoned, why fight it? As Randy saw it, this would be his legacy—his contribution, his moment of infamy. At the very least, he would ride on his chariot straight back to the glory of God, and wouldn't Daddy be proud then?

Tomorrow was the Folsom Street Fair, and so his research would begin. But for tonight, a Wednesday, he would slip into the local Bible study up the street, being careful to speak to no one. In the event that he somehow survived, it was best not to leave a trace.

An hour later, Randy was speeding along 101 North, wedged in behind two Asian business men, an aloof teenager glued to his phone, and two large older women from Oklahoma who were chatting loudly with the driver.

"We've never been to Frisco before," said one.

"Always been our dream," gushed the other. "Sixteen years we've been talking about it, isn't that right, Rosemary?"

"Yes, it is," Rosemary concurred.

"We want to walk across the bridge. If you can . . ." said the first woman.

"If you mean the Golden Gate, you can," the driver confirmed.

"I told you," said Rosemary to her partner. "Anyway, we're here for the FOLUC conference."

"That's the Feisty Old Lesbians United for Change."

Randy closed his eyes and attempted to breathe. *This too shall pass.*

Rosemary continued. "We're not sure what they're trying to change exactly, but it was an excuse to get out here. And we just got married . . . this is our honeymoon."

That did it. Randy had to speak up.

"God rejects the blasphemers," he said quietly.

Rosemary turned around in her seat and looked at him with a smile. "I'm sorry. Didja say something? I'm hard of hearing."

Randy cleared his throat and raised his voice. "God rejects the blasphemers," he said firmly, looking her straight in the eye.

The two women exchanged looks. The second woman now swiveled in her seat. Randy found himself looking at the two women who continued to stare him down.

"It's a fact," he said simply.

"Asshole," said the second woman.

"Prick," muttered the first. Then she turned to the driver. "Let us off here," she said loudly.

"Wait—Rosemary—" demurred the second. A look of panic crossed her face.

"We're getting out of here," Rosemary announced as she began collecting her things.

"Come on, honey," soothed the second. "We can't get out here. We have bags . . ."

Rosemary raised her voice. "Get me off this bus now! There's a hater onboard."

"I speak God's truth," interjected Randy. "Renounce your sinful ways and all will be forgiven."

"Shut the fuck up, you turd," retorted Rosemary. Then, turning to her new wife, she said, "We're going." She leaned forward to the driver. "Let us off here."

"Ma'am, we're on a highway," the driver replied.

The second woman laid a restraining hand on her wife's arm. "Rosemary . . . honey . . . we don't even have a map."

"Get off at the next exit!" Rosemary hissed to the driver. "I am not going to share the air with this fuckwad for one more minute."

"Ma'am, please—" said the driver helplessly.

"Come on, honey . . ." pacified the second woman.

"We'll take a cab!" Rosemary exploded as she threw off her seatbelt and began to strap on her fanny pack. "Exit!" she demanded to the driver, who meekly obeyed, joining the line of cars getting off at DuBose Avenue.

There was a frosty silence for several minutes in the van. Then the driver pulled over, jumped out, and opened the side door. The two women began to exit.

The first woman paused and looked Randy in the eye. "Fuck you," she said tartly. "I hope you rot in hell."

"I've got Christ on my side, so that's mighty unlikely," Randy retorted. "I believe you're the one who's going to Hell."

"As IF!" Rosemary said with a snort as she got out. She waved her fist at him as he passed. "Sonofabitch!" she screamed.

Sinners, thought Randy as he watched the two women begin a slow, trundling walk up the sidewalk, pulling their suitcases behind them.

There really was no hope for this world.

CHAPTER

6

B rill's was not one of those gyms loaded with stacks of fluffy towels. There were no yoga classes, blow dryers, or dispensers of lavender-scented hand soap. And there were almost no women—Frankie was one of the few.

SFPD Sergeant Frankie Kennedy hoisted her entire 124-pound frame up to the chin-up bar, and then peering over it, she paused at the top. Curly headed, lightly freckled, with the classic features of an English rose, she hardly looked like the kind of woman who could take out a sniper at one hundred yards. Rather, she seemed more like a woman one would find wandering the moors in her cape in some Edwardian novel.

Frankie held the position long enough that sweat began to break out on her brow. Then, slowly, she descended. The sergeant did another repetition.

Frankie liked to feel the steel rod in her hands and the strain of her palms against it. She liked the way her muscles burned as she pushed and the familiar smell of body odor that permeated every inch of Brill's. And she especially liked the *Dies Irae* pounding through her ear buds.

She'd been listening to the Mozart *Requiem* for more than six months now when she worked out, and she wasn't tired of it yet. *Funeral music,* she thought. Perfect.

So far everything was calm today, and that's just the way Frankie liked it. She woke up alone. Made the drive in alone. She would work out, put on her uniform, put in her ten hours reading reports, approving bookings and driving around her district in a black and white. Then she'd make the long trip home again. She would do it all pretty much alone.

Since Dree's death, it had been nearly a year of the same old same old. Except for one thing. She still hadn't gotten her original assignment back from the chief—the one about cleaning up the department—and at this point, it probably wasn't coming back. But who cared? The whole damn city was a mess as far as she could tell.

She should never have left the Navy. She could have been a Seal. At least, that's what Frankie always told herself.

Dree's death stopped all the clocks in Frankie's life. A blindsiding cancer diagnosis took both of them by complete surprise in a tsunami of brute force. The whole thing lasted four months from start to finish. But then, that was how pancreatic cancer was. It took no prisoners.

In the aftermath, Frankie was left to reflect on what had become of her life after losing her wife. All she had left was her job, her sister, and the home she and Dree had made together. So it was no wonder Frankie had chosen to live on their boat. She'd only been back to the house twice, mainly to get her stuff.

Dree's death had nothing to do with Frankie's transfer, of course, even though that was the official reason the department gave her. They could never admit that Frankie got moved because the new district commander was a corrupt idiot. Or because she was a so-called whistleblower who knew too much.

Just when things started getting tricky at work, her wife got sick and died. How convenient. So of course they wanted to get her out of there, giving her paid sick leave for months and months and then "easing" her back in with some remote station gig.

Fact was, she'd been hired out of the LAPD to come up here and do specialty plainclothes work. Then she got hired to clean up the department's rampant weaknesses, and now they were stuck with her, given how the city labor laws worked. They couldn't fire her, but they could make her professional life a living hell, which seemed to be exactly their intention.

Frankie lowered her feet to the mat and wiped her face with her hand. Picking up a pair of twenty-five-pound weights, she seated herself and began a series of lateral curls. *Where are your good friends when you need them?* she wondered.

Frankie had few friends; almost none, actually. Most of them were down in L.A., vestiges of her college days. But she didn't really need friends . . . did she? Frankie saw herself as an independent contractor in all matters pertaining to life these days. Don't count on her for much, and she won't count on you.

A tall, muscular man now waited patiently for the use of the straight-backed chair she was seated in. She'd seen him once before. Gay? Maybe . . . or what? There was something unusual about this guy. He always seemed just a little too relaxed.

Eyeing him, she kept up her reps. "I'll be done in a minute," she said coolly as she rested for a moment.

"No rush," said the man. He smiled at her.

Frankie did not return the smile. After all, one never knew what people were up to in a gym. It wasn't always just exercise.

Still, the man stuck around, waiting patiently. Frankie curled into the third set of reps as her biceps began to burn. She closed her eyes as the somber, haunting strings of the last section of the *Sequentia* filled her head, shutting out the pain. *This*, she thought, *is the most moving piece of music in the entire* Requiem. *Perhaps the most moving piece ever written.*

Choral voices began their tender lament.

Lacrimosa dies illa
Qua resurget ex favilla
Judicandus homo reus . . .

Frankie had looked it up, curious about the meaning.

Mournful that day
When from the dust shall rise
Guilty man to be judged
Therefore spare him, O God
Merciful Jesus
Lord Grant them rest

Tears suddenly sprang into Frankie's eyes. *Dammit*, she thought, clamping her eyes shut even harder to prevent their flow. This kept happening lately, and she didn't like it one bit. It had been more than a year, for God's sake—when was the grief going to stop? She fast-forwarded quickly to the next song on her iPod. This was not convenient.

A moment later, after regaining her composure, she opened her eyes. The dude was still standing there.

Jesus, she thought.

"You waiting to use this?" she asked after a moment.

"Yes," he said agreeably. "But don't rush."

"Oh," Frankie replied. "Thanks."

"Interesting they only have one of these benches," he remarked offhandedly. "You'd think a place like Brill's would have a few more."

"Yeah." She was relieved to be moving on to another subject in her own head.

"It's no frills," he continued. "That's what I like about this place."

Frankie continued her reps silently. The man leaned against the wall and, folding his arms, studied her as she worked out. She did not like to be watched at the gym, especially by men.

"What's your name?" he finally asked.

"What's it to you?" she replied curtly.

"Curiosity," he replied. "I'm Charley. Charley MacElroy," he continued.

Frankie was deep into a fourth set of curls now, and she grunted a response. Frankie came to a stop and looked at him. "Like the rum?" she asked after a minute.

"Yeah," he said lightly. There was a pause. "You're seriously not going to tell me your name?"

"It's Frankie."

He smiled. "Hey, Frankie."

"All yours," she replied, moving away from the bench. "Knock yourself out, Charley."

What is up with this guy? she thought curiously. *He doesn't roll like a guy. He's just standing there. He's actually being patient. And he's . . . observant. Like me.*

It occurred to her then that he might be trans, and suddenly she softened a little toward him. She wiped her face on her towel and lingered for a moment. The fact that he might be trans made her want to know more.

But then suddenly, Frankie felt shy. She hadn't actually made a new friend, or really spoken to anyone off the force, for a long, long time.

"Oh . . . here," she said quickly, moving back to the chair before Charley could sit down. She wiped the bench off with her towel.

"Don't worry about it," he said. "It's good clean sweat."

Frankie chuckled. "Yeah, but it still stinks," she said.

Charley began a set of overhead triceps presses with a forty-pound weight. Frankie lingered for a moment, and then she walked away, putting a little extra hulk in her step. This was the walk she used when she wanted to appear bigger than her 5'3" frame. *Just setting the parameters,* she thought to herself. She didn't want Charley to get confused.

<hr />

An hour later, Frankie picked up her gym bag, closed the old, battered locker, and headed for the exit. One minute later, she intersected Charley as he emerged from the men's locker room. Only, it wasn't exactly the men's locker room—it was the handicapped restroom to the right of it. *That confirms it,* she thought to herself. *He's a trans.*

Frankie flashed a smile at Charley. "Good workout?" she asked.

"Feeling like I can justify the next martini. How about you?"

"Same."

They walked together for a minute. "Where you going?" he asked.

"Work," she said tersely, bracing herself for his next question. News that she was a cop didn't always go down well in social situations. People usually got nervous, and then they stayed nervous. Some never actually got over it. Occupational hazard, she figured.

Charley sidled up to his bike and began to unlock it. "I'd give you a lift, but I don't have a lot of room."

Frankie laughed. "It's okay. I think I can get there on my own steam."

"Where is work?" he asked.

"The Mission," she said. "How about you?"

"Going home."

"Where do you live?" she asked.

"Nob Hill."

"Well, well . . ." Frankie exclaimed softly. "Don't usually meet a lot of Nob Hill types at Brills."

"Yeah, that's why I like the place," he said. "Let me ask you something."

Here it comes, she thought. She prepared to launch into a defense of the SFPD. "Sure."

"What were you listening to on your iPod?" Frankie felt a wash of relief.

"Mozart's *Requiem*."

Charley gave a nod of recognition. "Great piece of music."

"You know it?"

"Sure," he answered easily. "Though I'm more the opera fan." Charley began fastening on his bike helmet.

"Seriously?"

"Yeah," he replied.

"Where are you from?" she asked curiously.

"Honey Island, Louisiana. I don't expect you've ever heard of it."

"Oh . . . where the rum is made."

"Right," he said simply.

This guy was actually *from* the rum family. *So he is probably some kind of gazillionaire,* she thought to herself, *and apparently modest.* How likely was this?

"Where are you from?" he asked her now.

"Marin. Belvedere."

"Born and raised?"

"Yeah." They paused for a moment and surveyed each other, recognizing their kind. Charley nodded. "Glad to meet you, Frankie," he said.

"Yeah, me, too . . ." She watched Charley straddle his bike. "Wait," she suddenly said. Charley stopped and looked at her.

"Do you want to . . . get a coffee or something? I don't have to be at work for another hour."

Charley smiled. "Rain check?" he asked. "I'm on my way to the airport—have to duck out of town for a day or so."

"Okay," she said. "I work out here most days around noon or so."

"Excellent," he said. "We'll do that."

Frankie watched Charley ride away, feeling oddly relieved. Somehow she'd just managed to make a friend.

7

C harley walked down the hallway at Agency headquarters in suburban Virginia, and entered R.J.'s office suite. It was ten past ten. He'd been sitting on an airplane all night, but somehow he still managed to be almost on time.

"Hazel!" he said with gusto. He offered the secretary a kiss on the cheek. "Looking beautiful as usual . . . Hey, wasn't it your birthday last week?"

Hazel moved her cheek away quickly, busying herself with her paperwork. "Yep," she said lightly, professionally. "I think he's on the phone. I'll tell him you're here, Charley."

Charley paused. Something was wrong—he could feel it. He sat down on the couch and tried to imagine what could possibly be amiss. R.J. had been thrilled with his work on the Marseille job. He told Charley so in no uncertain terms.

Suddenly he felt like crying.

Charley closed his eyes, inhaled deeply, and focused on his breath. *Everything will be okay.*

The door swung open after a moment, and R.J. appeared.

"Charley," he said, motioning. Charley felt a small flicker of fear shoot through his gut.

Charley didn't like this at all. R.J. hadn't even looked at him. Charley moved in what felt like slow motion toward the door. Something was definitely off.

He sat down across the desk from his boss, who was shuffling papers. R.J.'s glasses were up on his head, and his shirtsleeves were rolled. That always reminded Charley of Grandfather. All that was missing was the Perique tobacco smoke.

"How's it going, boss?" Charley began tentatively.

"Could be better," said R.J. now, finally looking at him. "We've got a problem."

The fear in Charley's belly quickly coalesced into a tight knot. "Oh?" he tried to ask casually.

R.J. swiveled in his chair so his back was to Charley. This was a bad sign, and Charley knew it. R.J. was silent for a moment. "You know I think you are an exceptional agent— one of the best I've had," he began.

What the hell is this? Is R.J. about to fire me? "Can you tell me what's going on?" Charley asked.

R.J. ignored the question and continued, his back still turned to Charley. "You've got a weakness, son. And we can't have that."

"What weakness?" Charley asked numbly. But, of course, he knew. There was always the same weakness—his complete and utter inability to manage any kind of administrative detail.

R.J. swiveled back to face him. "Why'd you steal the money?"

Charley was thoroughly confused. "Wait—what? What are you talking about?"

R.J. cocked his head and softened his tone. "Come on, Charley . . . it's me you're talking to here. You can be honest. Who do you know better in the Agency than me?"

Charley opened his mouth to speak, but he was dumbfounded. "I . . . I . . ." he stammered. "I honestly don't know what you're talking about."

R.J. leaned forward across the desk. "Are you doing drugs, Charley?" he asked.

"Drugs! What? God no! Come on, R.J. . . .please. What is this?"

"Accounting says you never filed your taxes last year. An hour later, they called to say seventy-eight thousand dollars has gone missing from your account."

"Seventy-eight thousand dollars!" Charley burst. How could this have possibly happened? Something was very wrong. Charley closed his eyes, groping for an explanation. He couldn't even remember the last time he looked at his Agency checking account. *Shit.*

And . . . oh Jesus. Taxes. He *really* had to get to that.

"It didn't help that you were three months late submitting your expenses," continued his boss.

"I know, I know—I'm totally sorry. Honestly. Zorik kept pestering me—I just . . ."

"Can't handle numbers. I know," R.J. said drily. "Listen, this childish bullshit is hurting both of us. I had the fucking Secretary of State on the phone yesterday asking for you, specifically, on the Zurich job. And I can't deliver you on that job—and you know why?" R.J. leaned across the desk and fixed Charley in his famous icy stare. "Because you didn't pay your fucking taxes."

He sat back and sighed.

"You're suspended, MacElroy. Get out of here. You'll be hearing from accounting about the missing money."

Charley stood up abruptly. "Wait—please! I don't know anything about any missing money. Honestly. I'm not a thief, R.J. I think you know that about me."

R.J. just looked at him, nonplussed. "Maybe you're not, Charley, but how many times have we talked about your expenses?" he asked.

Charley was silent for a moment. His boss had a point.

"I mean, yeah, okay, I didn't check my account for the last few months, but I didn't take any money," he finally said. "Honestly. There has to be a mistake! And as for the taxes . . . well . . ." His voice trailed off to nothing.

R.J. sighed. "Tell it to accounting," he said. He scribbled something on a piece of paper and handed it to him. "You are officially under investigation by the Agency," he said. "This is the agent assigned to your case."

Numbly, Charley took the paper and stood up. "Please believe me," he said quietly. "This job means everything in the world to me. You know it does."

"I know," said his boss sadly. He strode over to the door and opened it. "You have too much talent to go on like this, Charley. Fly back home to San Francisco and get your shit together."

R.J. watched Charley leave, and then he shut the door softly.

He sat down at his desk, looked out the window, and took a long breath. That was one of the harder meetings he'd had in recent memory. Hopefully some kind of good would come from it.

Charley walked out of the SFO Arrivals terminal and stood there for a moment, hands on hips.

Now what?

The wind had been taken soundly out of his sails eight hours earlier. Now that he was back home, he had no idea what to do. There was no longer any job, purpose, or any real meaning to his life at all.

Charley had been resolutely benched. And all because of a goddamn tax return—and an expense report, potentially doctored.

A thought flickered across his mind: *Zorik.*

No, he thought. *He wouldn't.*

Charley knew Zorik didn't like him, that he was jealous of his relationship with R.J., and that he didn't like most of his own assignments. But why now, just after their spectacular success in France? His mind darted lightly to the Secretary asking for him on the Zurich job, most likely without Zorik.

Suddenly it was starting to make sense. Zorik filed their expense report. *That fucking asshole.*

Charley began to walk toward his car, his heart still beating wildly.

Dimly he remembered he had a date to see Electra in an hour. He was going to show her his favorite view of the city, the one up on top of Russian Hill.

Screw it, he thought. The company of a beautiful woman was just what he needed right now.

He bent his head and forged on. This, too, would pass.

Everything always boils down to clothing, thought Electra, surveying her wardrobe. Her date with Charley was in less than an hour, and she felt oddly confused.

Tasteful suits signaled philanthropy mode. All black, on

the other hand, said either funeral or "I am about to kick your ass." Her jeans-Burberry-cashmere combo, the weekend staple in Manhattan, did nothing out here but overheat her. A skirt and sweater seemed oddly prim, like the old days.

Electra felt stymied.

The women of San Francisco seemed to be fairly oblivious to dress codes. It really was each woman for herself. There were Tasteful Chic types who dressed like they were in Paris—all monochromes and classics. Then there were the Spiritual with Money types who looked like they'd come straight from yoga class, or maybe Tibet, with dangling pewter jewelry and necklaces made from seed pods. Then were the high-end East Bay intellectuals, usually Power Lesbians dressed in somber suits with greying, frizzy hair. There wasn't a pair of pumps in the bunch.

Marin women, on the other hand, were in a class of their own—fur vests, faux ammo belts, exotic bloomers, boots with lots of straps. Electra found them slightly scary. Yet now she was officially Electra—or at least as far as Charley MacElroy was concerned, she was. That meant she could actually be whomever she wanted and wear whatever she wanted. She liked this game.

Electra fingered a favorite corduroy jacket thoughtfully.

The old dress code had evaporated, along with the old habits and attitudes. Everything was new, and she felt oddly displaced. Was she still the same old aging preppy? Did she actually care about wearing the latest Marc Jacobs tweed V-neck sweater? Did it even mean anything anymore?

Out here, nothing meant anything. Or at least, that is how it seemed as Electra wandered, lost, through her first months.

Nothing about her old life was even remotely applicable now. So Electra was left with a mandate to reinvent, for what else was there to do? Which led to the vacuous question, what on earth did she actually want? At this point, all she could come up with was someone to have a few cocktails and a laugh or two with. Other than that, she had no idea. Charley seemed to fill the bill just fine for now.

Pulling out a silk shirt and a pair of jeans, Electra began to dress. He said they were going for a walk. Something about Russian Hill. Electra checked herself in the mirror and frowned a bit. Was she getting jowly? Now was not the time to worry about such things, even if she was about to go out with a man nearly twenty years her junior.

Taking the corduroy jacket out, she gave it a shake and put it on. Its soft sleeves wrapped around her just as they always had. She'd gotten this jacket in her thirties, and somehow, even now, it always seemed to soothe her. It was that kind of day, she realized as she looked at herself in the mirror.

She felt tender, strangely new, and even a little scared. *Better not to dwell on such things,* she thought as she took a scarf from her drawer and draped it around her neck.

Yes . . . Well, no, actually. No.

Putting the scarf back, she gave her hair a toss and took one more critical look. What in the hell did she think she was doing? He was thirty-five, for God's sake. Forget sex. Just forget it! She was not getting naked with this man—even if she wanted to. Even if he did have those serious bedroom eyes, and even if he did have a way of talking to her that was so disarming, so . . . personal. The other night, she'd felt herself relax completely in his presence.

Still, there would be no dating. Electra couldn't; she just couldn't. Even if she did feel an instant rush the minute she saw him.

Now was the time to rebuild, to resurrect, to pick up the

pieces and somehow forge ahead. A relationship could throw her seriously off track, especially with a man so much younger. Electra knew that script. She'd seen it a million times before, and it always ended badly. Being a cougar was not for sissies.

No, she would befriend this man; in fact, she already had. Electra loved the easy banter that sprung up between them, and she felt an instant chemistry. But couldn't chemistry lead to fast friendship? That's what she needed right now more than anything. That and a cave to hide in for a few decades.

Just friends and nothing more, Electra reminded herself as she applied her lipstick. After all, she could use a good friend.

———————

Charley was home again.

He walked up Taylor past the cream-colored Victorians, the endless corner stores, the modest laundries, the swank Italian coffee bars, and saw none of it. The usual consoling stroll through San Francisco's warm bosom did nothing to cheer him today. He felt like he'd just lost his best friend. In some ways, he had.

He'd never seen R.J. like this, all gruffness and ultimatums. At the same time, Charley felt ashamed. He'd let his boss down, let the Agency down, let his country down. And why? Because for one thing, he'd just totally spaced on his taxes—which the Secretary of State was about to find out. Oh God, he couldn't even let his mind go there. The Parade of Shame was a bad, bad train of thought. He had to get a grip.

Charley cleared his throat and, putting his hands in his pockets, began a low, whistled tune. It was nothing specific, just the meandering of a few notes. It consoled him. He nodded amiably to the old woman shuffling along Taylor toward him. "Afternoon, ma'am," he said softly. She smiled.

In the end, this world was a good one. People were kind. He was blessed with more than his share of gifts. Charley knew that. And he knew that ultimately he would be fine, Zorik notwithstanding. The truth would prevail, his taxes would get paid and penalties applied, and his record would be cleared. He would be exonerated.

Still, in this moment, he felt like he didn't have two sticks to rub together, emotionally speaking. Charley felt truly bereft, as if the rug really had been pulled right out from under him. He walked on.

Charley thought about Electra. He really didn't know what he expected here, and it hardly mattered. She was charming, beautiful, funny, all the things he loved rolled into one beautiful package. He found the idea of an edgy, exciting older woman fascinating, irresistible really. Or maybe it was just Electra herself. As for the whole dominatrix thing, it didn't intimidate him. Not at all—if anything, it challenged him, stimulated him, and made him intensely curious.

After all, he called himself a pansexual. So he was up for anything, right?

And yet . . . Electra could well be another one who would climb into bed with him and straddle the crux between strange and conceivable. Would she, too, have to get down and walk away out of sheer discomfort, even if she was fairly kinky herself? The no penis thing loomed as huge and intractable as ever.

On one hand, Charley knew he had to take care. On the other hand, he couldn't care less. Electra was one of those women he just wanted, pure and simple.

Some things really were out of his control.

8

The Ina Coolbrith Park tumbled down a San Francisco hillside with the casual air of a swath that had been there forever. It was here where Charley now waited on a green painted bench for Electra to show. Down below, the entire city stretched out before him, a languorous, waiting mistress with all of her rolling city hills and painted Victorians. The Bay Bridge glistened across the water, just one of her many bracelets.

Charley was early as was his custom. Usually it gave him time to tune in to a place and collect his thoughts. Today he simply attempted to hang on and quell the vice of anxiety that was closing in on him.

"Are you napping?" he heard her say. His eyes snapped open, and he jumped to his feet.

"No . . . no . . . Just collecting my thoughts," he fumbled. A surge of electricity ran through his body as he looked at her. Yes, Electra was stunning this afternoon. Charley leaned in to give her a kiss. She smiled at him and offered her cheek.

"Wow," she said, acknowledging the view with a gesture. "Spectacular."

"Come sit and enjoy it," he said. "But just for a moment, because there is something even better I want to show you."

She sat beside him, and they were silent for a moment. Charley found himself at a loss for words. Electra turned almost shyly to him.

"How have you been?" she asked.

"Fine!" Charley enthused. Still, his words felt empty.

Electra looked at him. She was on to him. "You seem distracted."

He shook his head lightly. *Come on, now*, he implored himself. *Get a grip, buddy.* "Just the usual stuff of life," he said lightly. "Here . . ." Charley rose and extended his hand, but Electra did not take it.

He dropped his hand, smiled at her, and they walked on.

They climbed the stairs behind them, a typical San Francisco staircase—aging steps of concrete that had been installed in an older, more gracious time and always seemed to lead to someplace special. One staircase led to another until they arrived at the tiniest set. Hand-laid stone steps led, improbably, to a small jewel of a lawn at the exact top of Russian Hill.

At its edge stood a pepper tree and a black walnut, each twining up toward the sky as they apparently had for decades. The green patch was framed with an elegant Italian balustrade, and just beyond it was a house one might see tucked away at the edge of an English village. It was a pretty shingled cottage. The whole place seemed to be some kind of aging urban fairyland.

They sat down on the grass and surveyed the even more spectacular view spread out before them. An orderly march of pastel sun-bleached buildings in blues, pinks, and creams worked their way toward the bay. It was one of those crystal clear fall days when nothing bad could ever happen. The Bay Bridge stretched out to the forested lump of Treasure Island, and beyond that to Mount Diablo. The bay was its usual iridescent blue. It was a scene that inspired nothing but optimism.

"Isn't this someone's lawn?" Electra asked.

"No, incredibly. It belongs to the city of San Francisco. And right now," he added, "it's all ours."

A large, greying man appeared just then, evidently the owner of the cottage. He was wearing a pair of Peal loafers and an expensive shirt, and carrying the garbage. He had the air of someone who was used to running things. The man gave them a gruff nod.

Charley rose and walked over to the balustrade. "Hi," he said easily, greeting the man. "How are you doing today?"

The man stopped and looked at him as if to say, *What on earth do you want from me?*

Charley stuck out his hand. "Charley MacElroy," he said in his soft drawl. "I just wanted to say thanks for being a gracious neighbor. May I ask you something?"

The man eyed Charley wearily, but he grunted his consent.

"I suspect you planted the pepper tree and the black walnut?" Charley asked.

The man smiled unexpectedly. "Yes, I did—thirty years ago."

"Good for you," said Charley.

The man put down his garbage and gave a little chuckle. "As a matter of fact, I've been trying to do the Oklahoma land grab on this piece ever since."

"Crazy how the city divides things up, isn't it? But then, that's history for you. Speaking of which, is your house Ina Coolbrith's former home?"

Now the man grew more talkative. "No, that was a place

down on Taylor, where that high wall with all the greenery is. Got completely wiped out in the Great Fire back in 1906. She lost the manuscript of her memoir in the fire, you know . . ." He rambled on, recounting the story of the first poet laureate of California.

Charley interjected a brief story of his own, about finding a copy of a long lost literary magazine that got started on this very street 150 years earlier.

The two men chatted along amiably as Electra lazed in the grass. She lay back, studying the sky in the branches spread above her. The men were just getting to the part about Ina Coolbrith being one of the few women admitted to the Bohemian Club when she sat up suddenly.

"Hey," she said. "There's a green parrot in this tree!"

The bird was eyeing her curiously. Looking up, Electra saw several more, and then even more on the branches just above. There had to be twenty. In an instant, the parrots rose up in the sky—a dense red and green cloud that set off a wild cacophony. It sounded like a chorus of intensely loud squeaky wicker baskets. The birds took off together.

"What was that?" she said, getting to her feet. The two men laughed.

"They live on Telegraph Hill, but we let them fly over here," the man explained. "They make such a racket that all those people who thought they would make great pets back in the nineties set them free . . . and, well, they're still here along with their kids. Turns out they don't migrate. Or die."

"How extraordinary," remarked Electra. "Wild parrots . . . here."

"I'm afraid I have to run," the man continued, sticking out his hand to Charley. "Come up for a drink sometime," he offered. "We'll have to talk more."

Charley smiled and gave him his card.

"A writer," the man said, inspecting the card. "MacElroy—like the rum?"

"The same," replied Charley.

The man looked at him with new respect. "I'll mind what I serve," he said drily.

After a moment, Charley joined Electra again on the grass. "You made a friend," she remarked. "I thought he was about to chew us out."

"I knew he wasn't."

"How?"

"I just sensed it. I know the type—probably divorced, lonely, looking for a good conversation but not just any old chatter. He needed proof that I was conversation worthy. Anyway, it's my business to know," he added lightly.

"Being a travel writer . . . or an MIA rum baron . . . or whatever you are."

"Yeah," he replied evenly. "It's all about talking to people. And they will open up to you, every last one of them, but only if you approach them correctly. You should try it some time. It's amazing the things you can learn."

"Share your technique?"

Charley looked at her. "Just tune in. Put yourself in their shoes. Spend a quiet moment sussing them out. Then ask them the things you really want to know about. Not the superficial stuff, but real things. Disarming things. You'll get it in a heartbeat."

She looked at the sky with a smile and then gazed back at him. "How do you know I'll get it?"

Charley looked at her. "Because you're a woman," he replied. "You're just naturally good at that."

"Then maybe this should be my new job," she teased. "Woman about town who gets strangers to spill their guts."

"You could do worse," he said, extending his hand. "Walk?" he asked.

"I'd love to," she said, taking his hand. Their fingers entwined for just a moment and then she dropped her hand.

Friends, remember? he reminded himself. "Lead on, MacDuff," she said.

"Ah," Charley smiled. "A woman who paraphrases Shakespeare . . ."

She really was just his type.

9

It was a beautiful day in San Francisco, just the sort of day for going out in your cock ring and your harness, which was fortunate as this was the first day of the Folsom Street Fair. The world's biggest leather fair, a non-stop orgy for every gay man in the Bay Area and all their friends, was bursting at the seams by 2 p.m. Randy stood across the street from the bulging, pulsing spectacle, mesmerized and a little scared.

Men and women of all shapes and sizes cued up to enter. They were checking clothing at a coat check, stepping out of jeans and shirts to reveal flesh, leather accouterments, and little else. Some were muscled, tan, and rippling, others were pale, flabby, and soft. A tired-looking bouncer, a large, bald man who had to be six foot seven, stamped hand after hand automatically. Several others were collecting fistfuls of twenties and tens. A long line pressed to get in.

Randy's heart pounded, and his ears already ached from the incessant, high volume house music. On top of everything, he had a sick stomach. That was what always happened at times like this. Randy sighed, lowered his head, and moved toward the entrance gate with resolve. He had to get this done. It was why he came. He invoked the Lord.

Randy had come dressed for the occasion. He thought he should in order to fit in, which meant getting rid of the wooden cross that usually hung around his neck, as well as his tie. Instead, he had his Casual Friday look on—a lightweight poly/wool jacket in a dusty cream plaid shirt, freshly pressed jeans, sturdy walking shoes. And he'd be keeping his clothes on, thank you very much. This was the best he could do.

Randy was nervous. Earlier he found himself trimming his mustache, fussing over it for nearly fifteen minutes in the hotel mirror for reasons he didn't fully understand. This was his first live encounter with the heathens en masse. Randy had never actually seen people like this. He told himself that the Lord was with him—and that he was just doing research.

Randy's aim was to observe the sinners in action, look for patterns, and mostly observe the onsite security and controls the SFPD put in place at the fair. He rightly figured that this event, with its 400,000 people and thirteen-block radius, would show him the extreme limits of festival security.

Taking a deep breath, he walked across the street and produced his ten-dollar bill. The bouncer stamped his hand, and he entered and rounded the back of a huge Jumbotron. A massive, teeming crowd of partiers immediately engulfed him.

Young buxom girls sported tight-fitting rubber dresses, orange hair, body-length tattoos. Others wore elaborate chain-covered corsets over fishnets and scanty leather panties. Masks were big: gas masks, horse masks, unicorn horns, devil horns. Compliant, trussed-up people were being led around by their masters on chains. Knots of men stood together wearing leather masks with floppy puppy ears and combat boots.

Two gay men in strange white face paint, elaborate eye shadow, and peaked Elizabethan hats swanned around together holding hands, dressed only from the neck up. Two others had assembled extreme Carol Channing costumes with matching green polka dot glitter swing dresses. They teetered around on six-inch sequined platform heels, their matching parasols adorned with black marabou trim. Another man wandered by dressed convincingly like Hagrid, the Hogwart's groundskeeper, complete with a huge beard and animal skins adorning his vast girth. He carried a leather mug of stout.

A massive handmade banner hung on the façade of a Victorian house beside a rainbow flag. "Revel in Your Faggotry," it said in gold letters. A young man in a leather thong and chest harness crouched in the house's open second-story windows, bobbing and weaving to the blasting dance music. In the other open window, another man rocked his naked hips to the music, as the furry tail protruding from his anus swayed to the music. Randy turned away, unable to watch any more.

Lord, help me get through this, he thought as a wave of revulsion washed through him.

Sweat broke out on his brow as Randy plunged further in. After a few moments, he found what he was looking for. A young girl was lashed to a tall wooden pole, her naked ass being paddled by a tough-looking lesbian in a leather vest. Eyes half closed, she had a beatific look on her face as a sea of men watched, captivated. A photographer was shooting the scene, apparently for Japanese media.

Standing on the outer edge of the scene were two SFPD officers, surveying the scene with an air of utter boredom.

One looked at his watch and sighed. Randy took up his post along the wall of a brick building and studied the officers, attempting to look casual. Pulling a tiny notebook from his pocket, he began to discreetly make a few notes.

———•◦•———

Electra felt the weight of the crop in her hand as she withdrew it from her tote bag, and it felt good. Very good. She pulled open the locker door, took off the Burberry raincoat, wadded it up into a ball, and stuffed it inside, along with her bag. Then she closed the door and locked it with a click. It was a risk coming here today, but already it was worth it.

Even going incognito in the elevator in her building was a problem, so she had to take the back stairs and slip out the side door. She just couldn't face Ricky, her doorman, and his eternal pony-tailed gladness. Today she intended to kick some ass.

Most likely there would be people who knew her at Folsom Street—gawkers, autograph seekers, even hecklers potentially. On the other hand, maybe no one would bother her. Maybe she could finally just bond with her tribe. Maybe she would even have fun. Either way, Electra knew she had to go. There really was no choice.

Her outfit had been carefully chosen for this important occasion. Breasts bared, she styled herself as a sort of high Wiccan priestess, even though she really had no idea what Wiccans did. She chose a long, diaphanous dark grey gown, a black leather bustier with spiked studs and chains that crisscrossed her naked breasts, and a necklace of decorative sharp objects. She'd topped it all off with a simple leather thong around her forehead festooned with a pointed pod she'd found in Golden Gate Park. That was the Wiccan part.

She looked like an elegant Mother Earth who regularly drew blood at Burning Man.

Now Electra began her slow, meandering roam through the festival. She had no idea what she was looking for, but it was something. Or someone, perhaps? She felt quite alone, though God knows she could have brought Charley along. She suspected he'd have been more than willing to come. Salivatingly so.

Still, Electra preferred to attend alone. That way if there was another interesting prospect, someone who was already in the tribe, someone she might even do business with, she could freely connect.

Electra wasn't cruising the Folsom Street Fair. Not really. In her mind, she was merely coming out to play for a while and reveling in this most San Franciscan of indulgences— costumes plus kink. She was testing the water.

For a while, Electra busied herself watching an Owari demonstration. A beautiful young woman was trussed up between two pillars in an elaborate net of intricately tied knots. Her naked flesh poured out of the tense web of cords that held her fast, and her hands were slowly turning blue. She writhed gently as a straight man tickled her skin with a feather. Finally, Electra moved on, past the whipping post and a booth for something called the San Francisco Bay Area Animal Role Play Society.

A man carrying a beer and wearing nothing but a diaper and sneakers tried to engage Electra in conversation, but she couldn't take him seriously. Just beyond him, there was an entire oversized crib of grown men also in diapers. Some were cuddled up sucking their thumbs while others sat up, crying. They all appeared to be pre-verbal. At least one of them needed a diaper change.

Electra tried not to be disgusted, just to go with the flow, but finally it all became too much. *Where in God's name are the normal perverts?* she wondered. Why did *everything* in this town have to be over the top? And why oh why was there so much pot everywhere? Or . . . wait . . . Weed. That's what people under fifty called it.

Instead of connecting with her tribe, Electra felt more out of place than ever. She finally felt some relief when she came upon the cage corner in which various doms tormented their subs, all housed in little black cages. One woman sat on top of her sub's cage and dangled her pinky alluringly. Every time he tried to lick or bite it, she withdrew it with a laugh. Their cat-and-mouse game continued until he started nuzzling her crotch. Instead of playfully pulling back, the dom simply hopped off, peeled off her tiny black rubber panties, climbed back onto the cage, and offered herself to him. Her sub leaped right into action.

At that point, a lurking SFPD officer intervened. "Sorry, miss. You can't do that here," he said. The dom looked furious for a moment, and then she backed off.

"Oh. Right," she mumbled, climbing back off the cage. "Forgot." Then she began the slow arduous process of pulling her little rubber pants back on again. "Hang on a minute," she squeaked as she attempted to pull the panties over one six-inch platform heel, and then another. She wiggled and squirmed inch after inch of leather up over her ample body. This was going to take a while.

The cop folded his arms and looked on, nonplussed, but Electra was amused. She continued to watch the scene for a while until she happened to notice a strange man who was also watching. He was leaned against a nearby wall.

He was strange merely because he was so conventional

looking. The plaid shirt and the bland beige jacket made him look like a dentist on a holiday—or someone's uncle in from Missouri. Electra couldn't help but wonder what he was doing here. She suspected he might be a willing customer, perhaps a tourist in town just for the fair. Meanwhile the dom was now leaning on the police officer's shoulder for balance as she struggled to put her latex pants back on. Her sub sat in his cage, looking mildly put off. The mood had clearly been broken.

The strange man pulled a tiny pad from his pocket and began making notes. *Crap*, thought Electra. *He's from the media.* There went her chance for an easy prospect. But instead of immediately leaving, Electra watched him curiously for another moment. He really didn't look like any media person she'd ever seen.

He was so . . . straight looking. Christian media, perhaps? She'd already been stung by a film crew from a TV show called the *Crusaders for God*. They'd camped out day after day in front of her apartment in New York, staking her out. After she hired a bodyguard, they finally gave up and went back to Missouri.

The man tucked his notebook away and stood there for another moment or two, hands in pockets, just watching. Electra was mesmerized; she couldn't take her eyes off of him. She'd find out in a heartbeat if he was media simply by making eye contact with him. She continued to look at him, and when his gaze finally met hers, he registered nothing. He just turned and walked away.

Apparently he had no idea who she was. Or even better, he didn't care. This was interesting.

Electra wandered through the fair several paces behind the man, ducking behind structures, walls, barricades, whatever she could find in order not to be noticed. He stopped at a smoothie stand, considered the options, and kept moving. Then he paused by a stage featuring a large drag queen belting out "Bippety Boppety Boo."

The performer waved his fairy princess wand at the audience as he removed his breakaway skirt. Meanwhile, a pair of police officers quietly conferred by the side of the stage. The man sidled up beside them and appeared to be watching the show. Electra had the sense that he was eavesdropping. Could it be the police he was researching?

Now she was seriously intrigued.

She ducked around the back of a building and hurried up an alleyway to position herself behind the two chatting police officers. She tried to overhear their conversation, but she couldn't make out what they were saying. Apparently the man was somewhere to their left now, just out of her sight. Electra edged a bit closer and tried to look busy studying something in the distance.

She heard the man approach the two officers. "Excuse me," he said. "Is there a medical tent here?"

The two stopped and surveyed him. "Are you having a problem?" asked one.

"I'm feeling a bit faint," she heard him say. "I think I just need to rest. I have . . . a condition," he finally mumbled.

One of the officers picked up his walkie talkie and radioed a message to the dispatcher. "Do you need a wheelchair, sir?"

"No! No. Heavens," he demurred. "Just point me toward the medical tent, please." The officers directed him to the other side of the fair, and slowly, he walked off. "Weird guy," Electra heard one cop say to the other.

"Yeah," said the first, giving a nod. The other ambled off after the man at a discreet distance.

Electra fairly ran down the alleyway, passed the building next to it, and managed to slip in just behind the following police officer. Just ahead was the retreating beige figure of the strange man.

Unaware he was being watched, he stopped once more, extracted his notebook, and wrote something down.

The police officer's radio suddenly sounded with the crackling voice of the dispatcher. "Copy," replied the officer. In an instant, he turned and took off in the opposite direction. Suddenly, Electra was following the strange man alone.

Should she stop? Or keep following him? He continued to scribble with his worn pencil. She neared him, unobserved, until she was standing just behind him.

"Excuse me," she heard herself say. "Are you a reporter?" *Holy shit*, she thought. *I'm talking to him.*

Randy looked up, startled, unsure where the question came from. Then he turned around. "Oh. No," he fumbled, stuffing the pad into his pocket. Clearly she was making him nervous.

Electra said nothing. The man had a distinct deer-in-headlights look on his face. "No, I'm not in the media," he repeated for emphasis.

"I just thought—" she began.

"What?" He looked at her curiously now. She could see him sizing her up and down. His eyes came to rest on her naked breasts. He looked away quickly. Now she sensed he recognized her.

Electra felt exposed. "Forget it." She shook her head. "Sorry to bother you." *Why am I even talking to this guy?*

But suddenly, he stuck his hand out. "Don't go away," he said. "I'm Roscoe. Roscoe Stevens."

Electra did not take his hand. "Are you sure you're not a reporter?" she asked.

"I promise I'm not."

"Then what are you?" Electra couldn't stop herself. *What in God's name am I doing?*

The man hesitated for just a second. "I'm a real estate broker."

"Oh, really," she said pleasantly. "Where?"

He looked askance and put his hands in his pockets. He coughed. "Here and there," he said. "Anyway, let me not bother you," he said with excessive gentility. *Clearly he is being evasive.*

"Don't run away so fast," she began, but he was already walking away quickly. *Damn it. I blew it.*

Electra hurried after the retreating figure of Roscoe, weaving her way in and around the gathering crowd at the center of the festival. Now she really had to find out where he was going.

Was he being evasive because he was afraid someone would know him at a leather fair? Maybe he had something to hide. *It is especially odd that he introduced himself,* she thought. She couldn't wait to Google his name. *Roscoe Stevens. Like hell he is in real estate,* she thought. And he had almost certainly given her a fake name.

He stopped and stepped into a porta potty at the edge of the fair. Electra waited behind the cover of the corset booth, where she watched one woman trussing up another.

"You'll want to stop eating lunch for a while," the trusser advised her subject. "Maybe dinner, too."

The man emerged, and Electra hurried right after him. She began to run Charley's question strategy through her mind. She had to unpin this guy, whomever he was. It seemed urgently important.

She caught up to him at the edge of the beer tent. "Roscoe," she called out, and he looked over his shoulder at her.

"What do you want?" he asked with a trace of annoyance.

"Just . . ." Electra was a little out of breath. "I just wanted to apologize. I sense you're from out of town, and I know the city can be overwhelming at times." She paused, panting.

He stopped and looked her up and down as if he was memorizing her appearance. "Hnnh," he replied noncommittally.

"Is there anything I can help you with?" she asked. "Correct me if I'm wrong, but you're not from here, right?" The man nodded. "I'm new here myself," she offered.

"Really?" he said with interest. "What's your name?"

Is it possible he doesn't know me? she thought with wonder. "Electra."

"Electra what?"

"Just Electra," she answered. Then she handed him her card. "Here. Not that you're looking or anything." The card gave her name and her email address, followed by the words "Dominatrix for Hire." She'd had the cards printed since Charley gave her the pep talk the night they met.

Now Roscoe studied her card. "I might be," he said as he pocketed it. "You never know, Electra."

"First time at the fair?" she asked him.

He didn't answer, but he smiled. Now she understood perfectly; his smile said it all. He was a sex tourist who was probably cheating on his wife back in Duluth. *But why is he checking out the police?* she wondered.

She noticed he wasn't going to the medical tent, even though he was supposed to be faint. In fact, he wasn't going anywhere near it.

"Where are you from?" she asked as casually as possible.

The two looked at each other awkwardly for a moment. He didn't answer her.

"Okay, Roscoe . . ." she finally said. Again there was a stiff silence. "Bye," she said lightly.

"Good-bye, Electra," he said blandly. "I enjoyed meeting you."

"Thanks. Me, too," she concluded with a wave.

She walked back toward the center of the fair. Every fiber of her body was now tingling with warning. Turning, she looked over her shoulder one more time. Roscoe was watching her walk away. She turned back quickly and hastened her step.

He is one weird dude, she thought to herself. *Even the police agreed.* Which simply made her more curious than ever. She hoped Roscoe would call.

Randy advanced rapidly up Thirteenth Street, leaving the fair in his wake. He couldn't believe his good fortune. He'd gotten far more than he came for.

He'd observed police interaction fully. He'd observed their numbers, their call and response system, and just how casual they appeared to be. Which, in his opinion, was shockingly so. After all, this was San Francisco.

But far better was the true gift from God—meeting Pamela Delacroix, the Society Dom, all dressed up as "Electra" no less.

Randy felt a burst of exuberance as he recalled how neatly and easily God's plan was already unfolding. She had approached him! He didn't have to do anything but receive. She'd even given him her card with her email address. He was filled with such gratitude, for here was his insect on a pin, his butterfly under glass.

His access to Electra would help him understand and destroy so many more of the hedonists. He and God were moving in perfect alignment for sure.

Now Randy turned and entered a soot-covered, nondescript church in the Tenderloin. He didn't care which kind. He simply needed a moment alone to give thanks. Slipping into a pew in the silent sanctuary, he fell to his knees and began repeating the Lord's Prayer followed by his own personal entreaty.

Lord, thank you for this unique opportunity . . . for bringing me this guide. Help me smite the blows of Satan in all that I am and all that I do. Help me eradicate the ways of evil that have tainted our pure land. Help me remain calm and courageous in the face of such degradation. May I serve your will as I eradicate this woman and all the other hedonists . . . please protect me as I do this good work.

Then, praying for one moment longer, he closed as he always did.

And thank you, Daddy, for being the role model you were in this life. I honor your will, so help me God.

10

"I'm Lou-Paul, and I'll be your waitperson today," said the slender African-American man. "May I tell you how insanely great the Prather Ranch short ribs are? They come with a sweet potato-apple-butternut squash hash, and they are just off-the-hook fabulous . . ."

Charley and Frankie had discovered they were both foodies. "Is the hanger steak Prather, too?" Frankie began. The conversation about the origins of their meat went on for several minutes until Frankie was satisfied. She was already blowing Charley's concept of cops.

Once the waiter took their order, they were alone again. Frankie sighed and sat back in her seat.

Charley looked at her. "Why the big sigh?" he asked. "Something bothering you?"

For a few weeks now, they had been bumping into each other again and again at the gym. Finally they were having brunch—a reward for a tough morning with the weights.

"No, no." Frankie waved her hand dismissively. "It's nothing."

Charley just continued to look at her.

Frankie shifted in her seat, finally melting under his gaze. "Okay—okay," she said. "But this is completely confidential." Charley nodded his consent.

Frankie looked around the restaurant uncomfortably. She leaned toward him and lowered her voice. "Work's like a nightmare these days," she said. "The chief wants me gone. Apparently I'm 'a troublemaker.'"

"Really?" Charley asked with interest. "What did you do?"

Frankie sighed and closed her eyes. "I got hired a while back to clean up the department. That was with the last chief. Then he took a job in Phoenix, and suddenly I was toast." Her eyes snapped open with a glare. "The new chief is a fucking sleazeball who wants nothing to do with me. But I can't help myself, Charley. I've seen the rot, and I want to expose it."

"Can't you fight him?" asked Charley. "You must have a union."

She glanced around the restaurant again and lowered her voice even further. "Sure we do. But the mayor appoints the chief, and those two are as thick as thieves. And I am fresh out of friends in City Hall."

Frankie was practically whispering. "There's some serious shit going on, Charley. I don't have proof yet, but I know what's happening. I was next in line for lieutenant when this guy arrived, and now I'm stuck processing paperwork all day. That way I supposedly can't make trouble."

"Wow," said Charley with real empathy. "So you're benched."

"Exactly," she concurred.

"I know how you feel," he said.

"Do you?" Frankie asked. Cocking her head, she studied him. "Do you really?"

Charley paused. "I've been in a similar position."

Frankie sized him up. "Since when do writers have to play office politics?" she asked.

"Sometimes I ask too many questions myself." He sighed. "I've been benched. Recently even."

Frankie regarded him curiously. "What happened?"

Charley had said too much already. "My literary agent's furious with me," he fibbed. "I'm way behind on a deadline. But hey . . . I was distracted!"

They were silent for a moment. Charley knew Frankie hadn't totally bought his explanation, but he also wasn't ready to drop his cover. Not yet, at least.

"We have more in common than you think," he added. They looked at each other and smiled.

———— + ————

The waiter put Charley's lavender French toast down in front of him with a wink. Frankie had gone to the ladies room, so Charley was momentarily alone.

"Titch, more honey mascarpone, honey? Or are you all set?" the waiter cooed. He smiled adoringly at Charley, who blushed a little, enjoying the attention.

"I'm good on the mascarpone," Charley cooed right back. "But maybe a little more syrup?"

"Now, now, now . . . that's bourbon syrup, you know, darling," gushed the waiter. "Wouldn't want you getting tipsy so early in the day."

"Why not?" asked Charley. "It's the weekend . . ." He held the man's gaze for a long, tantalizing moment and smiled. He always enjoyed a good flirt, regardless of gender.

Frankie suddenly appeared and cleared her throat, causing

the two men to look away. "Am I breaking something up?" she asked as she seated herself again in the booth. Charley smiled. "No comment," he replied.

The waiter appeared with her grilled hanger steak and eggs and put them down wordlessly at Frankie's place. She wasn't getting nearly as much love from Lou-Paul.

"Man," she said, picking up her knife and fork, "no one ever flirts with me in the Castro."

"I suspect this isn't your venue," Charley said with a smile.

Frankie gave a little grin. "Definitely not," she agreed as she tucked into her steak with gusto.

"Are you single?" he asked her.

"Yeah," Frankie said, adding nothing more. Charley waited a beat, and then he moved on.

"Me, too," he remarked. "I'm a transman."

"Figured," said Frankie.

"Not that it matters," Charley added. "Except when it does."

"When's that?" asked Frankie curiously.

"When you want to get married," he replied evenly. "I'm batting zero for four."

Frankie sliced into her steak. "You've got guts, Charley," she said. "When did you transition?"

"When I was ten."

"Ten! Seriously?"

Charley affirmed with a nod. Then he shrugged. "Twenty-five years later and I'm still working out the kinks. It's complicated."

"I can imagine," said Frankie. "It's hard enough being a vanilla lesbian."

Charley smiled. He genuinely liked this woman—she was forthright. Real. And apparently she had the gut of three men. He wasn't sure how, but he suspected that Frankie was going to be very useful to him.

"Anyway, here's to friendship," he said, raising his mimosa in her direction.

She raised her glass, and they clinked. "To friendship."

"Words are easy, like the wind," said Charley. "Faithful friends are hard to find."

"Shakespeare," concluded Frankie. Charley smiled and nodded.

Exactly.

Electra stepped into the shower and began to wash off the detritus of the Folsom Street Fair. She took some high-priced shower gel in her hands and began to spread it evenly across her body. She was troubled.

So far her research had turned up nothing. A preliminary check for "Roscoe Stevens," "Roscoe Stevens Real Estate," even "R. Stevens Real Estate," came up blank. As did "Roscoe Stevens Bay Area," "Stevens Roscoe Real Estate San Francisco," and all variants thereof. Google images had a number of Roscoe Stevenses, but not one who looked anything like the man she'd met at Folsom Street.

Electra checked Facebook, Twitter, Instagram, even LinkedIn. She had spent the last hour and a half hunting all over the internet for this guy. As far as she could tell, he simply didn't exist.

At the very least, she thought, *"Roscoe" should have been on LinkedIn*. He was totally the type. If he wasn't there, at least he might have had an ad in the Yellow Pages. But so far, nothing had turned up.

She closed her eyes and tried to relax under the steady stream of hot water. The guy was probably a tourist, but from where? Texas, Oklahoma, Florida, or Rhode Island, maybe. Or someplace like Ohio or Illinois. Hell—he could have been from anywhere, even Alaska.

She noticed he had no accent to speak of. In fact, he seemed utterly bland in a tense sort of way. She wondered now why he'd given her a fake name. Perhaps he was just being cautious about strangers in general? Maybe just one of those people who trusted no one, letting vague paranoia inform all of his decisions.

Or maybe it was something else. Electra closed her eyes as a small shudder passed through her body.

Stop overreacting. Just stop it right now.

He was probably just a passing weirdo. Electra had no reason to fear him. She should probably drop the whole thing and just forget about it.

But maybe he was faking the fact that he didn't recognize her.

What if he knew her, just like everyone else? Maybe he was faking it because he wanted to hurt her. Maybe he was the stalker who was always in the back of her mind. Perhaps he was that man they talked about on the six o'clock news— always described as "a quiet man." Maybe he was that guy who loved to observe BDSM scenes, and then when he finally got his big moment, he turned out to be a serial murderer.

Her mind flashed to her carved-up body, bleeding to death in an alleyway, her life slowly draining away. No one would care, really. Not even her daughter.

Oh, for God's sake! Get a frigging grip. You're wasting water.

Right. There was a drought on. Electra snapped off the shower and, stepping out, grabbed a towel. Drying herself off, she walked over to the computer on her bed and flipped it open. She clicked on her email inbox, wondering if perhaps he had sent her an email already.

He would; she was fairly sure of that. The real question was when. Though she had barely begun her life as a dominatrix, Electra could already tell when a connection had been made. She could feel it in her body.

On second thought, she knew exactly when he would contact her.

There would come a day when Roscoe—or whatever his name was—would rise up and realize that his time had come. Then the forces beyond his control would finally make him feel small, weak, and overcome with need. That's when he would pick up the phone or perhaps carefully compose an email. He would be unable to resist any further.

I'll have fun with this one, she thought, *even if he is a little strange.*

Electra gave her inbox a quick scan, seeing no emails from anyone resembling Roscoe. But one email caught her attention. It had the subject line, "Invitation to Speak."

Ordinarily she deleted all of these. She certainly didn't need any more publicity. But this time Electra stopped and checked the sender. It was from something called The Refuge.

Curious, she opened it. Her eyes scanned the email . . .

. . .now making your home in the Bay Area . . . obviously many invitations to speak . . . a real contribution to the sex positive community . . .

She read on until this stopped her:

We are hoping you will consider teaching our workshop on Fearless Domination. Our former dominatrix, Diamond Lil', 2012 Pacific Coast Power Exchange titleholder, has gone on to greater glory as she tours the country on her Taut Rubber Tour.

She left behind her curriculum if you wish to use it. It covers all the basics—spanking, chains, sensory deprivation, cuffs, collars, plus common fetishes, using costumes, role-play, domination communication tips, switching, bottom/top dynamics, and safety considerations. Or, of course, you are welcome to teach the class any way you wish.

Electra stopped short. They were asking her to teach a workshop.

This was not another sensationalized "interview" in which her life would be drilled into a thousand different ways until she felt like a piece of Swiss cheese. This time she'd be in charge. She'd be standing up there alone. She would be the expert. The Dominatrix.

Electra would have an entire room full of people under her control.

She smiled. This was exactly what she wanted—wasn't it? If she was going to seriously go pro, well . . . the door had just been opened.

She sat back and wrapped the towel a little more tightly around herself. Was she ready for this? A thousand ragged thoughts collided at once in her brain.

What if I'm not any good at teaching this stuff? What if I simply don't know enough? How many sessions have I led . . . a few dozen? Is that even remotely enough to qualify me to lead a class?

What will my sister and brother do when they find out?

And Peyton?

She could hear her now: Yeah, my mom's a professional dominatrix.

That would be the end of everything right there. Any slim chance Electra might have to reconnect with her daughter would disappear the minute she emailed back a "yes." It would be done.

Over.

Finished.

Electra reopened the email and read it once more. She would have to think about this. She hurried to get dressed now, lit up by her thoughts. She felt both confused and exhilarated.

She'd been waiting for something like this to happen, without even realizing it. It was perfect, this offer. Here was her calling card to the BDSM community, to the larger world beyond her grasp. Here was her entry point, her in. A small surge of joy spread through her chest as she zipped up her jeans.

Buttoning her blouse, she looked at herself. Hell, she was definitely ready for this. She'd pack the house. She knew that, too. They were smart to invite her, weren't they?

Electra paused and regarded herself one more time. Was she *really* ready to hang out her shingle and truly go public with all of the other "sex positive" freaks out there?

She sighed and looked away. This was going to take a little more thought, she decided. Still, she left the house with a spring in her step.

Someone actually needed her.

———•◆•———

"Okay, it's happening," Electra began, tucking herself into the banquette in the Vietnamese restaurant. She leaned across the table and gave Charley a kiss on the cheek. "And all I had to do was change my name to Electra, just as you predicted."

Charley smiled and lifted his scotch on the rocks. "Here's to your first paid client," he surmised.

"Well, no, not exactly. But I have been offered a workshop at a place called The Refuge. Ever heard of it?"

"I don't know much about it," he admitted.

"They want me to teach their class on 'Fearless Domination'. God knows how they got my email address."

"Will you do it?"

"I want to . . ." she began a little wistfully.

"But what?"

Electra grimaced. "Oh, who am I kidding, Charley? I'm a media splat, known for her bad behavior. Notoriety does not a teacher make. What if I can't actually teach?"

He peered at her over his menu. "I think you underestimate yourself, love. By the way, the tendon and brisket phô is the thing to get here."

A waiter paused briefly at their table. His pen was poised in midair over his order pad. "What can I get you?" he asked.

Charley placed their order, and a moment later, the phô arrived, steaming under its stockpile of bean sprouts, basil, and jalapeño. Charley picked up the lime wedge and began to squeeze it on the soup. "Did you know this stuff is the perfect cure for a hangover?" he asked, dousing the bowl liberally with sriracha.

"It's 5:30, Charley . . . What in God's name did you get up to last night?"

"Nothing to speak of," he said innocently. He certainly wasn't going to fill Electra in on a night that started with a Radical Faerie Thrift Fashion Show and ended in someone's hot tub on a rooftop overlooking Noe Valley as the sun was coming up.

"I think you should do it," he said as he tucked into his steaming bowl of phô. "Why on earth wouldn't you? It's what you want, for God's sake."

"Because—Oh, I don't know. I don't know!" Electra took a long pull on her drink. "Because my daughter would kill me," she finally admitted.

"You have a daughter?"

"Barely. Peyton hasn't talked to me since all hell broke loose eighteen months ago. That's a long time not to forgive your mother."

"Or a short time to grieve the end of your family."

"You think it's grief?"

"It is most definitely grief. Anger, too, probably, and all kinds of things. Her family just fell apart. How old is she?"

"Twenty-seven . . . Old enough to know better."

"Perhaps. But one thing is for certain, love. You're always going to be her mother. So why not give the girl some slack? She's just doing what she knows how to do. She'll be back sooner or later. When she's ready. "

"But in the meanwhile, my ex is filling her head with—"

Charley held up his hand to silence her. "You don't know what goes on in your daughter's head, Electra," he asserted. "I can promise you that. Mothers never do. They just think they do."

Electra just looked at him. "How do you know so much about mothers and daughters?" she asked.

"I know these things," he said with a shrug. "Now eat your phô."

She regarded him curiously one more time before she returned to her soup.

I really have to tell her, he thought. *It's just that she's so damn attractive . . .*

11

Electra pulled the ski cap down over her forehead and squinted at herself in the mirror. Tucking her blonde hair up inside of it, she looked a little pinheaded. But it didn't matter. The point was to be incognito. After all, she was heading into the belly of the beast—San Francisco's famed sex museum.

She put on her sunglasses but then took them off again. Too glam. People would recognize her in an instant. Pulling the men's camouflage shirt from its paper bag, she unbuttoned it and slipped it on.

That was better. She stepped into the black steel-toed work boots that completed her costume. Now she looked like a tall, thin butch who might have had a bit of work done.

Today Electra was going to walk the streets of this town without feeling like a target. Not a soul would know her. Too many times lately she had left herself open to pure and simple invasion of privacy, and frankly, she was sick of it. After a tourist followed her for eight blocks, calling her name and begging for a selfie, she took matters into her own hands.

From now on she would do things differently.

———•—•—•———

This was not the kind of place Randy ever thought he'd find himself—this library of iniquity. The Lord, as usual, had laid down a mighty challenge. Sometimes you just had to do what you had to do.

In general, Randy liked libraries. In libraries, the peaceful, natural pace of life was always observed. There was a blessed stillness, and only the turning of an occasional page to break the silence. Randy felt that people understood him here.

Like many other evangelical Christians, Randy relied on libraries heavily. It was a must given that he didn't own a computer or use a cell phone. This was a legacy from his father. There was no need for all the electronics, his father had said. "Technology is a fool's canyon," was how he put it.

So when he heard about the sex library, it was a natural choice to come here. Where else could he safely learn about BDSM, which seemed imperative for his mission now that he'd met Pamela? This was apparently what God had in mind next for him.

The librarian, a bespectacled woman with greying hair and a friendly, academic manner, pulled book after book out of the stacks. She topped the pile off with a dollop of vintage porn— a few glossy magazines called *Rough Play*. "These should get you started," she said with a smile. "Enjoy!"

Randy felt his face flush red. "Oh . . . no, these aren't for me—" he stammered. "No. No, they're for . . ."

Who? Could he even invoke the Lord's name in a place like this?

"Never mind," Randy said quietly, but she had already turned away. Apparently the librarian had heard it all before.

She returned a moment later with a small catalog in hand. "Do you know about The Refuge?" she asked. "It's our local BDSM 'school.' They're having an intro class in a week or so. Here . . ." She placed the pamphlet before him. Immediately the headline jumped out at him: "Rope, Gags, and Spanks; BDSM for Beginners with Pamela Delacroix (Electra), The Society Dom."

Randy could scarcely believe his eyes. *Pay dirt!* "Fantastic," he gushed. "Thank you!"

And thank you, Lord. As ever I bow to your divine will.

He sat back in his chair and marveled at divine providence—things were just getting easier and easier. Then he made note of Electra's appearance in the small datebook he carried with him. He would be there, of course.

Randy returned to his copy of *Rough Play* as the random moan issued forth from something called a Masturbatathon, in full swing down the hall.

What in God's name are these people thinking?

———•·•———

The sex library would have them, Electra was sure. The "them" in question were instructions for advanced Owari techniques. The curriculum notes left behind by her predecessor at The Refuge simply referred to that part of the workshop as "the Owari shit."

Not enough detail, clearly.

Electra made her way down-market past the once shabby, now venerable headquarters of Twitter. A scattering of twenty-somethings stood around outside smoking cigarettes and surveying their phones. A few wore sporty hipster glasses. They all looked tired.

Making the right on Ninth Street, Electra cut over to Mission and found her way to the door. The sex library was a somewhat secret place—or at least that's how the locals thought of it. And well it should be. It was probably the only library in the world that hosted its own Masturbatathon.

San Francisco's sex library was anything but a dusty old stack of sex manuals; heavens, no. Rather, it was part curio cabinet, part reading room, part shrine—all dedicated to eradicating any lingering squeamishness the world may feel about sex. Electra had no doubts they would not only have all the Owari instructions she needed, they probably knew, and even trained, her predecessor.

Electra buzzed and gave the fake name she had made her appointment with. "I'm here for the BDSM manuals," she said into the intercom. A sweet young Asian man in a Mickey Mouse T-shirt came downstairs and let her in. He said his name was Andy.

A few random moans of ecstasy could be heard issuing from a room at the top of the stairs as she ascended. "There are a few people here," he mentioned casually. "The Masturbatathon is on day three."

Sure enough, at the top of the stairs, a room on the right seemed to exude nothing but pheromones. Electra peeked in. Through the lowered, red light, she could see various people— nearly all of them men—spread out on mats around the floor. Most of them were frantically masturbating. The room stank of body odor and semen. She recoiled and backed away almost immediately.

"Wow," she said drily.

"Yeah, it's pretty intense," he agreed. Then he added on a chipper note, "It's an *awesome* fundraiser!"

They walked down a short corridor, its walls covered with posters for everything from erotic movies to AIDS prevention. A pair of passionately kissing women appeared in black and white behind the headline that said, "Read My Lips."

A jumble of books, dusty vases, and pieces of costumes dotted the hallway as well. A large stuffed hawk, wings akimbo, was mounted over a glass vitrine filled with small cylindrical objects. Electra looked more closely and saw they were aging dildos from another era.

They entered the main reading room of the library, and Electra stopped short. Sitting thirty yards away was Roscoe, absorbed in something he was reading. He did not look up. Immediately Electra backed into the hallway.

Shit, she thought, *he's here. He's fucking HERE.*

The young man turned and looked after her, confused. He poked his head into the hall. "Something wrong?" he asked.

Electra just kept backing down the hallway, trying to keep her expression as neutral as she could. "I want to go . . . to the Masturbatathon!" she said suddenly. "Can I buy a ticket? Right now?"

The young man brightened up. "Certainly," he said. "That will be seventy-five dollars. I can leave your materials on the table if you want."

"Fine," she said, practically running now toward the steamy room full of writhing, moaning men.

Electra paused outside the door and wondered how long she could linger in the hallway. She had to make a plan. If only she could see what Roscoe was reading. If only he would go to the bathroom or something. Then she could casually walk by and take a look. Thank God she was incognito.

Electra sauntered back up the hall a bit, looking for a hiding place, trying the various doors. She pulled open a door revealing a small bathroom just as the young man appeared beside her. "Here," he said, handing her a small towel. "For the Masturbatathon."

"Oh. Thanks," she said. They looked at each other awkwardly for a moment.

The young man cleared his throat. "That will be seventy-five dollars?" he said a little uncertainly.

Electra pulled her wallet out of her back pocket and peeled off four twenties. "Keep the change," she said.

"Just make a spot for yourself anywhere. Most people bring their own mats, but you don't have to," he explained. They hesitated again.

"Want me to walk you in there?" he suggested.

"No, I'm fine," Electra said. He watched her curiously for a moment until she turned, walked down the hall, and entered the Masturbatathon. "Have fun!" he called after her.

God Almighty, she thought as she walked in and surveyed the room. A few men looked up and one stopped, mid-stroke. "Over here," he said, patting the floor beside him.

Like hell, she thought grimly.

———•◦•———

Randy looked up from his reading. Something was happening.

The young Asian assistant was trying to coax someone into the library; it was a person he couldn't see. He took a deep breath. At such moments he could practically feel the Lord peering over his shoulder. He certainly hoped He wasn't offended by what he was looking at.

Returning to the pages of Rough Play, he stared dully at the leather-clad figure paddling a trussed, naked woman.

Randy flipped a few more pages, and then he suddenly stopped short as an unexpected shiver of lust passed through his body.

A double-page spread of BDSM partiers in various stages of undress spread out before him. One couple at the edge of the page caught his eye in particular—two barrel-chested, leather-clad men engaged in the act of fellatio.

Randy slammed the magazine shut and tried to ignore his own surge of excitement. He swallowed hard and counted to ten backward in his mind. This was his cure-all for unwanted bouts of lust. He would get through this.

Or maybe he wouldn't.

Turning the page, he stood up and headed for the men's room in the hallway. He could just about barely handle any of this.

———•◦•———

Electra had found refuge in the corner behind the lone woman in the Masturbatathon, a twenty-something MC named Jill who called herself "The Mistress of Orgasms." Jill's parents definitely did not know where she was.

"Come on, boys!" Jill invoked in a cheerleader voice. "Give it all you've got." She turned around and looked pointedly at Electra. "Someone in here's holding back . . ." she said in a playful singsong.

Electra was not only fully dressed but curled into a tight protective ball in her corner. "I'm just watching," she murmured to Jill, who smiled encouragingly. Twice already she'd tried to slip out, but the young assistant had been out in the hallway.

"I say your inner slut is aching to come out!" announced Jill. Then her look softened. "Maybe you need a hit of weed?

Or a cocktail? There's a bar around the corner . . ." she added helpfully.

Enough. Electra stood up and strode to the door. "Come on back when you're feelin' slutty," Jill intoned after her. "You're always welcome!"

Electra made her way carefully up the hallway and peered once again through the doorway of the Reading Room. A surge of adrenaline hit her as she noticed Roscoe was gone. In his place sat a stack of magazines and books. Beside them was a large leather datebook and a pen. He must have gone to the bathroom.

Quickly she made her way to his spot and surveyed the copy of *Rough Play* that was closed on the table. Electra surveyed his datebook, turning a page or two. It was crammed with all sorts of inscriptions, information. Odd pieces of paper were stuck in the pages here and there.

Something called "H.S." was inked in for three days the following week. *Hardly Strictly,* she thought to herself. Hardly Strictly Bluegrass was San Francisco's biggest outdoor event every year.

Putting down the datebook, she now noticed a catalog for The Refuge was open, facedown, beside a stack of books. Picking it up, she saw it was turned to the page about her workshop. Roscoe had apparently been reading all about it.

She closed her eyes for a moment. *He knew who she was.*

Andy the helpful assistant appeared once more by her side. "You're back!" he enthused. "How was the Masturbatathon?"

Electra just looked at him, casually replacing the catalog on the table.

"It's not for everyone," he prattled on lightly. "So your materials are over by the couch." He pointed to the velour divan in the shape of a large lavender high heel. "I found a few white papers on Owari I think you're going to love."

Then he lowered his voice. "I just want to say it's a real privilege to serve you, Miss Delacroix. I've been following your work for the last year, and I'm just such a big fan."

Electra rolled her eyes. Roscoe was due back in at any moment. Clearly she had to get out of here. "Thanks," she said tartly as she headed back toward the door.

"Oh. Wait! Did I say something wrong? I'm really sorry! Hey, Miss . . . uh . . . Electra? What about your materials?" Andy's voice trailed after her forlornly as Electra made her way fast down the stairs. She'd have to learn all about Owari some other place. Like online.

If it isn't one thing, it is always another, she thought grimly.

12

R andy flipped through the pages of his datebook. It was a small, leather-bound book, like the one given to him years ago by his father. He carried it whenever he traveled. It had his life in it.

Notes adorned every page—things he ate, quotes from Scripture, locations, appointments, ideas, insights, observations. All were recorded faithfully in the lined pages for each day in his slightly shaky, spidery handwriting.

Randy was not a believer in electronica in any form—nor did he need it. He got along just fine with the good old-fashioned telephone, the newspaper, his datebook. In fact, he didn't actually know how to use a computer.

Something called smartphones seemed to run the world now, but not to Randy. He preferred the connection to a live human on the telephone—and if he had to talk to a few robots to get there, it was worth the effort.

Randy made all his calls from a wired phone for good reason. No cell phone was going to track his comings and goings and dump them in the big universal database. He'd read all about that kind of surveillance in his favorite newspaper, The Christian Reporter.

Now a robotic female voice periodically advised him that his call was very important to them while a mellow samba intermittently came on the line. After several minutes, an agent finally picked up.

Randy didn't mind. He'd been praying. "Good morning, ma'am. I need to change my plane ticket," he began.

All he had to see was the notice that Pamela Delacroix was leading a class at The Refuge and he was in.

Even if he had to pay extra for a new plane ticket.

———•◦•———

"So what is so urgent that we had to meet live?" Charley began as he slipped into his seat. "You got me worried—I pedaled over here as fast as I could. Are you okay?"

"Yes, yes, I'm fine," Electra said, waving her hand dismissively.

The waiter set two steaming glasses of smoky Russian tea before them and retreated wordlessly. Around them, the good people of Hayes Valley chatted over steaming cups. The tea house was becoming Electra's local bar.

"It's this guy . . ." she began. Charley immediately raised his eyebrows.

"No, no—not like that," she added. Electra took a deep breath and continued. "Twice now I have run into the same very strange man. So strange I'm a little scared," she admitted.

Charley just looked at her. "I'm listening," he said.

"I mean, I have no reason to be worried about this guy. None at all. He's just some quirky person, but I keep running into him. And the last time . . ." She hesitated.

"Go on."

Electra took a sip of her tea and regarded Charley. "For better or for worse, I'm a celebrity now, and celebrities have stalkers, you know. This guy's a little too interested in me and my gig at The Refuge."

She went on to tell Charley about meeting Roscoe at The Folsom Street Fair and then finding him again at the sex library. "There was the brochure for my event right on the table in plain sight. Clearly he recognized me at the fair even though he pretended he didn't."

Electra paused, her tea cup in hand. "What if he's one of those quiet guys who turns out to be an axe murderer?"

Charley tilted his head. "Sweetheart, I think you're getting a little ahead of yourself," he said gently. "What makes you think he's a stalker? Maybe he genuinely wants to learn about BDSM. Why else would he have the books and magazines? Maybe he didn't recognize you at all . . . maybe it was just a coincidence."

"Charley, he gave me a fake name. I ran searches for Roscoe Stevens everywhere. On Google, Facebook, Instagram, even those cheesy background check sites. I looked for him, for his business. Nothing. I must have spent hours searching. There is no Roscoe Stevens in real estate anywhere, not even on LinkedIn."

"Unless he isn't online," Charley remarked. "Tell me more about what you think is so weird about this guy. Acting paranoid at the Folsom Street Fair is no guarantee of anything wrong, you know. I mean, it *is* Folsom Street."

"True. But I followed him that afternoon, Charley. He was clearly casing out the police."

"How do you know?"

"He kept following them, making notes on a little pad and pestering them for details. Then he pretended he was sick, but after they told him where the medical tent was, he went the other direction. The police even started to follow him until someone radioed and they got diverted. I'm telling you, Charley, this guy is a bona fide weirdo."

"And . . . ?"

Electra narrowed her eyes and leaned in to him intensely. *"He's coming to my workshop."*

"Ah." Charley nodded his head understandingly.

She rolled her eyes in frustration. "Is that all you're going to say? Must you be so typically male?"

The waiter placed the Russian Tea Service before them. It was a silver tray containing pickled beets, smoked salmon, horseradish, pickled eggs, and rye crackers.

Charley picked up a cracker. "Actually, I'm not typically male." *Here we go*, he thought. But then turning on a dime, he abruptly changed course. It occurred to him that now was not actually the time to come out to Electra. "So you think the dude's casing you out because he looked up your gig at the sex library?"

"Of course I do!" she burst. "I know he is. I can feel it!"

"Okay. So say he is a weirdo and a stalker of sorts, but he doesn't know that much about you. All you gave him was phone and email, right? You haven't been getting any strange phone calls, have you?"

"No," she admitted. In fact, part of her wished he would call. Then she could at least learn more about him.

"But what if he figures out where I live, Charley? Then . . . well . . . hell . . ." Electra's voice wound down into a small, sad whimper. She seemed near tears.

Charley reached across the table and took her hand. "I've got your back, love," he said. "Nothing bad is going to happen." Her hand was warm; it trembled slightly. She released it after a moment.

Electra wiped at the tears in her eyes furiously. "He can find my address online, you know."

"Are you sure?"

"Totally," she moaned. After the piece in the *Chronicle* appeared, anyone could find out she lived in San Francisco. "Remember the *Chronicle* piece?" she asked, and he nodded. "It even mentioned my neighborhood."

"All right, so that's a risk. But honestly if you're worried about it, hire security. It's a business expense," Charley added sensibly.

Electra closed her eyes. "I don't want some security guy," she said. Then, suddenly, her eyes flashed open. "I want you. Help me, Charley. Come to Hardly Strictly with me. He'll be there. Then you can see what I'm talking about. You need to do this with me." She looked at him beseechingly. "Please?"

"But, honey, Hardly Strictly is an absolute zoo—"

"I know. Seven hundred and fifty thousand people."

Charley gave a shrug and smiled. He really did have a hard time resisting this woman. "Okay. Sure," he said. "Count me in."

Electra was about to continue, but then she stopped, slightly startled. She wasn't expecting him to agree so quickly. "Oh— Okay! Great!" She paused to double-check. "Really?"

Charley tucked into his smoked salmon. "Sure. I'm convinced."

"We'll have to go all three days until we find him," she continued. "But if we scope out the police at various stages, we may find him sooner."

"Sounds like a plan," said Charley with a smile. "You are really invested in finding this guy, aren't you?"

"I have to be for my own safety," she said a little gruffly. "Anyway, it just feels right." Electra picked up a pickled beet with her fork. "I would love to get a picture of him."

"Hmm . . ." said Charley. Frankie came to mind. "Then we could use face recognition software," he said.

"Good idea—know anyone who has some?"

"Maybe," he murmured, returning to his salmon. This idea was taking shape. Of all the paths he thought he might get on with Electra, this was not one he had considered.

The coming out will have to wait, he thought to himself. There were bigger matters at hand.

13

Frankie stood in the latte line, feeling like warmed-over dog shit. Maybe she was getting a cold. On the other hand, maybe this was just more of the usual bleak unfolding, the numb feeling she always had moving through life without Dree. So far the day was not going well.

A couple in front of her was taking an incredibly long time to decide what the hell they were ordering. She felt like shaking them. *It's just coffee, people.*

Finally it was her turn. Frankie stepped up to the bored-looking young woman on the register just as a voice boomed out behind her left shoulder.

"I'm having what she's having." It was Constantine, from the CHP. "It's on me, Frankie," he added.

"Hey! Thanks!" she said, turning around. *Constantine is always such a nice guy,* she thought, *and definitely not in a creepy way.* Connie was the real deal—a colleague, a professional, a family guy with two little kids. It was people like him who made her want to be on the force in the first place. He never made off-color jokes. Never gave her shit about her size. Why were the Highway Patrol guys always like this?

"I'm having an iced venti latte, Connie," Frankie said with a grin. "It's got three shots—sure you can handle it?"

"I'll try," he noted wryly.

A few moments later, they walked up the street to his waiting patrol car, coffees in hand. Today Connie was directing traffic at a PG&E construction site near Mission and Second. "So you heard about Linsky?" he asked.

"Jerome Linsky? What?" Linksy was a well-regarded informant for the narc squad, among others. Many of the cops knew him, simply because he was so very good at getting the info that no one else could. Linsky was legendary, in fact. So legendary, even CHP folks like Constantine had heard about him.

"Dead," said Constantine. "Hit and run."

"When did this happen?"

"Couple days ago."

"Huh," she said. Frankie hadn't heard this, which was a little surprising. This was the kind of small talk that was always filtering through the station. Linsky was a well-known SRO dude who lived in the Tenderloin. His ear had been burned off in a meth accident many years earlier. He was one of the few who'd actually tried to clean up, but somehow never managed to. For a junkie, there was something honorable about him.

The police generally looked out for Linsky, and everyone knew it, mainly because he was so helpful. On the other hand, being an informant was a good way to get yourself killed.

"Any leads on who did it?" she asked.

"Nothing," said Constantine. "No witnesses so far. But no one's investigating. Seems a shame, you know? Like . . .

where's the respect? You'd think the department would feel . . . I don't know . . ."

A small, white-hot thought ricocheted through Frankie's brain. *Cover up?* She immediately dismissed it. "Yeah, I hear you," she said, switching gears. "So how long are you going to be around this part of town?"

"Month or so."

"Well, you know where to find me. I'm here every day at three getting jacked up before my shift starts."

Constantine smiled. "Hang in there, Frankie," he said after a moment.

"Right," she said. Connie was one of the few cops who knew about her funk. "Next one's on me," she added.

He nodded and was gone. Frankie turned to walk back to the station, full of thoughts.

———•◆•———

An hour later, Frankie was deep into an SFPD database. Specifically she was looking through the registry the DA kept on informant payments. She'd gotten it from one of her plainclothes friends who owed her one.

Back in her own plainclothes days, Jerome was always referred to as "Tenderloin Informer, disabled male, 47" in the registry. No one else got that particular description—this way everyone would know it was Linsky. His age was always the same; "disabled" was some kind of unofficial code for disfigured.

But there were no listings in the log for Linsky for at least the last four years. Frankie knew for a fact this was wrong.

She'd never actually looked through the back pages of the informant registry before. And she, herself, hadn't logged anything in since she stopped working as a plainclothes officer a few years back. Frankie flipped through page after page, moving backward through time. There was nothing there.

Draining the last of her iced coffee, she sat back to think. Then Frankie clicked to a new page, one that listed all the various department heads. She clicked through the various stations, noting who'd made it to lieutenant lately. One of them had been promoted from plainclothes to lieutenant in just the last year. Another made it to commander from plainclothes, skipping lieutenant altogether.

She knew for a fact that last dude, O'Leary, had screwed up his test. Conveniently, he managed to skip being a lieutenant. Of course, he still got to double his salary.

Like everyone else, Frankie had been patiently waiting for forever to apply for lieutenant and take the test. Now, armed with new information, she opened the registry and began combing through its back pages once again.

Fifteen minutes later, Frankie was satisfied. *Jerome Linsky did not die in vain,* she thought to herself. At least, not while she was sitting at an SFPD desk.

———•◦•———

My name is Charley, and I'm . . . well . . . I guess I'm not great with money.

This is how the meeting began for Charley. He shifted uncomfortably in his seat. He wouldn't even be here except that his Agency-appointed therapist insisted he go.

Even after three meetings, he couldn't see how not knowing an account balance or avoiding paying taxes meant you were an addict. Did this mean he was no better than all those people who took crystal meth or gambled compulsively? Charley tried to listen with an open mind.

A heavy, middle-aged woman shared about how she overcame her need to shop, about her garage full of unopened merchandise, about her out-of-control credit card bills. "In the beginning I was so ashamed," she said. "I just couldn't help it." Then she paused. "But the truth is I was really lonely. So instead of feeling my feelings, I shopped."

Charley shifted uncomfortably in his chair and glanced at the clock. Fifty-seven minutes to go.

The man to his left raised his hand and began to speak. "I know I have to open my mail every week," he said, "but somehow I just can't get myself to do it. It's . . . scary," he said. "My bills are overwhelming right now. I probably don't have enough to pay them—but I'm not really sure. So I'm asking for an action buddy who wants to bring their bills over. I figured we could open them together. See me after the meeting if that's you." He sat down.

Now Charley noticed he was beginning to sweat slightly. He closed his eyes.

Someone else began speaking about their tax troubles. "I haven't earned any money for fifteen months," he began, "but the IRS is about to put a lien on my bank account for all the back taxes I owe, which is . . . uh . . ." The man's voice became inaudible for a minute. Then he cleared his throat. "It's about $75,000." He paused. "I know I have to surrender here, but I just want to be done with this, you know? Apparently Higher Power has other plans for me. So I just need to say I'm going to call the IRS today. And I'm praying for guidance."

Charley thought to himself about his own meeting with his accountant yesterday. It had been like torture preparing for it. It had taken all week just to get himself to sit down and do it. Even with a deadline. Even with the Agency suspension. He'd been deluged with shame all day. Unlike the rest of these people, he had plenty of money.

"Are there any newcomers who wish to share?" a small, grey-haired woman in the circle asked.

No one raised their hand for a moment or two. Finally Charley raised his. *Might as well get this over with*, he thought.

"I'm Charley," he said again. "And I'm a . . . well, I don't know what I am. The fact is I've been suspended from my job because I didn't pay my taxes." He was silent for a moment. "I need help, I guess . . . I just . . ." He stopped wordlessly. Then, suddenly, without warning, Charley began to cry.

"Wow," he said shakily. "I can't believe I'm crying." He stabbed at his eyes with the back of his hands and rubbed them on his expensive jeans. He paused for a moment, trying to compose himself.

"I love my work. I live for it. Honestly. I do . . . and I don't know why I didn't pay my taxes. I guess there must be some reason. There has to be, right? I have the money. I just . . ." His voice drifted off uncertainly. "I don't know what's going on," he finally admitted.

The group was silent, waiting for him to finish. Charley sat down. "That's all," he said quietly.

"Welcome," intoned the group. "Keep coming back."

Charley knew he would, of course. Apparently he had no choice.

———•◆•———

Frankie did not scare easily—seldom, if ever. But at this moment, she was feeling an intense surge of adrenaline. She swallowed hard against it and looked the other sergeant in the eye as evenly as she could, trying to steady her breathing. No shootout was happening. There was no barricaded suspect, bomb threat, or natural disaster to deal with. They weren't even on the street. Instead, she was simply speaking to a fellow sergeant, right here in her own station.

"I thought you'd have heard about Linsky," she said as casually as she could.

The sergeant in question, Mulroney, shrugged noncommittally. "Nope. What did you say the name was? Pinsky? Never heard of him." He picked up some of the papers on his desk dismissively.

Yeah . . . right, she thought. This was, of course, obtuse bullshit.

"Sure about that, Mulroney?" Frankie asked. She remembered one Thanksgiving in particular about two years ago. She and Mulroney were the only sergeants on duty that day. She'd seen him walking up Market Street with Linsky. She remembered noticing the way they walked, almost as colleagues. Even then it struck her as odd. Such an out way to be with an informer, even if you were a sergeant.

Mulroney just glared at her over his papers. "You done?" he asked stonily.

Frankie pulled back. "Yeah, I'm done," she said. "Whatever."

Mulroney kept his focus on the file open before him. Frankie turned to leave. "Don't fuck with me, Kennedy," she heard him say as she was walking away. His words were barely audible.

Frankie turned around. "Did you say something to me?"

Mulroney looked up, half-surprised. "Huh?"

"What did you just say to me?"

"Nothing," he replied pleasantly before turning back to his

paperwork. Mulroney mustered a half-smile. "Have a nice night, Sergeant."

Frankie didn't reply. Instead, she stepped out into the night air. Reaching reflexively for her baton on the left and her firearm on the right, she began to walk.

Market Street was pretty much deserted at 1:15 in the morning, save for a few passed-out drunks lying facedown on the sidewalk. Frankie walked on and let them be. She had to calm down right now. She didn't doubt what she had heard, not for one moment. Mulroney was one of them. That was definite.

The only question was how many more were involved.

14

The N Judah train chugged along toward its eternal destination, the ocean. Randy sat wedged in between a grim Chinese woman and a chubby high school girl on the phone with a friend.

The teenage girl twisted her hair and snapped her gum. "I wouldn't trust the dude," she kept saying. "No way. No frickin' way."

Randy closed his eyes and touched the large wooden cross that hung from his neck. His mind darted randomly back to the night before—in particular, to the full-body sensations he had as he left Friday-night vespers. They were like chills as the Lord's presence cascaded through his body. It was an almost unbearable feeling, filled with portents.

Emerging into the settling night fog that night, he'd crossed Van Ness, passed by the village shops of Hayes Valley, and walked on. All he seemed able to do was walk.

The words of the Magnificat rang through his head as he pushed along, block after block.

He hath shewed strength with his arm: he hath scattered the
proud in the imagination of their hearts.
He hath put down the mighty from their seat: and hath exalted
the humble and meek.
He hath filled the hungry with good things: and the rich he hath
sent empty away.

As he climbed the twisting hills above the Castro, Randy's heart beat faster and faster. He passed simple, elegant lace-curtained windows glowing yellow and white, beaming interior life and light. He passed families having dinner, couples washing dishes, people attending to all the details of life. He, too, had a mission now—to serve the humble and the meek. Something was happening for sure.

Randy found his way to the pocket park called Mt. Olympus, and when he climbed the concrete steps to its pinnacle—a stone pedestal topped with nothing—finally he stopped. He sat down on the steps and surveyed the tiny lights of a hundred thousand lives spread out beyond him. Then, silently, he began to sob.

The Lord's message had become undeniably clear, and he felt its enormity. Randy understood exactly what he must do. Not only was he to annihilate the heathens gathered at the Bay to Breakers footrace, he was to begin that day by murdering Electra herself.

He could do this thing. He could do it and he would do it, for nothing less than God himself had given Randy this resolve . . . and this command.

He had been given the task of liberating the poor and downtrodden, and he would do it by first destroying the woman who symbolized the arrogant, the elite, the wealthy, the corrupt. What better way to send his message to the world than by murdering the Society Dom?

Sitting there in the darkness, Randy dried his eyes and shook his head at the incredulity of his life.

His time had truly come.

The idea was a picnic—which was great in theory. Except for the teeming life force that packs the Hardly Strictly Bluegrass Festival beyond capacity, all apparently with the very same plan. Not only was there no exposed patch of grass to sit on . . . there was scarcely anywhere to stand.

Electra and Charley backed away from the Banjo Stage in mild overwhelm. Walking into Golden Gate Park had been a tipoff, of course. All around them hordes of people streamed toward one central point, bearing picnic bags and lawn chairs, their Chardonnay carefully decanted into plastic and metal lest it be confiscated. The locals knew the deal.

Charley and Electra had never been to Hardly Strictly and were ill prepared for what lay ahead. Music boomed in the distance. Hardly Strictly Bluegrass was a wealthy philanthropist's parting gift—a completely free, unsponsored music festival that would just unroll, day by delirious day, until everyone finally dragged themselves home, exhausted, hung over, and saturated with music.

At this moment, Electra and Charley were heading for the Bonnie Raitt concert, which, they figured, would attract the most people at this hour.

The sheer masses of humanity were overwhelming as they neared the stage. People spread out in all directions, peppered only at the outskirts by blue-uniformed members of the SFPD.

Electra was beginning to feel hopeless already. "This was a ridiculous idea . . ." she began.

Charley stuck his hands in his pockets as he surveyed the crowd. "Not necessarily," he said. His gaze traveled up to the massive oak tree just above them. "Just a sec," he said. "Can you hold this?" He handed over the picnic basket and blanket to Electra.

She watched as he nimbly jumped up, grabbed the lowest branch, swung his legs up the trunk, and hoisted himself up onto the V in the tree trunk. Charley stopped and surveyed the crowd.

"How's it look?" she asked.

He reached out a hand. "Come on up," he said.

Electra hesitated, and then, kicking off her shoes, she grabbed on to the lowest branch and swung a few times before she got her own leverage against the trunk. She crawled up as far as she could. Then Charley braced himself, reached down a hand, and pulled her up the rest of the way.

They stood, bodies pressed together, surveying the massive crowd. Charley casually slipped an arm around Electra. "I don't see any grass, how about you?"

"To hell with the grass—I'm just trying to find Roscoe."

"Might be tough," murmured Charley, clinching her a bit closer. Electra did not resist. "What's he look like again?" he asked.

"Sandy hair, neatly dressed," Electra continued evenly, though she noticed her heart was beating a little faster. Actually, it was beating a lot faster. "And a mustache," she continued. "Also sandy. If this is anything like Folsom Street, he'll be checking out the police again."

"Good point—let's just watch them for a while." Charley looked over at her. "Comfortable?" he asked with a smile.

"Yeah," she said. "Just don't get any ideas."

They looked at each other. Electra glanced away shyly. "He's got to be here somewhere," she murmured.

"Quite so," Charley answered, his embrace tightening just the tiniest bit.

----•◆•----

Why in God's name does everything always have to be so loud? Randy thought to himself irritably. He could already hear the music blaring from the park all the way back at the N Judah stop, blocks away. He trudged on, resigned.

It was bad enough with all the liquor and lawn chairs and the endless sea of people that streamed up the street. But then Randy arrived at Hardly Strictly Bluegrass. When he saw the wall of speakers beside the stage as the first rock 'n' roll act began to play, his entire body reverberated with the sheer sound of the thing.

He had sensitive hearing—and this was far worse than Folsom Street on that scale.

Please, God, give me strength, Randy prayed. *Help me overcome the many obstacles ahead of me, including the large cloud of marijuana smoke I'm about to breathe.*

He wondered vaguely if one could get high from second hand pot smoke. To be on the safe side, he held his breath as he moved away from the clusters of twenty-something stoners just ahead of him.

Randy scanned the crowd with mild overwhelm, looking far and wide for a single uniformed police officer. Hell—he was scanning for anyone over fifty. Then his eyes hit on something unexpected. Up in a large tree less than fifty feet away was someone he recognized.

It was Electra.

Randy pulled the small binoculars he'd bought for the occasion from his fanny pack, focused them, and looked again. Then he lowered them, unable to believe what he'd just seen.

Once more he looked at the tall, blonde woman just ahead of him in the crook of a large oak tree. A tall man had his arm firmly around her, and the two appeared to be scanning the crowd together, waiting for something to happen. They were talking and laughing. He paused, rubbed his eyes, and peered at them once more just to be sure.

Randy stood stock still, his focus unwavering. Putting the binoculars back to his face, he clamped his protective sunhat down just a little more tightly. This was the perfect time to make contact, to learn more about her. He needed every bit of information he could get about this woman.

One more little gift from God, he thought. How much more obvious was the Holy Spirit going to have to get?

———•◦•———

"No dice," Electra said after a good half hour in the tree. "I want to get down now."

"Are you sure? The music's probably going to end soon and everyone will shift. We've got such a good vantage point up here."

"I just watched a dog pee on my shoes, Charley. Anyway, we're not going to find him this way. We'll have to try something else."

"Okay," Charley said easily. "Just watch yourself on the way down."

But Electra was already descending easily. *How many fifty-something women would hang out in a tree with him, let alone climb one?* "Are your shoes okay?" he asked as he saw her inspect them delicately, one by one. They seemed expensive. "Really sorry about that . . ." he added.

"Don't worry about it," she said with a shrug. "What's a little Jimmy Choo in a lifetime of good shoes?"

Exactly, he thought.

———————

Randy pressed himself up against a gated barrier and tried to keep his eye on the tree Electra was in, which was no small task. At this exact moment, a drunken, hollering, half-naked man covered with tattoos was coming his way—handed deftly overhead by a crowd who seemed to know exactly what to do as they passed him along.

Randy ducked and scurried to the right, pushing his way into the middle of a family of four. He was not going to be manhandling some bare-fleshed degenerate. "Sorry. Excuse me . . . sorry . . . just need to . . . move," he intoned firmly as he pushed along blindly into the crowd.

The drunken young man passed overhead to Randy's immediate left; the Gothic cross around his neck dangled and flashed in the sunlight as he screamed something loud and unintelligible. Meanwhile, Randy's foot landed squarely in a container of potato salad as he bashed his way through another picnic and somehow kept on going.

"Fucking asshole!" fumed the owner of the potato salad. Randy looked back, wordlessly. He had to keep moving. A moment later, he remembered Electra. Craning around a gaggle of swooning women sitting on their boyfriends' shoulders, he trained his binoculars on Electra's tree just in time to see her companion drop from the tree.

Electra was nowhere in view.

Randy pushed on in their general direction, stepping in and around as many people as he could worm past. He would find her—no, them—again. He would find them if it took all day and half the night.

Please, Lord, he prayed. *Help me now as you've never helped me before. If you want me to be your vehicle of justice, your street sweeper of the heathens, please show me now. Show me, Almighty Lord—show me that I am your messenger of light.*

Up ahead, he saw a flash of blonde hair. He could see a very tall woman from the back. That had to be her. Or was it? It was hard to tell. His heart speeded up as he stumbled over another twenty people in legal lawn chairs. He simply couldn't look down or he would lose her. That much he knew. Randy advanced blindly on the blonde woman, intoning another prayer under his breath while calculating what he would say.

"Hey, man! Watch it," he heard someone say just to his left. And then . . . just as he looked up, the blonde woman turned around. His heart sank. It wasn't Electra.

Randy stopped stock-still. The crowd was now on its feet, giving a standing ovation. People whistled and stomped, and screamed with all their might. Randy stumbled and fell as he pushed vaguely on toward the edge of the crowd. He landed near an especially muddy pair of black sneakers as a helping hand pulled him up.

"You okay?" asked the man with a thick accent. "You okay?" he repeated.

"Fine! Fine," Randy flustered as he dusted off his pant legs and pushed on. There was no time to talk, no time to think. There was no time to do anything right now except find Electra. *Please, God, please, God, please.*

Out of the corner of his eye, he spotted the man Electra had been with in the tree. He appeared to be lingering on the edge of the crowd, talking to a police officer, of all things. Randy turned and hung back instinctively, backing toward the nearest tree. And just then, Electra came into clear view.

She joined the man she was with and began listening to what the police officer was saying. She had her back to him, but occasionally she turned. He could see from her profile that it was definitely her. Though he was only twenty or thirty feet away, Randy could not hear what was being said.

For an instant, he froze, unsure of what to do.

Help me, Lord, he prayed. *Tell me how to use this moment to our best advantage.* Then the answer tumbled down as it always did: *Kneel down.*

He followed obediently and knelt right there on the trampled grass of Golden Gate Park, beside two retirees in their low lawn chairs who looked at him curiously over their camping mugs. Clamping his eyes shut, Randy raised his hands in prayer.

I am kneeling, Lord. I am here. I am your missive, your vessel, your vehicle. Do with me what you will, my God. Use me as you will. Tell me what to do . . . please, tell me what to do.

"Roscoe?" His eyes sprang open. It was Electra, standing right in front of him. The man she was with strode up behind her as he slipped a cell phone into his pocket.

Slowly, Randy rose, brushing the mud from his trousers. "Electra! Hello," he said as casually as he could. "I was just . . ."

What—praying? Randy didn't finish his sentence.

"You remember me," she remarked.

"Oh, yes . . . yes," he murmured. "Indeed I do."

"I thought you were going to call me."

"Yes, well . . . maybe. I said maybe I would." He nodded.

"You still have my number, right?"

Randy found himself oddly tongue-tied. What should he say? He had no idea, so he said nothing.

"Why don't you give me your number as well?"

"No—I—" Randy stopped short of saying he did not have a cell phone. "I'm leaving tomorrow," he suddenly announced.

"Oh." A flicker of disappointment crossed Electra's face. "Good visit?"

"Yes. Oh yes. It was a fine visit."

"Back to Ohio, then?"

"Illinois." *Wait—why did he say that?* Randy's mind scrambled and spun as he tried to backtrack. "Or the . . . Midwest. You know . . ." he added weakly.

"Okay. Well, you take care now. Come on back and visit us again in the Bay Area," she said jauntily, and she stuck out her hand. He took it, and they exchanged a limpid handshake.

"Bye, Roscoe." She simply stood there, looking at him, as did her companion. He could tell they were studying him for some reason, and immediately he felt a flicker of discomfort.

"Bye," he said. Then they turned and began to walk out of the crowd of concert-goers. How he wanted to run toward them at that moment, screaming for them to stop. All of his denial, his lust, his rage, his sheer fear boiled up into his heart like some massive, intractable Gordian knot.

He found himself wanting to warn her just as much as he wanted to kill her.

Seeing her live and in person—all six feet of her—had been an oddly disquieting experience. Who was he to murder this woman, or anyone for that matter? Who was he but a broken, sad son of a once great man now dead? Randy suddenly felt very small.

Ashamed, he gave a shuddering sigh and slowly walked back to the N Judah. He would find sanctity at the Mariposa, the Chinese cafeteria he'd been going to night after night. There he would eat his dinner and wait patiently through the night for Sunday services.

As ever, His will would be done.

Electra and Charley stood looking at his phone. There it was, in perfect technicolor—a full frontal of Roscoe looking mildly embarrassed. He was half-crouching, as if he was straightening his pant legs, and a large wooden cross dangled awkwardly from his neck. He gazed up at Electra whose back was to the camera.

"Nice," she said simply. "That should get us somewhere."

"Yeah," Charley concluded. "Let me see what I can do with it."

"You do get what I meant about the guy? He's weird, right?"

Charley nodded. "Yeah, he's weird," he said. They looked at each other. The sun touched on her blonde hair for a moment, illuminating her face with a near halo, and he felt something in his solar plexus shift slightly.

"The cross is new," Electra conjectured. "Do you suppose he's an evangelical?"

A fan clutching a cell phone suddenly appeared beside them. "Are you the Society Dom?" she asked Electra. Electra glanced over and shook her head. "No, I'm not," she answered evenly.

"Sorry," the young woman said.

"Don't worry about it—happens all the time," Electra said dismissively. Her eyes returned to Charley. He nodded slowly. "He could be an evangelical," he concurred. "It's worth checking out."

Electra was softening toward him; she could feel it. "So are you going to help me or what?" she asked.

"Yeah," he said softly. "I am. But first, can I walk you home?"

Electra smiled and put her arm in his. *This is going to be fun,* she thought to herself with a smile.

Hell, it already was fun.

CHAPTER

15

"Electra, quit being weak."

Intoning these words was a small, thin woman with large eyes, long mousy hair, and bad teeth. Small silver studs pierced the nipples of her breasts, which were clearly visible in the cutaway vinyl corset she wore as she circled Electra. She carried a crop behind her back as she strode around the room in her black motorcycle boots.

Miss Kitty was Electra's dom coach. And today she was taking no shit.

Electra swallowed hard. "What?" she said a little tremulously.

"You said you don't know if you're good enough to do paid gigs. You're the Society Dom, for fuck's sake. A million doms would pay to be in your shoes . . . and you're practically throwing it away. I mean—be responsible!" chided Miss Kitty.

Now she stopped behind Electra and ran the tip of her crop along her spine, just visible above her camisole. "You know exactly what I'm talking about, sweetheart . . ." she cooed in a softer tone.

"Well, no, I don't," concluded Electra. "That's why we're sitting here, Kitty."

"Miss Kitty," the coach warned. She circled around and bent over to look into Electra's eyes.

"Yes, ma'am," Electra answered compliantly.

Miss Kitty dropped into a chair opposite Electra and crossed her legs. "Electra, you don't really have a choice here," she said. "What can I tell you? They want you."

Electra inhaled and closed her eyes. "God," she said.

Miss Kitty rolled her eyes. "Oh boo hoo hoo. Get over it, honey. You know what the truth is?" Miss Kitty continued. "You could be the world's worst dom and they wouldn't even care. Once you get plastered all over *People, USA Today*, and the *National Enquirer*, you're the flavor du jour. You're the friggin' Society Dom. Whether you like it or not, you now have an obligation to the public."

"Jesus! Okay, okay, *okay!*" Electra muttered. How was she going to turn this woman off? Even though she'd stopped smoking long ago, suddenly she craved a cigarette. Or a shot of vodka. Hell, even a hit of pot would do right now.

"I mean . . . what's the big problem?" Miss Kitty rattled on. "You don't even have to know what you're doing. You just put on the clothes, get out the cuffs, the manacles, the chains, the flogger. You get your—"

"Stop!" Electra stood up. Suddenly she was boiling with anger. "Just fucking stop, would you?" she shrieked, her voice ratcheting up in anger. "Just . . . leave! We're done here."

Miss Kitty sat back and looked at her admiringly. "Now that's more like it," she said, breaking out in a grin. "It appears my work here is finished."

Was it? Electra stopped, mildly confused. When she'd hired a dom coach, she'd imagined she'd be showing her . . .

well, at least where to buy better stilettoes. She had no idea it involved ritual bullying.

"Nothing like a little humiliation to rev the engines, huh?" said Miss Kitty, buttoning up her lacy little blouse. "Works every time."

"Whatever," said Electra, holding the door open. "As you know, I've got a signed NDA from you, so don't even think of talking to the press. My lawyers know how to draw blood."

"Not to worry," said Miss Kitty with a smile as she exited. "Looking forward to our next session."

"As if," Electra hissed.

The door clicked behind Miss Kitty, and Electra sat down again on the wooden chair. She had to admit it; she did feel remarkably better. Maybe there was something to this life coaching. She reached for her cell phone. Charley was going to love this one.

<hr />

R.J. popped on Charley's computer screen, looking slightly distracted. The crummy government web connection always made him look slightly pixilated on Skype. "What's up?" he asked gruffly.

Charley did his best to keep the conversation moving. "Hey, boss!" he began as cheerfully as he could. R.J. did not reply but just sat there looking at him.

"So I have a lead that might be worth pursuing here, and I need an in at the FBI," Charley continued. "It's more of an enforcement issue. A possible terror suspect."

R.J. was not impressed. "Charley, you're still suspended. Your security clearance is toast."

"I know, I know, but this is for real, R.J. Technically it's not spying; it's enforcement. I have a friend who happened to find this guy at this big leather—well, never mind where . . . Anyway, the dude stood out in a crowd." Charley found himself talking faster and faster. "He's an oddball, loner, totally fits the profile. Definitely worth watching, R.J.," he finished a little breathlessly.

"Enforcement is not our gig and you know it, so give it a rest, Charley. Go spend a little more time at Debtor's Anonymous." Clearly R.J. had been checking in with Charley's Agency-appointed therapist.

"I got a picture of this guy, R.J. If I could just get into some face recognition software, I could find him. I know I could. He's totally off the grid otherwise."

R.J. coughed and looked away. He busied himself with the paperwork on his desk. "Can't help," he said without looking up. "Is that all?"

Charley felt stung. This was not the reception he'd been hoping for. "R.J.—please. This is for real."

"So were last year's taxes. How are they coming?"

"Filed. Paid. Done. Complete . . . and I'm working with the forensic auditor. I just have to find some . . ." Charley's voice faded. He hadn't been able to locate the requested paperwork, and frankly he was a little scared of the auditor. The guy was a total automaton.

R.J. stopped and looked directly at the camera. "You just have to find *what?*"

Charley shook his head. "Oh, nothing. Just some paperwork that's in storage in my house. Really. It's no biggie. I've got it, boss."

R.J. sighed. "Get with it, MacElroy. The jobs are piling up here, assuming we can even get you back. So quit fucking around, okay?"

Charley said nothing.

"I'm sorry, Charley," R.J. said with a glimmer of affection. "I wish I could help." Suddenly the screen went black. R.J. had clicked off.

Charley sighed and looked out the window. He hadn't expected R.J. to be quite that cold. Closing his eyes, he fought the approach of tears. The Agency was family to him, and suddenly the family wanted nothing to do with him. *Shit.*

He seriously had to go find that paperwork.

Pulling himself off the couch, Charley stood up, put his hands on his hips, and thought about where it might be. He had no choice; he had to tear apart the attic. And if he didn't have the fucking paperwork, there had to be some other way out. He'd pay the goddamn $76,000 himself if he had to.

No asshole in accounting was going to keep him from doing his job.

"Why couldn't we just meet at a restaurant?" Frankie asked as she walked up to Charley. "Anyway, why are we meeting here?" They were standing on a deserted street corner in the middle of the Sunset, a largely Asian enclave on the cold, foggy side of San Francisco.

He turned around. "Hey!" he said pleasantly, giving her a pat on the shoulder. "Shall we walk?"

"Sure," she said. They began to walk toward the reservoir. "So there's something about me you don't know," he began.

"Beyond being a transman?"

"Yeah."

"Go on."

"I'm with the Agency," he said simply. "Covert operations, usually in Europe."

Frankie looked at him with eyebrows raised. "And why are you telling me this?"

"Because I need your help, Frankie. I've got an enforcement issue—it needs a delicate touch."

Now she understood why they were going for a walk. Frankie sighed. "What did you do, Charley?"

"Me? Nothing!" He laughed. "No, no. I have a friend who keeps running into this very weird guy. He may be stalking her or possibly planning a terrorist action. I don't have anything real—not yet, at least. But he totally fits the profile, and I'm dying to get a wire on him."

"So wait a minute. Stop. Why do you need me? Why can't the Agency hook you up with the FBI?"

Now Charley sighed, and his voice dropped a little. "I'm suspended," he admitted. "I didn't file my taxes last year." He didn't bother to get into the part about the expense report.

Frankie raised her eyebrows. "Jesus—you mean you got benched, too?"

Charley nodded, and now Frankie laughed out loud. "That's incredible!" she burst. "How did we ever find each other?"

Charley shrugged and pointed to the heavens.

Frankie gave a snort. "That's enough of that! So what do you want from me exactly?"

"Help me out. Let's find out what this SOB is up to," he said. "Let's get a wire on him either through the SFPD or the FBI if you know somebody. Someone in law enforcement has to care."

"The NSA has wires, but I don't know anyone there. And my FBI connections are all in bed with my commander who hates my guts right now. So I can't help you there either."

"So I'll get one online."

"But if he hasn't done anything yet, I can't stop him. I have no jurisdiction. I can only tag along while you plant the bug, and we can watch him. If we get him making a confession or there's clearly a life-threatening situation, then . . . sure, I can help. And I can get backup."

"Awesome," Charley said. "I know I can't do this alone."

They reached the reservoir and sat down on a bench. There wasn't a soul around at that moment. The Pacific was visible from their berm, a great blue swath, vast and glittering in the California sun. To their right, the Golden Gate Bridge was a burnt orange footnote.

"So you think this would help you get your job back?" Frankie asked.

"God only knows. I paid my taxes—I'm being a good boy. But there's some bullshit going on about my last expense report. My partner on that job screwed around with the numbers so it looked like I stole some money. They've got a forensic accountant who wants every receipt I've ever had." Charley sighed. "I'm just hoping I even have them."

"Oh, Jesus," Frankie commiserated.

Charley scratched his beard. "Right now, my boss is so pissed, he'll barely speak to me. But if we get something on this dude or force a confession, well . . . it's *got to* help."

"Why not just deal with the fucker who doctored the books?" suggested Frankie.

"Nah," said Charley. "That's not going to get my job back. I've got to keep it clean, you know?" He turned to her. "If this guy is for real and we can stop him and prove it, it will help us both. I imagine you can take it straight to the top, right past your so-called commander."

"Maybe," said Frankie reflectively. "Stranger things have

happened." She sighed just a little wearily. The commander and his cronies really did seem like an insurmountable monolith at that moment. "Let me think about it," she demurred.

Charley nodded and turned back to their view of the sea. She would come around in time, he suspected.

He knew there was a reason they met.

16

Randy poked at the remains of his breakfast with his spoon. Two organic blueberries and a few stray buckwheat flakes floated around in the remaining pool of skim milk. He felt listless, and he really didn't know why. He wondered if he had been in San Francisco too long. Was it time to go home?

He looked around at the would-be trendy furnishings of the Napier Hotel. The formerly dingy room had been upgraded with hip checkered carpet, modern light fixtures, and paint in colors like espresso and tomato. It was clean, cramped, and clearly not home.

He missed his bed and his vegetable patch—God knows whether his pole beans were still alive. And he missed Thumper. How he missed that dog. He picked up his worn copy of the King James Bible and thumbed through it. Then he put it down on the bed again.

Randy began to pace.

Tonight he had to go to a BDSM club called The Refuge to see Electra do . . . well, whatever it was that she did. She was teaching something called "Ropes, Gags, and Spanks." *Sounds just lovely*, he thought grimly.

Frankly, he was sick of the gritty, down-in-the gutter feeling he got every time he went to one of these dens of iniquity. There was something so bleak, so heartless about it. Yet, it was all so utilitarian and matter of fact. It made him feel physically ill.

Still, at the same time, he had to admit there was something secretly thrilling about it as well. Randy couldn't quite tease out whether it was the prospect of serving God so completely and fully that filled him with wonder—or was it something else? There was that somewhat giddy feeling he'd gotten when he was dressing for the Folsom Street Fair. He'd shaved and dressed so carefully that day. Yes, there was excitement in doing God's bidding. Yet, there was also a dark, forbidden sense to it he could scarcely acknowledge.

The sight of the men in their harnesses and their boots excited him. But, of course, that was just the shock of the new, wasn't it? He wasn't *really* moved by it at all, was he? How could he possibly be? They were the vilest of sinners, for Lord's sake! At the same time, he wondered, what about all the young girls in their vinyl dresses?

Why weren't the girls turning him on?

Could it be all those tattoos?

No, no, no, Randy decided. One couldn't help but be swept along by the tsunami of degradation that seemed to be everywhere in San Francisco. But, then, that was the Devil for you, always working himself in around the edges. This was merely what it was like to be a tourist in Sodom and Gomorrah just before their day of fire and brimstone.

Straightening his tie in the mirror, Randy checked himself once more and decided to go for a walk in Union Square.

He'd been in this godforsaken city for nearly six weeks, and he had yet to do anything resembling fun. Maybe he'd take a cable car ride.

Either way, he had to get out of this hotel room. The knot of anxiety in his gut was threatening to become more than he could take.

It really was time to go home.

Charley chewed the tip of his pencil and contemplated the empty notebook before him. Then he took another long swig of the pale ale he was using to get through his Forth Step. A grey-bearded biker ambled in and took a seat at the bar. Charley listened idly as he chatted with the bartender. Apparently his name was Tiny, and his usual was a Dewar's neat.

Charley had chosen an ancient bar in North Beach to work in simply because he needed to be alone . . . but not too alone. A pale ale was going to go down a whole lot better than some designer latte made by a Mission hipster. Anyway, these days SF coffee bars were always so packed with coders, it was hard to get a seat. On a Saturday afternoon, Charley knew the only place to find a little peace and quiet was at one of the city's crustier bars.

At the moment, he was supposed to be filling out a workbook assignment for his DA sponsor. It was a grid listing the people or institutions he'd had a grudge against, the cause of his resentment, and what his part was in that conflict. Charley thought and chewed his pencil a little more. The problem was that he didn't have a lot of resentments. He just . . . didn't. His parents didn't even fit into those narrow crosshairs, despite the fact that he seldom saw them while growing up.

After a few moments, Charley decided to move on to the section where he listed all his fears. That seemed easier somehow. Several minutes later, however, he still hadn't written anything. There was always his perennial fear of spiders, which probably didn't count. He couldn't seem to come up with another.

Charley took another long sip of his ale. He had to get serious here. His sponsor was going to be looking at this grid in less than twenty-four hours and expecting results. In the absence of finding any fears, Charley moved on to the section on pride. How did he demonstrate pride, the workbook asked, and how did this lead to denial and excuse-making?

Denial. There was that word again. As in the denial of reality—like *none of those U.S. laws about paying taxes actually apply to me*. Charley sighed. Okay, okay. Denial was an issue for sure. He didn't pay his taxes because he found things such as administrative details unconscionably boring.

Charley swallowed and thought of his accountant's secretary, Rosemary, leaving entreaty after entreaty over the phone. Each one had sounded more and more desperate. He sighed as a surge of shame poured through him. This was becoming un-fun. Which was probably the point.

"What fear created this act of pride?" asked the workbook. *Hmm*, thought Charley. There was that fear business again. Something fluttered in his chest and threatened to well up.

A waitress walked by and plunked a plastic basket of Ritz crackers and a block of orange cheese onto his table. At 3 p.m., the bar was populated by a handful of funky misfits. Two aging men played checkers at the next table, while a woman in a hat decorated with rows of playing cards sang loudly to herself, her song unrecognizable. A younger man quietly read a paperback at the bar. The Weavers could be heard playing softly in the background.

What in God's name was he so afraid of that he would willfully break the law and lose his security clearance? He had to be afraid of something.

Fear of intimacy came floating into his mind. Which seemed right, given his track record and his on-going, endless deliberations about getting a penis.

Enough of this, Charley thought, draining the rest of his ale. "Check, please?" he asked the bartender abruptly.

A moment later, Charley wandered out, blinking, into the sunlight. *Fear of intimacy* continued to ricochet through his brain as he walked, hands in pockets. He was going to Electra's in just a little while to teach her how to use the fountain pen recording device he'd just purchased. Then they were going straight to her BDSM workshop.

He noticed he felt the slightest bit nervous.

Actually, he felt seriously nervous. As far as Charley could tell, his affection for Electra was not being returned. Which simply made him want her all the more. *Did* he have fear of intimacy . . . and if so, was that why he was so hot for a woman who professed no interest in him?

Is that why he liked to lie awake at night and think about her? Or why he checked his phone several times a day to see if she'd responded to his texts? Was that why Charley wondered at any given moment what Electra was doing or where she was?

Maybe there is *something to this so-called fear of intimacy*, he thought to himself. But what in God's name did it have to do with not paying his taxes? Charley was confused.

Still, the sun was shining, and he was soon to see Electra. And it was Saturday.

That was certainly good enough for now.

———————

Electra began to pace. Charley was fifteen minutes late. *Where the hell is he?*

She tugged at the corset she was wearing. She was wearing her classic black velvet today, and its steel bones were beginning to warm and expand. It was time to yank the laces ever so slightly tighter. It was the first time she'd appeared in front of Charley, or the general public, in her full dominatrix regalia. She wanted to look as perfect as she could. Her workshop was starting in exactly seventy-nine minutes.

Electra undid the bundle of tightening loops. Then, isolating the center laces, she yanked up the lower one to squeeze her ribcage just a little tighter. Her bosoms pressed forth slightly. As they did, the buzzer sounded.

Shit.

Grabbing the center laces with a death grip, Electra toddled over to the intercom and answered that she'd be there in a minute. Then, locating the top lace, she yanked it down and felt her waist contract ever so slightly. She inspected her more defined curves in the mirror. It was always worth it to tighten up her corset, despite the feeling that she couldn't quite breathe.

Tugging here and there to even things out, she finally tied the excess laces in a neat bow and admired herself one last time. Now she could let Charley in.

———————

Charley looked mildly shocked when Electra answered the door. Stepping inside, he couldn't help but look at her body pouring forth from her corset, and the long legs that followed, encased in black hose. He seemed temporarily dumbstruck.

"This is just for work," she said lightly, offering her cheek for a kiss. "You know, the workshop and everything."

"Yeah . . . oh, wow," he managed to murmur as he gave the required peck on her cheek. He didn't know what else to say. There was no end to the surprises with this woman.

Charley could feel his heart pounding. There was a brief, awkward silence. He had to calm down. He swallowed hard and followed her into her kitchen.

"Did you bring the wire?" she asked.

"The pen! Yes!" Charley whipped the fountain pen out of his pocket, relieved to have something other than Electra's spectacular body to focus on. He pointed out the tiniest of microphones on the tip of the cap. "It's voice activated," he said. "All you have to do is slide the clip up to turn it on before you approach him. Then it will just start recording on its own."

"I thought I'd carry it with a notebook—as if I'd been making notes."

"Yeah, yeah. Perfect," he said. Charley swallowed again. Suddenly he felt unbearably shy with Electra. He hoped he wouldn't start to sweat.

"Does it work?" she asked.

"Huh?"

"The pen—does it work?"

"Oh, you mean as a pen? Yes! Absolutely. It works just fine. It's . . . blue," he concluded. *Is my voice shaking?*

She stopped and looked at him curiously. "Are you okay?"

Charley stuck his hands into his pockets and, nodding his head, mustered up a smile. "Totally! Everything's great."

They walked into the kitchen where she'd gathered her materials for the workshop. The studded black leather handle of a cat o' nine tails protruded from her Prada tote bag.

Jesus, he thought to himself. *This is for real.*

He watched Electra take her trench coat from the closet and put it on over her lingerie. She poked at her hair in the mirror after she buttoned up her coat. Then she reapplied her lipstick. "Nervous?" he asked.

"Mmm-hmm," she said lightly. Then she looked at him. "Don't bring it up again."

"Oh. Sure . . . fine." Charley cleared his throat. "Shall we go?"

Electra glanced at her watch. Sixty-three minutes to show time. "Yeah." She picked up her bag. "Let's walk."

Less than fifteen minutes later, they rounded the corner of Sixteenth and Mission and Electra let out an audible gasp. "Oh, Jesus," she said. A huge crowd had assembled outside The Refuge. She wondered how they would get through it.

Charley looked at her wide-eyed. "They're all here for you?" he asked.

Electra stepped out of sight into a nearby alley. "Just ask someone," she hissed. "I'll wait here." *Fuck,* she thought miserably. *This is much worse than I expected.*

She glanced at her silenced phone as she waited. There were at least four messages from The Refuge people. *Bouncer in black will bring you inside safely,* said the last one.

Charley returned in less than a minute. "They're in line for you, but no worries," he said. "I used to be an offensive lineman."

Electra put on her sunglasses and pulled up her collar as Charley slipped a protective arm around her. "Okay," he said, pausing. "I'll be between you and the crowd. Just tuck your head and move fast. Ignore everyone. Don't turn your head. Don't look at anyone. Just keep on moving." Before she could answer, they were off.

She felt almost weightless by his side as he muscled her up the street. Her feet were barely on the ground as they rushed the length of the block. Predictably, the crowd spotted her and started calling after her. "Society Dom!" shouted some, while others screamed and whistled.

Charley tightened his grip around her as the din from the crowd got louder. She glanced over her shoulder. The crowd had begun to move up the street after them.

"They're moving in on us," she murmured.

"Hang tight," he said as people seemed to converge on them from every direction. She could feel a hundred hands reaching for her, touching her, pulling at her clothing. Cell phones were waving everywhere. "Hey, Electra!" someone yelled. At least they were learning her new name, she noted.

Meanwhile, Charley was doing his best to push the offenders away. "Head down," he barked at Electra. Putting out his hand, he pushed her through a knot of paparazzi photographers who suddenly appeared. They scattered like ninepins, flashes popping as they went. She felt limp and trusting in his arms, like a rag doll being dragged to the playroom.

The entire crowd was chanting her name in unison by the time they reached the door:

So-ci-ety DOM!
So-ci-ety DOM!
So-ci-ety DOM!

An enormous black-clad bouncer at the door grabbed Electra's free arm and pulled her and Charley inside. Then he closed the door and locked it behind them. The crowd began hammering on the door, screaming for her.

"Jesus," he said. "It's like the Beatles at Hollywood Bowl." Shaking his head, he unlocked the door and once again slipped out into the fray. "Quiet down, people!" they heard him bellow to the crowd. "No one's going anywhere until you all stop."

Electra took a deep breath and leaned against the wall. She was completely unprepared for this.

———•◦•———

Charley stood at the edge of the audience with his hands in his pockets. The place was packed, and the crowd was growing impatient. Electra still hadn't emerged. He scanned the crowd for Roscoe. He found him sitting up front in the third row, arms folded across his chest.

Now the owner of The Refuge took the microphone and gave his introduction, citing Electra's long list of media appearances. "This is," he said soberly, "a historic event." The crowd stamped and whistled and began shouting her name again. Still Electra did not appear.

Finally the bouncer appeared and repeated his message to be quiet.

The crowd stomped and whistled, refusing to be quiet. Until finally, after several more agonizing minutes, Electra came striding up the center aisle to thunderous applause. In an instant, the crowd was on its feet, cheering wildly.

She was stunning as she stood there on the small makeshift stage, holding her black leather riding crop. Electra did not speak, but instead she simply surveyed the crowd for one moment, and then two. Then three. The room became increasingly quiet as the crowd watched her curiously.

She began to tap the crop slowly against her hand as she walked into the audience. Slowly, she walked down the length of the center aisle and back once again. Another moment ticked by. Still, Electra didn't say a word.

The crowd was completely silent now, watching her every move. Suddenly, Electra slammed the crop down on a Formica table near the stage, making the two people sitting in the front row jump. Then she turned to the crowd.

"Good," she finally said. "I'm glad you're behaving yourself. Because . . . really . . . you wouldn't want to get punished, would you?"

The audience roared its approval. Electra was on, and she was hot.

She ran her riding crop around the head of a young man sitting at the table. "You wouldn't want to get punished, would you?" she asked him. The young man swallowed. He looked both terrified and delighted. Quickly, he shook his head.

Electra turned to the crowd. "How many people found that thrilling?" she asked. Nearly everyone raised his hand.

Everyone, Charley noted, except Roscoe.

———•◆•———

Ninety minutes later, Electra was a hot, sweaty mess. The line of ardent fans eager to speak to her snaked through the space and back out the door.

Meanwhile, assorted screams, moans, and cries from the dungeon drifted up through the balconied hole in the floor. The section on whipping had been particularly popular. Randy waited in line to speak to Electra and found himself glancing over the railing to see a man suspended upside down in a web of intricately tied ropes. He was being flogged by a smaller man dressed in little more than a pair of leather chaps and a pair of nipple clamps.

The hanging man was literally crying for mercy as bleeding welts covered his slowly rotating body. A crowd of spectators cheered him on.

Randy winced and turned away. How in God's name could this possibly be fun? He turned his attention to Electra who was just ahead. He wasn't sure exactly what he'd say to her. He just knew God had told him to come—and that this would somehow inform his plans. The more he knew about her, the clearer her murder would become.

Meanwhile, that younger man he'd seen her with in the park was lingering nearby. Randy had watched him pushing photographers out of the way as he rushed Electra up to the door. Maybe he was her bodyguard. On the other hand, he could be her boyfriend.

A moment later, Randy approached the table Electra sat at. She looked up wearily, and then her face changed completely. "Roscoe!" she said brightly. Picking up her pen, she asked, "An autograph for you, too?"

"No, no," he said. "I just wanted to pay my respects."

Electra leaned toward him and looked at him almost perniciously, her pen still poised in midair.

Electra dropped her voice. "I'm so glad you came, Roscoe. I wanted to add you to my contacts, but I couldn't find your card anywhere," she said. "You know I'd love to have you in my Rolodex," she finished almost breathlessly.

"Oh . . . I don't carry a card," he replied tightly.

"No worries," she said, pulling her phone out of her bag. "What's your cell phone number?"

Randy was momentarily dumbstruck. "I don't . . . I don't

have a cell phone," he finally stammered. This was not going well. *Why did I have to tell her that? Please help me, Lord . . . help me.*

Suddenly, a wave of inspiration poured through him. "I had no idea you could do so much with ropes," he said. "You're very good with knots."

"We used to own a sailboat," Electra said dismissively. "But let's talk about you. I thought we were going to meet sometime . . . maybe just for a coffee?"

An opening, he thought. *A blessed opening.*

"Yes . . . a coffee is a grand idea."

"When?" she asked.

"Well, I don't know . . . but I have your number."

"Of course you do. Call me, Roscoe. If you can find your way to a phone, that is," she added. Taking his hand for a moment, she looked deeply into his eyes. "I'm looking forward to it so very much."

Still, she did not release his hand.

"Yes," he intoned gruffly. They gazed at each other for one more moment. He felt like he'd taken some sort of strange drug that was pulling him tightly into her gaze. *Was this what it was like to surrender utterly and completely to God? To know only God's will?*

Or was something else going on?

Randy released her hand and moved on.

———— ·•· ————

Randy stepped outside in a mild daze. He was completely unaware that Charley had taken several photographs of him. Or that Charley slipped out the front door behind him.

Instead his mind was focused on what had just happened.

He had been blessed by the most visible sign yet that he and God were moving as one, and that he and Electra were now moving as one. From here on, there would be no going back.

Thy will be done, not mine, Randy thought as he drifted down the street.

———•–•———

Charley stood in the doorway of a shuttered deli, watching Roscoe enter his darkened hotel room. A moment later, a light came on in a room five stories up. Roscoe appeared by the window. Charley watched him remove his tie and loosen his collar. Then Roscoe left the room, as the light in the bathroom came on.

The Napier seems like a fairly simple place to infiltrate, Charley thought. He could get into Roscoe's room easily enough, and at the very least plant a bug. It would be harder without the right credentials, of course, but it could be done.

Hell, he could probably just get in through the service entrance. He'd come back tomorrow and stake him out. Roscoe seemed to move around the city a fair amount. This would be a breeze.

Charley walked away whistling under his breath, his mind on Electra in her corset.

Some things in life were just . . . well, perfect.

17

Frankie walked down the hall feeling physically ill. Her meeting with the lieutenant did not go well. But then she knew it wouldn't the minute he called her in. Her mind flashed back to his face leaning in toward hers, flushed with anger. "Your actions are under review, Kennedy," he practically spat at her.

Frankie still had no idea where the so-called actions came from—but then that was how it was with trumped-up charges. They came out of nowhere, and if you were lucky, they retreated back to nowhere. Unless they took you all the way down and got you fired.

As she walked back to her desk, Frankie studied the cracked linoleum floor of Northern Station, her home for the last seven years. Now that she was put on review, she figured she had two choices. She could put up with the review process and the coming months of humiliation, defending herself and who knows what else. Or she could simply surrender, quit, and go find some other line of work.

Like . . . what? Waitressing?

Screw that, she thought furiously. Frankie had worked far too long and hard to let go of the pension that lay ahead. And what about the retirement plan she's been slowly piecing together in her mind? Furthermore, she hadn't done anything wrong. The charge was killing a dog.

First of all, there was no dog. For God's sake, she would have remembered! It had been seventeen months since she even discharged her weapon.

But no—the lieutenant had a report sitting right there on his desk that named her as the dog shooter. It looked real enough. So now the Firearm Discharge Review Board would have to get involved. Christ, the media might even get trotted in. Knowing her luck, it was probably some seeing eye dog that went down. There would be meetings, public disclosure, and the rest of it. And why?

Undoubtedly it was her conversation with Mulroney—the one in which she let him know she was on to him. The charges were nothing less than harassment. And while she hadn't been suspended, she now was going to have to put up with this major, if not catastrophic, pain in the ass.

Frankie sat down at her desk with a sigh. Someone had killed a dog and it wasn't her, but she was going to have to pay. Exactly where in the rule book was shit like this allowed? Grabbing her phone, Frankie strode out of the station and walked up to the pocket park on the corner—her favorite place to think.

She let herself through the gate and sat on a bench beneath a jacaranda tree, abundant with purple flowers. For a moment, she closed her eyes and tried to feel the peace of so many living things around her. Then she took a few deep breaths to try to calm herself, but that didn't help either. She was just so sick and tired of everything about her life.

She was tired of being understanding, mature, and thoughtful. She was tired of following rules no one else seemed to give a damn about. She was tired of being fucking circumspect. And she was colossally tired of being the one square peg who had to continually jam herself into the straight, male round hole that was the SFPD.

Fuck all of this shit. And fuck the fucking lieutenant of police.

Frankie reached for her phone and texted Charley. It was time to marshal all of her resources.

Okay, I'm in, she typed. *Let's get this party started.*

Charley slipped down the alleyway of the Napier and tried the emergency exit on the side of the building, which was predictably locked. His real goal was to find the service entrance, talk his way into the building, and then slip into a service elevator to get up to the fifth floor. He nervously jiggled the gardenia he was carrying.

A young Latino man in a maintenance uniform was on his phone outside the kitchen door as Charley approached. "Hi," he said. "I'm looking for the service kitchen?"

The Latino man glanced up, slightly confused. "La cocina de servicio," Charley said.

The young man nodded through the open door, and in Charley went. *That was easy,* he thought.

A dishwasher looked up as he passed by. Charley smiled. "How you doin', man?" he asked genially. The dishwasher nodded and kept on rinsing dishes. There was no one else in the kitchen.

Charley peered into the lobby through the round hole in the service kitchen door. A bespectacled Asian woman in a dark suit and pumps was on duty behind the registration desk. She was simply standing there, looking off into space. The lobby was annoyingly quiet.

He waited one moment, and then two. He could feel the dishwasher eyeing him curiously. Charley turned his back to the dishwasher and busied himself stacking and restacking some teacups on a nearby shelf.

A service person suddenly entered the kitchen, bustling through the door just next to him. He glanced over at Charley. "Can I help you?" he asked.

Charley looked at him conspiratorially and raised a finger to his lips. "Shhh," he whispered. "I'm with her." He pointed to the young woman behind the registration desk. He held up the gardenia in its small plastic box, clearly a love offering.

"For Jee Won?" the porter asked in mild amazement. "Seriously?"

Charley nodded and once again put his finger to his lips.

"Okay, whatever," said the porter as he went off to locate a mop.

Charley peered through the round window again. The stairs to the rooms were just ahead. He had fewer than thirty yards to traverse once he was in the lobby.

Just then a large pack of English teenagers loudly poured into the lobby, hauling backpacks and wheeling suitcases. There had to be sixteen of them. *Bingo*, he thought. Charley slipped through the door and up the stairs as the entire knot of them converged on the woman behind the desk.

Charley found Roscoe's room with no problem. He paused for a moment outside the door and listened. The crack at the bottom of the door indicated the room was dark. There wasn't a soul around; blissful silence ensued. It was even the right make of lock for his equipment.

He pulled the microcontroller out of his pocket and was fishing around for the socket wire when suddenly a woman inside started speaking Italian.

Charley paused.

This was definitely the right room. It was the same one he'd seen Roscoe moving around in from the street. Could Roscoe actually have a visitor, an Italian speaker at that? Highly unlikely.

Charley leaned in to listen for one more moment. The woman seemed to be talking on the phone.

Charley sighed and stuffed the microprocessor back into his pocket. This was shitty luck. He wouldn't be breaking into the lock after all, as Roscoe had most certainly checked out. He thought for a moment longer. If only he knew his real name, at least he could verify it at the desk.

On the other hand . . . maybe he could.

A moment later, Charley waited patiently behind the last of the English teenagers. Finally it was his turn. The slightly bedraggled hotel clerk looked up at him. "Can I help you, sir?" she asked flatly.

"I'm so sorry to bother you," he said in a hushed, notably Southern tone. "Really, I hate to be an agitator but one of the other guests has been . . . well . . . ." Charley hesitated.

The hotel clerk's expression now shifted from exhaustion to concern. "Yes, sir?" she asked.

Charley rolled his eyes and grimaced, looking as pained as possible. "Oh, it's nothing. Honestly, I shouldn't have bothered you," he said as he started to turn away.

"Please, sir . . ." The hotel clerk reached out to stop him. "If there's something I can do, sir, I'm happy to help."

Charley turned and looked into her eyes. Her badge identified her as Jee Won. "Oh, Jee Won," he said more softly, laying on his drawl just a titch more. "Honestly, I find this all a bit distasteful. I am not a snitch. But I do believe in telling the truth about certain things . . ."

The hotel clerk dropped her voice and nodded encouragingly. "It's okay," she said. "Anything, sir. I'm here to help."

"Well . . ." Charley hesitated. "There's a man I kept hearing . . . I think he was in Room 523. And . . . I'm almost certain he's had a . . . a prostitute in his room."

Jee Won immediately began clicking through files on her computer. Then, pausing, she grimaced slightly. He could see she was determined to maintain her composure. *A direct hit,* Charley thought to himself. *Roscoe has clearly left a trail.*

"Thank you for letting us know. I'm so sorry for your inconvenience," she said tightly. "May I have your name, sir?"

"Charley MacElroy," he said smoothly. "I'm not staying here. I attended a series of business meetings in one of the other rooms on five. But you know who I'm talking about, right? That very odd fellow in 523? I saw him coming out of that room."

Jee Won continued to study her computer screen. "That guest is no longer with us," she said simply.

"Oh, Lord Almighty! The bugger died?" Jee Won half hid a smile. "No, sir, he just checked out. Is there anything else I can help you with?"

Charley exhaled and leaned on the desk conspiratorially. "Well bless your heart, Jee Won. I'm up there trying to sell software at three in the afternoon, and he's knocking that poor girl six ways to Sunday." Standing up, he rubbed his hands together. "I won't trouble you further, my dear. Thank you, and have a stupendous afternoon. And here . . ."

Reaching into his backpack, Charley produced the gardenia in its clear plastic box. "Please accept this small gift with my compliments, Jee Won."

The young woman was visibly taken aback. "Oh, I couldn't," she murmured.

"Have you ever smelled a gardenia?" he asked, opening the box and lifting the flower toward her face. Jee Won closed her eyes for the briefest moment and inhaled with a slight smile.

"Take it, please," he said. "A gift from an admirer."

The young woman smiled and blushed a little. "Thank you," she said as she took the flower in its box. "And do come again, Mr. MacElroy."

"I believe I will," he said with a smile.

Jauntily, Charley strode out the door. Now how the hell was he going to find Roscoe?

Randy leaned back and savored his last sip of Coke, enjoying the caffeine buzz that ensued. He felt good . . . very good. The trip to San Francisco had succeeded beyond his wildest dreams. *If the research went this swimmingly, the attack itself is going to be a piece of cake,* he thought giddily.

First of all, he'd found Pamela Delacroix. The Society Dom had basically been delivered to him on a silver platter. He even had her contact info in his pocket at that very moment. Randy carried it everywhere now as a talisman of the Lord's faith in him. Furthermore, he now understood the basics of the SFPD's strategy for crowd control at large outdoor events. So Bay to Breakers was bound to be a breeze, especially if it was anything like Folsom Street.

Finally, in a relatively short time, he'd built up an iron-clad resistance to all those sinners. He'd even been to a sex museum and managed to keep his cool. Somewhat.

Randy didn't like to think about that part. Instead, he focused on the giddy sense that he could do pretty much anything. Because that was what happened when you surrendered to God's will, no matter how outrageous the request. Mountains moved. Doors opened. Miracles occurred.

Okay, other things happened too . . . like getting arrested. He didn't mean to run that red light, for which a California highway patrol officer pulled him over. Wildly, Randy had gotten out of his car and ran, knocking the officer down in the process. If only the officer hadn't insisted on tackling him.

Randy reflectively rubbed his left knee where he still had a small Band-Aid. If only he'd somehow managed to get away. Hitting the sidewalk was painful, but worse . . . he was now in their records. Ultimately, the police let him off without much of a fuss, but he did have to go into the station and get fingerprinted.

That was a mistake—but maybe his only mistake on this trip.

Randy tried not to think about it. They'd never find him until well after the attack. By then, he could well be dead.

A male flight attendant reached past him to serve a second martini to the frazzled woman by the window. Randy noticed that he smelled slightly of aftershave, and it turned him on slightly. He closed his eyes, breathed, and tried not to notice.

Yet here was another piece of the San Francisco trip that had revealed itself: a strange, insatiable lust that was now riding shotgun in his psyche twenty-four seven. Randy certainly didn't plan to act on it. *He* wasn't going to be tempted by the Devil. No way!

Satan was tapping on Randy's shoulder, just as God had. This came as no surprise. For the more urgent the mission, the more likely the detractors. Here was the spiritual lesson of the moment: not only was Randy being challenged to step up and eradicate other sinners, he was being asked to ignore his own sinful impulses as well.

But then what did one expect from hanging around in a place like San Francisco and frequenting leather fairs and such? Randy needed a long, hot spiritual shower.

He gave his empty plastic cup a shake and drained the last of his Coke.

Maybe a ten-day fast was in order.

———◆———

Frankie slung herself into the front seat of Charley's car. "Thanks for waiting up for me," she said.

It was well past one a.m. The city was quiet as they drove down Fillmore toward the Mission. The fog left the streets with a greasy sheen as they drove nowhere in particular.

"So?" Charley asked simply.

"It's disgusting," Frankie began, shaking her head. She exhaled slowly and looked out the car window, uncertain where to begin. Finally she turned to him. "I've found an undercover extortion ring that includes one of our new lieutenants. The fucker's right in there with the rest of them. They've been at it for at least four years. Hence our two new captains."

Charley whistled slowly under his breath. "Brazen," he said.

"Yeah, you think they'd be at least a little more subtle, right? Who knows how much more rot is just underneath . . . I mean, it's sickening. Apparently I'm the only person who thought to look any of this up in the department records. Anyway, they know I know. So now they're trying to get me suspended for shooting a dog."

"A dog?"

"Don't even ask . . ." she muttered. "Animal shootings are a lot harder to prove or dispute. And they still have to go before the Review Board, which takes frigging forever. It's harassment, plain and simple."

They drove on in silence for a few more moments. Finally Frankie spoke up again.

"So yeah, Charley, I'll do anything you want," she said. "Let's nail your suspect. I think I'm going to need it if I want to keep my fucking job."

Frankie turned back to face the red light ahead of them. "Sons of bitches," she muttered.

"Great," Charley replied. "Once I can actually find this guy, we'll have our work cut out for us."

Frankie looked at him. "I thought you knew where he was staying."

"He checked out. Now he could be anywhere."

Frankie threw up her hands in frustration. "Oh, Jesus!"

"But we do have a picture of him, if we can get into some photo recognition software."

Frankie shook her head. "I don't know, Charley—even I could, what good would it do? I've got nothing on him. Anyway, if he went back home to Minnesota . . . well, then end of threat, right?"

"For now," said Charley.

"I mean, it's unlikely we'll be able to track him down now unless we run into him somewhere."

"Like the next big outdoor event, which seems to be his pattern."

Frankie tapped her chin thoughtfully. "The big events are all done till Bay to Breakers in the spring. All we've got till then are Giants games *if* they make the Series."

Charley turned and looked at Frankie encouragingly. "So I say let's spend the winter getting our jobs back. I'll help you. You help me. Deal?"

"What about the dude?" Frankie asked.

"See if he surfaces. Electra can keep an eye on him. Meanwhile, I'll give you whatever I've got. Then we'll turn your steely mind to getting me out of lock up."

"Sounds fun," she said. "I'd love to bust the shit bag who set you up."

Charley smiled. "Thought you'd think so," he said. Turning onto Fillmore, he was almost back at the station. "So keep in touch, Frankie."

"No problem," she said. "But first, send me the suspect's picture. Let me see what I can do."

"Will do," he said as she got out of the car.

Charley watched her walk into the station, marveling at his luck. But then that was how life was. Why *wouldn't* there be an angry cop dying to help him expose the rot in the world?

Grandfather would be proud.

18

"What I'm really interested in, Electra, is building your brand, because that's the opportunity here. There's money on the table!" declared Miss Kitty as she tucked into her Neapolitan pizza with gusto. She was one of those people who could eat like a truck driver and still fit into her corset at 6 p.m.

They were now into the business-building segment of Miss Kitty's highly expensive Dom-in-a-Month coaching program. So far it wasn't going well.

"I thought *People* and *Good Morning America* had already built my brand," Electra replied a little testily.

"Exactly my point. So what are you doing to monetize it?" asked Miss Kitty. Then she answered her own question: "You're doing shit."

Electra closed her mouth and decided to listen. After all, Miss Kitty did know more than she did about such matters.

Miss Kitty continued. "I say do it all. E-courses, webinars, a streaming video instruction series with actors. A podcast is a must, of course. 'Society Dom Rants,' perhaps? And then there's your social profile: blog, Instagram, Facebook page, Twitter, YouTube, the works. Hell, we could probably even get some traction on Pinterest. Bottom line is we have to build your email list. Do you even have one?"

Electra's head was swimming. But then she knew it would be like this.

"No," she said in a tired voice.

Miss Kitty put down her knife and fork and gave her a look. "Really, Electra. What are we doing here, anyway?"

There was a moment of silence, during which time Electra took a long sip of her Chardonnay.

"You are training me to be a kick ass dominatrix and build the business I deserve," she said, parroting the web copy that promoted Miss Kitty's services.

Her coach shrugged. "I can only take you as far as you're willing to go," she said evenly.

Electra closed her eyes against the truth. *What is my problem, anyway?* This woman was well qualified to help her build the business she kept saying she wanted. Electra swallowed. In her head was the cacophony of the past, a pastiche of her mother's rigid mold-making, her father's dialogue of shame, and the general restraints of an ordered caste she did not believe in.

Could she really do this to everyone who'd ever loved her? Was it actually true that she could be herself, finally, for once in her life? Was that option even safe to begin with?

"Look," Electra began uncomfortably. "I want this. I truly do. But I'm afraid. Massively, massively afraid," she admitted.

Miss Kitty just looked at her. "And what bogeymen are we so afraid of exactly?"

Electra gave an embarrassed grimace. "Look, I know it's ridiculous, Miss Kitty, but my mother would be rolling in her grave right now. She's not even alive! And then . . . then there's my daughter. I'm just not sure I can do this to her."

Miss Kitty leaned in to her. "Electra," she murmured. "You're already doing it to her. You're already out there as the Society Dom. The damage is done, honey."

Tears sprang into her eyes. This was undeniably true.

"If your daughter can't get with the program now, perhaps she will in time," continued Miss Kitty. "After all, life is change, which means you don't have to be that suppressed baby-dom who has to sneak around behind people's backs anymore, right? We're talking about creating the life you want—and deserve—Electra."

Electra took a shuddering sigh and blew her nose. "Yeah, yeah, I know," she said. Accepting Peyton's rejection of her was the hardest thing she'd ever done. "But maybe I have to get over this before I can build a brand."

"I understand," said Miss Kitty more gently, "but your moment is now, sweetheart, and your brand is already built. In fact, you are rapidly becoming yesterday's news and our window of opportunity is closing."

They were silent for a moment.

"Can you just allow this to unfold as it is meant to?" asked the coach. "Can you relax into the idea that you were given the Society Dom for a reason? There are people like you out there waiting for liberation. They need a role model, Electra," she said. "That's why so many of them showed up for your workshop."

Again, they fell silent.

"Your people need you," concluded Miss Kitty. "And they need you now."

Electra sighed. She knew the time had come.

"All right," she said quietly as she opened a notebook and took out a pen. "Where do I begin?"

They sat on Charley's terrace overlooking the city, mojitos in hand, surveying the burgeoning sunset. It was the best hour of the day—Magic Hour, photographers called it—that time when light turned to gold and everything was tinged with possibility.

The patchwork of buildings before them led an orderly progression up to Telegraph Hill. There, a broad cluster of wooden houses circled its base, old San Francisco style. This was topped by a cluster of trees and the Coit Tower, which stood up gleaming against the sky. The view was breathtaking.

Charley had called in the early afternoon with his dinner invite, and so far the visit had been quiet. Electra was still in the raw funk of her coaching-slash-therapy session with Miss Kitty, and Charley was oddly circumspect. She found herself genuinely glad to see him.

As they sat there and watched the sunset, Electra realized how precious his companionship was to her at this moment in her life. Never had she felt so alone, and never had she actually been so alone. All those Thanksgivings, birthdays, Christmases, soccer games, benefits, lunches, dinners, cocktail parties, school plays, arguments, reconciliations and the early morning sex that followed folded into an indelible tapestry in her mind.

The stuff of her marriage and her family followed her like a ghost through her days. And now it was over. In a very short time, Charley and her dog had become all that she had. For this, Electra was supremely grateful.

Charley was grilling marinated lamb chops tonight, along with a cluster of baby artichokes. He poked at the grill distractedly. But for now, it just felt so good to sit with Electra. He really couldn't say what it was about her that he found so intoxicating, but that was how it was at this point: *intoxicating*. He wanted to study everything about her so he could find more and more to appreciate. She was twice the woman Allegra was, or any other lovers he'd had, for that matter. That much was clear.

He glanced over at her, sitting in the last rays of reflected sunset. She seemed serene and unspeakably beautiful in the last of the daylight. Yet, the question still loomed—was she even interested in him?

His mind had catalogued and reviewed nearly every moment they'd spent together. Was her willingness to stand so close in the tree at Hardly Strictly an indication of interest—or was it just her zeal to find Roscoe? And the lingerie display before her workshop, was that some kind of pre-seduction choice or legitimately what she needed to wear to work?

Would she really have come to the door dressed in a corset and black stockings if she didn't want to be at least a *little* seductive to him? Like a Chinese puzzle, each delicious moment was either rich with possibility or completely meaningless. For the first time in his life, Charley was flummoxed.

In fact, he was feeling fairly nervous in this moment. He was never good at delivering unwanted news. He was quite sure Electra would not warm to the idea that he wouldn't be helping her further with Roscoe. In fact, she was likely to be angry.

On the other hand, Electra could be relieved to know Roscoe was gone. So he'd couch that little fact as "good news." *Timing is everything*, he thought to himself.

Charley turned the chops and considered things.

There was also the matter of coming out to her. That had to be dealt with as well. Then there was his cover and explaining why he would not be pursuing Roscoe but helping entrap a bunch of cops instead. Tonight he intended to fold these various pieces together into some kind of intimacy stew that would knit them even more closely together.

If he could.

At the very least, Charley figured, he'd learn where he stood. The prospect was tantalizing.

He returned to the seat beside her and began again. "How was your day?" he asked.

"I have to tell you something," she replied. *This is interesting*, he thought.

"Go ahead."

Electra turned to him. "I feel like you're the only person in the entire world who understands me right now, Charley." They looked at each other for a moment, and he felt his heart skip a beat. "I've had an especially shitty day today, and it made me realize you're all I've got," she said.

"I'm so very, very glad," he said gently.

Charley took her hand, and for once, it felt soft and willing. He could feel her relax into his touch. He had no words at that moment. Instead, he did what he'd wanted to do from the moment he met Electra: he pulled her close to him and kissed her. She unfolded willingly into his arms, and her lips responded to his.

Is this really happening? he wondered. Charley pulled back and looked at her for a moment. Her eyes were still closed. "What?" he whispered.

"I'm just hanging on to the feeling," she said.

"There's more," he replied.

"I know," she said simply, but then she opened her eyes and looked at him. "But it's not time yet, Charley."

Now he felt confused. "What do you mean?"

"I mean I'm all screwed up. I'm sorry . . . I just can't. Not yet. Maybe soon, but not now."

He grimaced slightly and turned away. *And she doesn't even know my story*, he thought. "It's just as well, Electra, because there's something I need to tell you, too."

She looked at him with mild surprise. Then she smiled. "Have you got a secret?" she said teasingly.

"Yes," he replied evenly. "Several, actually. I'll tell you the first one right now."

Settling back against her chair, she looked at him and her smile broadened. Electra liked secrets. And Charley liked kissing her. He took her hand again.

"The truth is I'm a different sort of a man," he began. "Back on Honey Island, I started out my life as a girl named Charlotte. My grandfather helped me transition by the time I was ten. And all the parts are there . . . except for one."

Electra's eyes widened, and she said nothing. Emboldened, Charley continued. "I don't have a penis," he explained, "but I do think a lot about getting one."

Electra remained silent as she processed his news. It was always like this, telling his potential lovers. First came the shock of the news, and then the sad settling in of his "otherness."

"What do you think?" he finally asked.

"You're the first trans . . . whatever . . . I've known."

"Transman," he corrected. "I'm a transman."

"Yes," she said. Then, reaching out, she touched his hair lightly. "And you are quite a man," she said. Running her hand down his cheek, she paused with her fingertips against his lips. "You don't have to say anything more," she told him.

"Have I said too much?"

"No, I just need to take this in. It's a lot, Charley."

He nodded. "I understand. But I wanted you to know. Just in case . . ."

"In case we fall in love?" she asked with a smile. "It's okay, Charley. I'm glad you told me. Let's just see how it goes," she said lightly.

Electra rose with her empty glass in hand. "The mojitos are in the kitchen?" she asked.

"I'll make you another," he said. Relief poured through his body as he followed her inside.

At least it wasn't a solid no.

———·◆·———

Now for Part Two, he thought as they sat in the afterglow of dinner.

The grilled lamb was perfect, as was the Sangiovese. He had not touched Electra since their kiss a few hours earlier, and at times it seemed almost too much to even look at her.

Charley perfectly understood her restraint. Not surprisingly, it just made him want her more. For now, she seemed even stronger and more judicious than ever. She was a woman who knew exactly what she wanted, and she expected nothing less.

Now that *is hot,* he thought with pride.

"So, Electra . . ." Charley began. "Do you remember earlier when I mentioned I had more than one secret?"

She stirred her coffee. "Mmm-hmm," she said almost dreamily.

"I'm going to tell you something that could get me killed. So before I tell you, you must promise never to repeat it to another living soul."

Electra sat up a little straighter. "Oh," she replied. A look of concern passed over her beautiful face.

He continued. "If it feels like too much responsibility, we can drop it right now."

"No," she said, composing herself. "Tell me. I know how to keep my mouth shut."

"Good," he replied. "Do you remember when I gave you the wire to wear at the workshop?" She nodded. "And how I taught you to talk to people so you can get all kinds of handy information from them?"

"Yeah."

"So I'm not actually a travel writer," he said.

Electra looked at him incredulously. "Wait a minute. You're not a spy, are you?" she concluded uncertainly.

He nodded. "CIA covert operations, working mostly in Europe," he said. "Sort of."

"Sort of?"

Charley exhaled and rubbed his chin. This was the part he really didn't want to tell her. "That's why I'm stuck at home. I got suspended because of . . . well, call it a financial mix up."

Her eyebrows shot up.

"I didn't pay my 2014 taxes, and I lost my security clearance," he admitted miserably. "Anyway, I just paid them, and I'm in the process of getting my clearance back. So . . ."

"Does this have something to do with Roscoe?"

"It does," he said, "but first I have some news for you. He's actually gone. He left the hotel where he was staying."

She stood up. "What? What else do you know?"

"Nothing, unfortunately. I tried to break into his hotel room and plant a wire, but he had just checked out. So he's either moved to another room in town or he's gone back to

Ohio or wherever the hell he's from."

"Wheaton, Illinois. Along with all the other evangelists," she said. "Why are you telling me this, Charley?"

He looked at her with genuine remorse. "Because I can't help you with Roscoe. Not right now, at least. I have to focus on getting my job back." He paused. "I'm really sorry, Electra. I'd love to help you."

"Wait a minute. First of all, how do we know he's actually gone?" she asked with real alarm. "He probably *is* in some other fleabag in the city. Christ, he's probably figured out where I live by now. He's probably actively stalking me."

"I'm sure he isn't, Electra."

"You don't know that!" she spat furiously. Electra clamped her arms across her chest. "Are you for real?" she burst. "First you invite me over and wine me and dine me. Then you *kiss me* and then tell me you have no penis. *Then* you decide to tell me you're a spy—and that you're not going to help me with Roscoe . . . I mean, *WHAT THE FUCK*, Charley?" She glared at him. "Or was tonight all about letting me down gently so you could still sleep with me?"

Shit, he thought. *This seriously is not going well.*

Electra began moving fast now, stuffing her sweater and her reading glasses back into her bag and heading toward the front door. "I'm done here," she said angrily. "I've had quite enough for one night!"

Charley rushed past her and blocked the door with his body. She couldn't leave like this. Not yet, at least. "Just wait. Please hear me out. Let's at least talk about this . . . Please!" he implored her.

Electra stopped and waited impatiently for him to get out of the way.

"*What?*" she practically spat at him.

"Just wait. Just calm down," he said, taking her arm. Electra angrily yanked back her arm.

"Don't touch me," she snarled. "And *don't* tell me to calm down."

"I need to tell you about Frankie."

"Oh great!" she burst. "Who the fuck is Frankie? Your gay lover?"

"No! Frankie is a lesbian cop I'm friends with, and she's going to help us trap Roscoe when he comes back. She's an SFPD sergeant who agreed to help us. But first I have to help her with something."

"Oh, GREAT! So some lesbian cop is your new best friend while I've got some fucking lunatic stalking me. I thought you understood women, Charley. I thought you understood me! Especially if you're some trans-whatever-the-hell-you-are . . . But you're just like all the other men out there. You think of nothing but yourself. Get out of my way!" Electra roared as she pushed him out of the way. Then, grabbing the front doorknob, she yanked it open and retreated fast down the steps in front of Charley's house.

"Electra . . . wait! Please!" he cried. But he did not run down the steps after her. Clearly, the horse had already left the stable.

Electra turned around at the bottom of the stairs and glared up at him. "I am seriously disappointed in you," was all she said.

Crap.

Charley stood there helplessly. "I'm incredibly sorry," he replied.

"I bet you are," she retorted. "Well, don't bother helping me anymore, Charley. And don't bother calling me, either. I'll handle Roscoe myself."

Slamming the door of her car, Electra pulled out of her parking space with a screech and took off down the street. Charley just stood there and watched her go with a sinking feeling in his gut.

Then, slowly, he turned and walked inside. Now what the hell was he going to do?

19

T*hank God for the U.S. Army,* Randy thought to himself as he counted his cash. At this exact moment, he was bent over the small briefcase open on his bed, sorting through the last installment of $100 bills. All he needed was an even hundred thousand in cash and he was set. The money would be used to pay his friend Irwin for twenty sealed glass vials of sarin packed into a small steel carrying case.

While Randy had never been in the military, he was extremely grateful for the vast array of experts it produced—people well-trained in things like weapons of mass destruction. Fellows like his friend Irwin spent years honing their skills on the U.S. military's highly expensive equipment. Irwin, for instance, had once regularly destroyed stockpiles of chemical weapons, or CW's as they called them. During the Gulf War, he drove around a handy little field lab he jokingly called "Hydrolysis to Go."

Now, some years after the Gulf War, Irwin wasn't laughing, and he was no longer in the Army, either. He'd developed a nervous head twitch that the VA wasn't doing much to help. So now Irwin was angry. Conveniently, he was also a member of Randy's church. All Randy had to do was share his vision and Irwin was in, but he figured he'd be. Irwin was known to be not all there. In fact, he relished the idea of whipping up a lethal chemical weapon for a good cause.

The most difficult part was actually getting hold of the cash. The money was in Randy's trust, but he certainly wasn't about to write a check. Nor would he transfer the cash into Irwin's bank account, as that would be traceable, too. So yet again, Randy found himself whistling "Blue Danube" under his breath and counting out bill after bill.

The ease with which this entire process was rolling was remarkable. Even lining up Arthur Dimsdorff, the young man who lived in his spare room, to drop the vials at the attack site had been a breeze. All Randy had to do was promise Arthur life everlasting and a spot in the Kingdom of Heaven, and he handily agreed. Arthur wasn't disabled, exactly; he was just slow. This made him the ideal man for the job: fully compliant yet still sharp enough to deliver the vials to their target.

Good old unquestioning Arthur. He really was the perfect accomplice.

The bigger question Randy was wrestling with now was Electra. He was clear that her murder was supposed to be part of the overall plan . . . but how exactly? That part the Lord had not been specific about yet.

Sarin was out, as Randy could easily be killed as well. He had no interest in handling the stuff, and had designed the whole sarin drop scenario to happen without him. Sure, he was willing to tote around a little steel suitcase full of the poison and pass it along to the right person to deliver, but would he ever open it? Certainly not.

That would be Arthur's job.

Still, the question of Electra's death tugged at him. Obtaining and carrying a gun seemed problematic to Randy. He didn't have a gun permit and he didn't want one—just one more place to put his signature in plain view of the government. And guns were . . . well . . . loud. And potentially bloody if he hit his target.

Something quieter and less violent was called for now. He'd considered morphine. It would have been so easy to get together casually with Electra, lace her drink with a tranquilizer, and inject her with morphine after she passed out. He liked this scenario. It seemed clean and efficient.

He even had some morphine, dating back to the weeks before his father's death. But he suspected he did not have enough to actually kill someone. Lately he'd been pondering an unlikely weapon: a few plastic grocery bags. He'd gotten the idea after reading about a prison suicide.

In the meanwhile, the final glory hole of hell he would personally reap upon the blasphemers was nigh. The sarin would soon be in hand, and perhaps his murder weapon as well. All he had to do was train Arthur to be his delivery boy, and the rest would take care of itself.

Really Randy could scarcely believe how smooth and easy that entire project had been so far. Counting out the last of the hundred dollar bills, he tidied up the final pile and tucked it into the last corner of the briefcase. The cash was all here. He was ready for Irwin.

Snapping the case shut, he rose and touched the wooden cross hanging around his neck. Briefly Randy closed his eyes. *Thy will be done, not mine,* he incited. And then, opening his eyes, he smiled as he looked out on the sunny day.

Life was truly good.

Electra pushed through the water, hand over hand, trying to lull herself back to calm with a swim. This was her Thursday ritual, and it was always the same. Ease into the water, clamp on the cap, the goggles, the fins, and then just let go. The day's cares would disappear reliably as she pushed through her yardage.

But this day was different. She was really bugged. Charley's unexpected advance and then retreat hit her much harder than she would have expected. She was angry. And she was hurt.

It didn't help that a several-hour hangout last night on various evangelical Christian websites yielded nothing. But what did she expect? There were hundreds of thousands of evangelicals in the U.S. What were the chances she'd run into Roscoe online? Hell, she didn't even know his real name, so how would she know if she found him?

She wouldn't. Yet this was all she wanted to think about. She'd tried imagining where he'd be right now if he was still somewhere in the Bay Area. She'd conjured and thought and projected and still come up with nothing. Electra felt like she was hitting her head against a brick wall. Still, she could not stop trying.

Electra gritted her teeth in frustration as she came up behind a slower swimmer plodding along in her lane. She neatly swam around the woman, gave a quick flip turn at the wall, and headed back to the other end.

Slacker, she thought was a sniff. Electra had no patience for much of anything at this exact moment, and she hated feeling this way. Yet here it was: the sickening sense that she was spinning her wheels. And not only that—now she was doing it entirely alone.

Screw Charley, she thought for the hundredth time that morning. *Screw him!* If he couldn't see the vast opportunity at hand, well, then, he just wouldn't reap the rewards, would he? He and his so-called security clearance could just go rot in hell.

She thought of the seven texts and fourteen calls he'd made to her in the last two days that had gone unanswered. *Make him sweat*, she thought. She wasn't talking to him until she was damn good and ready.

On the other hand, how exactly was she going to deal with Roscoe by herself? This was the piece she couldn't quite sort out. She couldn't exactly take her theories to the cops—the SFPD weren't interested in a bunch of theories. She had nothing specific on Roscoe, and she knew it.

Electra pushed through the water, willing herself to relax, to forget. To just let go and stop the relentless ranting in her head. Reaching the other side, she checked the clock. She'd been at it for the requisite hour. Slowly, Electra climbed out of the pool, wandered over to the spa, and lowered herself into the hot, bubbling water.

Maybe Miss Kitty was right. Maybe all she should focus on right now was building her brand, or at least capitalizing on it. The clock was ticking, after all. The thought made her more tired than before. Did she have to be a dom who knows marketing? Perhaps her brand was already built. Maybe Miss Kitty was wrong.

Really, what she needed more than anything right now was a nice long primal scream.

Then she needed to find Roscoe.

"Okay, okay. I made a mistake. A big mistake," Charley admitted.

It was a relief to talk about his botched evening with Electra, even if it was with the Agency-appointed shrink. "I mean, I honestly thought that telling the truth would bring us closer," he said. "I just didn't do it right," he added in a smaller, sadder voice.

Brunni, the therapist, regarded him quietly. She was an older German woman, empathic and completely grounded. Charley found himself trusting her despite his initial resistance to therapy.

"Maybe she just wasn't ready to hear the truth," suggested Brunni. "I can feel your sadness," she added.

I am sad, he thought to himself. Damn sad. Suddenly, unexpected tears sprang into Charley's eyes. "I'm so goddamn tired of being the freak, you know?" he croaked as a few tears trickled down his check. Charley wiped them away with his sleeve. "I mean, what's the big fucking deal? Why did she have to leave? Why does *everyone* have to have such a big reaction? Transmen are all over the place!"

Tears continued to roll down his cheeks as Brunni looked on compassionately. She handed him a tissue. Finally she spoke. "Maybe she was just triggered because you told her you wouldn't help her."

He closed his eyes. This was true; he knew it. He'd anticipated a big reaction from Electra. Now he was only surprised that *he* was taking it so hard. Charley began to cry more intensely. Sobs overtook him, and for a full moment, he could not speak.

After a moment, Brunni offered him another tissue. Finally, Charley gathered himself together and blew his nose. "I'm sorry," he said, somewhat embarrassed. "I don't know what got into me . . ."

Brunni waved away his concern. "You're supposed to cry, Charley. This is where the truth lives."

He fell silent. There was that damn truth again. "So what's this all mean?" he finally asked. "That I'm in love with her?"

"What do you think it means?" she asked.

He sighed and looked out the window. "I'm just so tired of being alone. I finally thought I'd found something with this woman—she's so magnificent."

"And . . ."

"And I blew it! She wanted me to help her, to protect her, to really take care of her . . . and I blew her off."

"So do you need to apologize?"

"I've tried," he said miserably. "She won't return my calls or my texts."

"Okay, Charley, but you pulled back from helping her for a reason."

This was true. The exact reason ricocheted through his head for a moment like a hard bullet. Oh, he did not want to admit this at all. A flash of serious pain crossed his face.

"So I would just do anything to get my job back, you know?" Brunni nodded compassionately. "And another friend in law enforcement is having some issues with an internal corruption case—not at the Agency, somewhere else. So I figured if I helped my friend and I was a hero and all that . . ." Charley hung his head miserably. "I just didn't think helping Electra was going to get me anywhere."

"Go on," Brunni urged him after a moment.

He raised his head and looked at her. "I was just trying to get my job back."

Brunni smiled. "And you thought you could end run around the problem by being impressive."

Charley looked at his hands, folded in his lap. "Yeah," he admitted.

"I think they're too smart for that, Charley. And apparently so is Electra."

"Right," he agreed miserably.

"You know what you have to do. Step work. Meetings. Keep your numbers. Submit all your records to the Agency. Start showing up like an adult."

"Right," he said softly.

"And then . . . then you'll see how it all turns out. Maybe you'll get your clearance back. Maybe she'll decide you're worth another try. Or maybe she won't."

"I know, I know," he said, putting up a hand. "Don't tell me . . . 'God's will,' right?"

"Something like that," Brunni said with a smile.

Charley sighed. He had his work cut out for him. He stood up. The clock was nearly at fifty minutes. "Thanks, Brunni," he said. "I'm on it."

"Keep the faith, Charley," she concluded. "Stranger things have happened."

He took one last long, shuddering breath and walked out to his chained-up bike. He wondered if other men took a little rejection this hard.

Randy snapped open the small metal suitcase on the table, and Arthur's eyes widened. The two men silently surveyed the twenty vials lined up on their velvet padding. Lying there they looked innocent enough, despite their collective ability to kill hundreds of people instantaneously.

"Don't even think of touching one of these vials until the

right time, Arthur," Randy began. "This is the only time this suitcase will be opened before the attack. I'm locking it in just a moment. You won't get the key until it's time to do the drop. Do you understand?"

Arthur nodded. He felt almost numb with excitement. This was by far the most amazing thing that had ever happened to him. Here was his ticket to ride straight up to Heaven.

"Do you promise me?" asked Randy gravely. And once again, the young man nodded profusely. "Yes?" Randy urged. "Say it out loud."

"Yes," Arthur replied obediently. "I promise not to try to open the suitcase."

"Okay, good. Because we have a lot to cover and I don't want you to get confused on the basics. Just remember that whatever happens, it's paradise on the other side. And you'll have the express ticket to get in because you're helping so very much, Arthur. A lot of bad people are going to die, and you're going to be the hero who makes that happen, right?"

Arthur, still wide-eyed, nodded eagerly. "Right," he intoned softly. He imagined himself walking out of Randy's house carrying the suitcase and his heart skipped a beat. He could scarcely believe it. "Can I take it home tonight?" he asked.

"No, not yet," Randy said. "Let's get out to San Francisco first. Then I'll give you the address, the sarin, the whole shebang, okay? First, I just want to make sure you understand how you're going to deliver it."

"Okay," the young man replied. "Want me to tell you what I'm going to do again?"

Randy nodded, and Arthur began his carefully rehearsed litany. "I push all the buzzers until someone lets me in, I walk all the way up the stairs to the top floor, and I walk down to the end of the hall and look for the door to the roof. It can be a little hard because it's heavy, so I may have to give it an extra hard push."

"Good," said Randy, encouragingly. "Keep going."

"After I climb up onto the roof and shut the hatch, I walk over to the side of the roof and look for lots of people down on the ground. When there's a crowd, I open the case, take out the vials, and drop them over the side where they will smash on impact." Arthur looked at Randy expectantly.

"What are you wearing the entire time?" Randy asked.

"Latex gloves," Arthur answered, and Randy smiled. "What's next?" Randy asked.

Arthur's face clouded over a bit. "I'm not sure," he said slowly. Now Arthur began to rock back and forth on his heels, and Randy sighed. He knew it would be like this, which is why they would continue to rehearse their plan, over and over again, until he got it right.

"You leave the suitcase lying there and quickly walk back to the hatch. Calmly you open it, climb down the ladder. Then you take off your latex gloves, put them in your pocket, and walk all the way down the stairs to the garage. Then you let yourself out the side door and walk calmly down the adjoining street away from the site. You ignore everything that is going on, you keep your head down, and you keep walking."

"Where do I walk to?" Arthur asked.

Randy was momentarily silenced. He had no idea mainly because he assumed Arthur would be dead by this point. "I'll let you know," he said.

A shy smile crossed Arthur's face. "Tell me the rest," he said. This was his favorite part.

"You may live or you may die, Arthur, and that is just as it is meant to be. For this is God's will we are acting on—and thy will be done, not mine." Randy paused. "Oh, I almost forgot the most important part. If someone catches up with you and starts asking questions, what do you tell them?"

Arthur thought for a moment. He was starting to ask for help when Randy interrupted them. "You tell them you are acting on instructions from God, right? And that you know nothing further."

In fact, the word would be out by then, plastered across YouTube that he was doing this spectacular attack in memory of his father. But he wanted to be the one to break the news . . . not Arthur. They would both go down together, he figured.

But this, too, was just part of God's will.

20

E lectra tossed and turned. Again. But then what did she expect? Between menopause and the Roscoe threat and now Charley being such a twerp, there was a lot to think about.

She rolled over and hugged her comforter tightly for a moment. Then she gave up, flung back the covers, and went directly to the refrigerator and opened it. Honestly, she wasn't one for middle of the night feeds. But right now even Xanax wasn't helping. It appeared only Ben & Jerry's or possibly straight vodka would do the job.

Screw Charley, she thought grumpily for the fourteenth time that night. Or maybe it was the fortieth? Who knew and who cared? She had to eradicate this man-slash-whatever-he-was from her system completely. It was simply too dangerous since he had proven unreliable.

No, she wouldn't be responding to his texts or his sad little phone messages. *Too. Fucking. Bad.* Bailing on her in her moment of need was not what friends did—and certainly those who even had the tiniest interest in becoming lovers.

Lovers. Such a loaded word, she thought. She hadn't even begun to contemplate sex with Charley now that she knew he had a vagina. Or did he? The entire matter was completely confusing. He might not have a penis . . . but did he have anything at all in the nether quarters? Do transmen magically lose their vaginas somehow after taking all that testosterone?

Perhaps he was simply gender-neutral, like Ken and Barbie.

For the briefest of moments, she imagined herself in bed with Charley. Kissing Charley, pulling him tight to her, and reaching . . . for . . . what?

The thought stopped her cold.

Electra slammed the refrigerator shut. There wasn't one iota of anything delicious or sinful in her refrigerator, only a stick of butter, and she wasn't about to stoop that low. She opened a cupboard. There had to be some peanut butter in here somewhere. It was her go-to sin in emergencies. Then she suddenly remembered.

Somewhere in this kitchen she'd also hidden a bar of chocolate. Could she possibly remember where?

Electra's hand groped around the back of the top shelf, finding nothing. *Damn,* she thought with annoyance. It had to be here somewhere. Dragging over a tall stool, she climbed up to really get a look at that top shelf. Just then her phone pinged. A middle of the night text. Electra glanced at the kitchen clock.

1:43 a.m. Undoubtedly it was from Charley.

Forging ahead, she ignored the text as her hand located something smooth with a telltale bit of foil around the end. Excellent: 78% dark chocolate from Madagascar. *Thank fucking God.* Electra extracted the chocolate bar and tore open the wrapper greedily. She began to scarf large amounts of the bar, and as she did, two more texts came pinging in.

Climbing down off her stool, she picked up her phone and glanced at them. They were indeed from Charley.

"I miss you. I miss us. Yes, Electra . . . there is an us," read the one.

Then another: *"I do want to protect you. I made a big mistake, and I deeply apologize. Won't you please forgive me?"*

These were all variations on a theme that had been playing for the last two days in his texts. Redemption, love, reconciliation. And always protection. That was the law enforcer in him, she suspected.

And honestly, she wasn't immune. Electra sat down on her stool as a large piece of dark chocolate slowly melted on her tongue. She considered adding a spoonful of peanut butter to make her sensory oblivion complete. Instead, she pulled the open bottle of Chardonnay from the refrigerator door and took a swig.

Electra could barely bring herself to acknowledge it, but she wanted him. Something in her animal brain had connected deeply with his, whether he had a penis or not and whether he even helped her with Roscoe or not. On some basic level, she had already surrendered to him, and she knew it.

Electra was all his whether she liked it or not. Okay. *But not yet,* she told herself, taking another pull on the bottle of Chardonnay. How in God's name was she going to manage sex with this man?

And another thing: was it actually okay to date a covert CIA agent? Weren't there protocols around this sort of thing? What if some terrorist found out about her and started stalking her? Electra worried on this for a moment. Then it occurred to her that a terrorist already was stalking her, which oddly improved her mood.

She closed her eyes against the intrusion of too many images bombarding her at once. All she knew was that when she looked into Charley's eyes, she saw another person who understood her perfectly. And she saw herself as well.

So when Charley told her he wouldn't be helping her find Roscoe, she was taken aback. Until that exact moment, she'd felt completely seen, heard, and taken care of by Charley. But now it had all gone to dust.

Except that it wasn't. His ardent apologies actually were having some effect, and she could feel herself weakening. *All that has to happen next is the armload of roses to arrive,* she thought. Then she might have to look twice in his direction, regardless of his nether quarters.

Electra ate the last piece of chocolate with a sigh. *It is hard being a celebrity dom,* she thought to herself.

No. Strike that. It was hard just being her.

———·◆·———

At this moment, Charley was walking the dog again. It didn't matter that it was the middle of the night. Nor did it matter that the dog had been out three times in the last six hours.

He needed the consolation of the fog. He needed the refreshment of the cool, misty air as it wrapped around him. He'd considered all the many reasons why Electra wasn't responding to his voicemails and texts. She'd lost her phone, perhaps. Or she left it somewhere. That happened to people all the time, right?

Maybe she just didn't get any of his texts or messages. Could he have her number wrong in his phone? (This was, of course, technically impossible given that they'd been texting and calling steadily up until their recent disaster.) Charley was doing his best to stay positive. After all, maybe Electra *wasn't* getting any of his missives. More likely, though, she wasn't responding because she was pissed and hurt.

The mere idea of this made him recoil. Charley sighed deeply and surveyed the skyline below him as the dog peed yet again on his favorite tract of yellowed grass. There was no getting around it.

Charley had fallen in love with Electra, and he wasn't going to feel whole and complete until they had at least talked. Would she ever forgive him? Possibly not. He recalled the sight of her in her corset, with her long legs encased in sheer black stockings, and his stomach gave a twist. Could he have seriously screwed up his one true chance for happiness in this short life?

Fuck.

The dog whined and tugged at his leash. Even Buster had had enough and yearned to go home. "Okay, okay," said Charley as they made their way back to his house. Even he had to surrender sometimes.

Roses, he thought. He'd send her two dozen long-stem roses in the morning. Maybe even three. What woman could resist that? Already his mind was darting ahead to what color would be the perfect choice.

It occurred to him that she might be playing him. Perhaps Electra already decided she would come back to him. If so, he didn't even care.

Somewhere deep in his loins, Charley wanted this woman as much as he'd ever wanted anything or anyone. He wasn't going to be the sorry loser this time.

Charley had made up his mind: he was going to give this relationship everything he had. *Everything*. This much he had learned from the current debacle. Electra was, indeed, worth fighting for.

———— •+•+• ————

Over at the Northern Station, Frankie was not having fun. About the last thing she wanted to do right now was sort through the arrest files. These were the records of all the people arrested in the last three months who were either vagrants, tipsy overseas tourists, or people who lived somewhere other than San Francisco county.

Four times a year, someone had to re-file these people and either send copies of their records back to their home counties or put them in the No Jurisdiction files. *Being a cop is a lot like being a doctor,* she thought. There was always an endless sea of paperwork to fill out.

These arrests were never extraordinary, just vagrant runaway kids who hung out near the park and shoplifted or sold heroin. There was the occasional kink tourist from Europe who got picked up in an orgy raid. Sometimes they got hotel guests, like the guy with the high heel fetish who started breaking into the other guests' rooms.

Then there were the traffic violations that became arrests. Mostly DUI's and ragers who were just plain inappropriate. These records were kindly provided by the CHP officers who didn't like processing the records any more than she did.

Why, Frankie wondered, did these tasks always wind up on her desk?

Oh yeah, that's right, she thought sourly. *I'm being screwed.*

She sighed as she scrolled through screen after screen, diverting herself by studying the booking photos of the arrested, until a face appeared that stopped her cold.

Frankie sat up and reached for her smartphone. Scrolling rapidly through her texts, she looked for the picture Charley had just sent her. Holding the phone up beside her screen, she looked once more. Then she looked again.

There was definitely something there . . . it was vague, but it was something, possibly even the beginning of a positive ID. The man on her screen looked remarkably like the one Charley had photographed at Hardly Strictly. Could he possibly be their would-be terrorist?

Scanning the arrest record once more, Frankie read the man's name: Randy Tytus, DuPage County, Illinois, born 1964. But then squinting at the picture again, she tried to ID it and she just couldn't. Charley's picture was just a little too fuzzy and out of focus.

Frankie read the record of the arrest. *Arrested for assault on an officer after being stopped for a red light violation.* They let him go after a lengthy questioning. God knows what that was all about . . . but it made sense, if he was the same guy.

Sitting back for a moment, Frankie contemplated the screen. Then, scanning the document, she found the arresting officer—an officer named Nobello. Grabbing her phone once more, she began texting Connie. Connie would get her the complete report—she knew he would, no questions asked. Ideally she could get notes on why he was released. If Connie was in the city, maybe he could even get it to her tomorrow.

Now she considered texting Charley. But then Frankie stopped herself. *It is better to wait,* she thought prudently—at least until she had a little more of the story.

———————

Electra was up at dawn despite, or perhaps because of, her sleeplessness. By 7:30, she'd already walked the dog, eaten an egg, scanned the paper, and secured her Blue Bottle coffee.

Now what? she thought with dismay.

Sitting down at her desk, Electra began to look for Roscoe. *He has to be out there somewhere,* she thought. But then that's what she always thought.

On the other hand, maybe she'd never find him. Maybe he wasn't actually a threat.

Maybe she'd just imagined the whole thing.

Maybe he was just some kind of sad, horny man she'd exposed in an uncomfortable way. What evidence did she have that he was stalking her, anyway?

But what if he did actually know her? What if Roscoe was no more than just another dazzled follower of her strange and intractable brand, like all those kids who needed a selfie with her?

On the other hand, what if he did intend her harm?

Still . . . what if her obsession with Roscoe was just a distraction from the real matter at hand, building a business and getting on with her life?

What if she was just chasing after this guy to avoid the massive, aching hole in her heart left by the person who was once her daughter?

No, today is going to be different, Electra thought to herself. Today she wasn't going to wander helplessly through website after website, vainly searching for the stray evangelist. Today she was going to get down to work. She would hire a web developer. She would arrange for new headshots.

Maybe she'd even come up with her tagline.

Maybe.

Electra sat at the opened laptop, but her fingers did not move. Instead they lay helplessly in her lap as she felt her heart beat faster and faster. Panic was closing in on her, and the only thing she wanted right now was to search for Roscoe. The searching, alone, provided her with a strange sort of comfort. At any rate, she had to do something so she could stop panicking and simply sleep at night.

She got up and wandered into the bathroom, where she counted out her remaining Xanax. There were twelve. She hadn't taken any since she'd arrived in San Francisco, mainly because she was waiting for things to get to the point where she needed them.

It could be argued that they were needed now.

She took one of the pills with a swallow of water and walked back to her computer. Opening up a blank document, she began to tap out possible taglines.

The Society Dom. Good Girl Gone Bad.

The Society Dom. A Whole Lot Tougher Than She Looks.

The Society Dom. Kink Made Respectable.

Sitting back, Electra surveyed the list and sighed. *Shit. How about this?* she thought bleakly. At least this one was true:

The Society Dom. Fucking Scared.

Randy adjusted the angle of the camcorder in the tripod and smiled into the camera. He glanced over at the flip screen to the right of the lens. Everything appeared to be in order.

Then he poked at the home screen with a hesitant finger until the volume meter appeared. Magically this thing seemed to be working today—but then what did he expect? God, as usual, was in charge.

"Testing, testing, testing," he said awkwardly into the mic. The levels were fine.

It was time to begin. Randy looked at the camera and sighed. Then, taking a deep breath, he squared his shoulders and pushed the record button. The red light above the lens began to flash.

"My name is Randy Peter Tytus, and I am responsible for—" He glanced over at the flip screen and stopped. He hadn't noticed the plaid shirt he'd left hanging to dry on his closet door. It was visible in the background of the shot. Since this was going to be on national and perhaps even global news, he should put away his laundry, right?

Randy returned a moment later, task completed, and settled himself before the lens once more. This time he took an additional step, and, closing his eyes, he prayed to God.

Lord, please help me find the words to say that will sanctify this act of righteous vengeance. Speak through me that those who are sinners may see and hear this video and come unto the flock. May they know their wrong doings, and may the world be eradicated of their toxic sin.

Squaring his shoulders once again, Randy looked at the lens, swallowed hard, and began.

"My name is Randy Peter Tytus, and I am responsible for today's attack on the sinners of San Francisco as well as the murder of Pamela Delacroix, the Society Dom. These murders I committed in the name of our Lord Almighty."

Randy's heart was beating wildly. He took a deep breath and, closing his eyes, he steadied himself once more before he continued. Now he glared into the camera.

"Isaiah 65:5 says, 'Stand by yourself, come not near to me; for I am holier than you. These are a smoke in my nostrils, a fire that burns all the day.' Sinners of San Francisco, you are the smoke in our nostrils that burns all day, as are *all* who imbibe alcohol, appear naked in the streets, fornicate recklessly, and practice deviant sex."

A light sweat broke out across Randy's brow. Still, he continued, his voice rising with fervor.

"People of San Francisco and deviants everywhere, this is your day of judgment! Your perversion is a mortal sin for which you are finally being punished. For this, you will go straight to Hell. You who kill the hearts of man with your evil ways must die as well, and today is the day."

Pausing for only a second, Randy tried to collect himself, but it was impossible. He continued loudly, ire rising through him like a red hot column of flames.

"I have staged these attacks in the name of the Father, the Son and the Holy Ghost," he burst. "In memory of my father, Rudy 'Evangelical' Tytus, may he rest in peace." Unexpected tears sprang into his eyes, and his throat caught slightly as he said his father's name. "Rudy 'Evangelical' Tytus," he cried again, this time with more fervor. "May his name be sanctified with this act forever."

Trembling, Randy reached over and turned off the camera. Then letting go, he bent his head and broke down into sobs.

This is impossibly hard, he thought. But what choice did he have? Once the Lord had spoken . . . well, that was that.

After a moment, Randy stopped crying. Sighing, he wiped his tears on his sleeve and took the camera off the tripod.

Arthur would be here soon to pick it up and turn his little video into something that would be seen the world over when the moment was right. Apparently it could be preloaded on the World Wide Web days ahead to be released just after the attack. Just like that, Randy would be an instant celebrity.

Daddy, I'm doing this for you, he prayed silently. *May it bring you peace.*

21

Connie sat back in the chair in Frankie's office and thought for a minute.

"I actually remember the guy. He was a certified nut job," he verified. "I happened to come into the station while he was being booked that day. And he was wearing one hell of a big wooden cross—that I remember for sure."

"Yeah, the cross is visible in his mugshot," Frankie remarked.

"We don't usually get those types," he said, pulling out the paperwork he'd brought for Frankie. "I'm not sure how much this will tell you. It appears the guy wasn't intoxicated. Didn't have a weapon. No record of any kind. He just . . . freaked out. After he got pulled over, he got out of the car so fast he knocked the officer off his feet. Then he ran. Basically he just screwed up.

"We kept him for a while. Then we finally gave him a citation and let him go. I mean, all he did was run a red light and bump into the officer. He only made it a block before the officer got him. We brought him in just to be on the safe side.

He was actually incredibly apologetic. Kept saying 'bless you' to everyone after he got released."

"Was he in his own car?"

"A rent car."

Frankie looked at the report. "And he was wrestled to the sidewalk?"

Connie shrugged. "Apparently. There was no reason, but you know how people are sometimes." Connie leaned back and put his hand behind his head. "Why so interested, Frankie?"

Frankie was non-committal. "His name came up."

"Hnnh," said Connie, looking at Frankie curiously. He waited for a moment for more information, but there was none.

Frankie shoved the papers into the top drawer of her desk. "Thanks, Connie. I owe you one," she said.

"Two," he said with a grin. "Technically speaking, you owe me two."

"Got time right now?" she asked with a grin." I'll treat you to a double."

"No time like the present," he replied easily.

"Starbucks or Peet's?"

"Let's go for the high test."

"Starbucks," declared Frankie as they headed for the door of the station.

This was just a little too good to be true.

———— ·•·•· ————

"No fucking way," was all Charley could say. Repeatedly.

"Way," Frankie replied.

At this moment, they were sitting at Charley's computer, gazing at the website for the Evangelical Church of Christ in

Wheaton, IL. All Frankie had to do was Google Randy Peter Tytus and she found him immediately.

The site featured a portrait gallery of their recently deceased minister, Rudy 'Evangelical' Tytus. It showed pictures of him and his son, Randy, taking communion together, distributing cans at a Food Bank, and greeting parishioners at some kind of church social.

"Jesus," Charley said, turning to Frankie. "I can't fucking believe this. You know who this is, right?"

"Oh, I know, all right," Frankie spat. "'Kill the fags.' Rudy 'Evangelical' Tytus. There isn't a queer alive who doesn't know about that asshole."

"And this guy is his *son?*"

"Yeah."

Charley threw his hands up in the air. "Well then, it's obvious why he's here. This is San Francisco, for fuck's sake. He's not here for some Bible Conference!"

"Well, don't get too sure yet, Charley. I mean, we don't know why he was here. He could have been a sex tourist just here to cheat on his wife, right?"

"He has a wife?"

Frankie shrugged. "I have no idea. This is all I could find on him.

It's weird because there's nothing else—like *nothing.* No social media, no other web pages, no photographs besides those two . . . even in the county records. No house, no mortgage, no job—it's like he barely exists. I did find his birth certificate, but you know, I couldn't even find a bank account."

"No bank account?" Charley exclaimed.

"It was a ridiculously lucky break that he ran that red light," Frankie said.

"Yeah," agreed Charley. "So we can assume he has no cell phone, he lives off his father's income, and rents or lives in his father's house. The dude's untraceable. Which, if you're a domestic terrorist, is probably a reasonable choice."

The two looked at each other, and Charley sighed heavily.

"So Electra was right?" Frankie conjectured.

Charley exhaled slowly. "Christ," he said. He looked at the ceiling. "Now we're doubly fucked."

"Because . . . ?"

Charley held up a hand and quickly fired off another text to Electra. "Because she won't respond to this text—or any of the others I sent today or yesterday or the day before. She's mad at me," he explained.

Frankie looked at Charley with dismay. "Don't tell me you—"

"No! It's not what you think. It's . . . complicated, but mainly she's mad because I told her I couldn't help her."

Frankie stood up. "For Christ's sake, let's help the poor woman!"

"We are! I mean, I'm trying to, at least. She's just . . ." He looked forlornly at the phone. There was no reply. Now he typed another message, this one all in caps.

That ought to get her attention, he thought. And if it doesn't . . .

Well, it has to. That's all.

———— ·•·• ————

Electra's entire kitchen now smelled of roses and her bedroom of gardenias. The floral arrangements Charley sent arrived just after her morning coffee, and she was pleasantly surprised.

In fact, she'd almost called him . . . until his most recent texts arrived.

But Electra wouldn't be calling Charley because now he was screwing with her.

URGENT, the last one screamed. WE'VE FOUND ROSCOE. *Call me immediately.*

Honestly, she'd expected more from Charley. Did he have to be a drama queen, too? She doubted he'd actually found Roscoe. How could he? The timing of his texts was just a little too frequent and a little too desperate. So no, she wouldn't be calling him.

Why should she? After all, as he'd carefully demonstrated to her, Charley was a master manipulator on top of everything else.

No, Electra would hunker down right where she was and keep on searching, and he could text all he wanted. Her door would not open again, at least not to him.

She'd warned herself not to get involved back at the beginning. But as usual, Electra hadn't listened.

"Screw it, I'm going over there," Charley announced.

"Whoa, whoa, whoa. Charley—I mean, buddy, this is not the way to get a woman's attention. You should know that." Frankie put a restraining hand on Charley's arm.

Charley threw up his hands. "Why, because I'm a trans? Frankie, for God's sake! The last time I was female was ten years old," he protested.

Frankie sighed. "She's playing you, Charley. And yeah, she's connected with a potentially dangerous guy. But who knows where he is? So let me deal with her. Your job right now should be to respect the boundary she set. Electra doesn't want to hear from you, remember? Give the chick some space."

Charley buried his face in his hands. "Dammit," he mumbled.

Frankie stood up. "I'll go over there," she offered. "I'll talk to her."

Charley looked up hopefully. "Put in a word for me?"

Frankie rolled her eyes. "Jesus, Charley! Get a grip. I'm going over there to take care of Electra and let her know what we found. That's all."

"Are you going in uniform?"

"Probably not," Frankie said. "It will just be a social call. We'll see how far I can get, because the fact is we need this woman. If Randy Tytus comes back to SF, it's possible he actually is planning something. Apparently he's interested in her. So if he comes back, he'll probably cross her path. Then something may be in motion, and we have to be ready to act."

"Don't forget we have the wire audio . . . not that it's worth much. They're just saying 'blah-blah-blah-be-in-touch-sure-okay.' *Fuck.* I wish we had something real."

"Well, the arrest is real. It just isn't linked to anything. Yet," Frankie pointed out. "What we have is solid proof that this guy's both erratic and highly religious."

"And highly religious people sometimes commit massive hate crimes." Charley sighed. "Okay. Go over there, see what you can do, and I'll give her some space."

"Sounds like a plan," Frankie said, rising. "For now, as far as we know, the dude is staying put."

"Maybe," said Charley.

"Yeah . . . maybe." Frankie put on her hat and headed for the door. "Don't worry," she said, turning back to him.

"We're going to be okay, Charley. You. Electra. Me, too. This is all going to work out. I just have a feeling."

"Thanks," he said, feeling a genuine wave of gratitude for his friend.

Charley watched Frankie head out into the night as the door clicked shut. He realized he felt utterly powerless, which was just plain strange.

A phrase drifted through his mind, something from an old childhood prayer he used to say at bedtime. That was back when he was just a little girl who wanted to be a boy with all her heart.

God's will be done, not mine.

In this moment, it felt oddly comforting. Charley inhaled deeply and closed his eyes, repeating it one more time.

"No, no, no," Randy began again. "You don't tell anyone where you are going, before or after we get to San Francisco. Even if you're just going out for a walk. You don't talk to people, remember?"

"That's going to be hard to remember, boss," the young man said.

"Well, try, Arthur," Randy said. *He really is incredibly thick sometimes,* Randy thought with annoyance. How many times had they been over this?

At this moment, they were driving through a small town outside of Lincoln, NE, looking for the Motel Six where they would spend the night. They were driving to California, simply because it was the only truly safe way to get the sarin to San Francisco. They'd been on the road since early that morning.

It would take thirty-one hours, according to the big book of maps Randy had purchased for their trip. They were on mile 492.

Randy had known Arthur for most of his life through the church. After both of his parents were killed, Arthur became a ward of the state until Randy and his father intervened. That was seven years ago. Now Arthur would do any old thing Randy asked, making him the perfect choice for delivering the sarin attack. Not only could Arthur be counted on to execute basic commands, he was unflaggingly loyal, and he was a team player as far as Christ was concerned.

"When are we going to get there?" Arthur asked. "To California, I mean."

"Two and a half more days . . . Saturday, I expect," said Randy. He pulled into the Motel Six parking lot. "We're going to go into the hotel and check in now. And you remember what you can't say to anyone, right?"

Arthur put his arms around his ribcage and began to hum quietly in his seat. "Can't tell anyone where we are going, right, boss?" he said after a moment.

"Right, Arthur. I'm going to go check in now and you sit here." Carefully, Randy removed the car keys and left Arthur in the car, waiting obediently. Thankfully, the sarin was locked—not that he thought Arthur would get into it.

Still, one never knew. Even after all their years together, he still surprised Randy sometimes.

God's will, Randy reminded himself as he headed into the lobby. That and a suitcase of sarin and he was all set.

22

"This time I've got something solid. Honestly, R.J., just give me two minutes," Charley urged into the phone,

His former boss had picked up. At least that was a good sign. Now Charley was doing his best just to keep him on the line. Or at least he was trying to.

There was no immediate answer.

"R.J.?" he asked again.

"I'm here," R.J. said wearily. "Come on, son. You know there's only one thing we can talk about."

Charley closed his eyes in frustration. "I'm doing the therapy. It's going fine. I'm going to meetings. They're going fine. I paid the taxes. I talked to the forensic accountant. I'm looking for the receipts. What else can I tell you? That shit's in motion, R.J."

A pained silence followed.

"Look, I have a positive I.D. on this guy," Charley exhorted. "He's a religious fanatic, a right wing Christian fundamentalist. His father was a big time evangelical who started the 'Kill the

Fags' campaign and picketed the funerals of gays in the military. I think he's potentially violent."

Charley could hear R.J. breathing on the other end of the line.

"Charley . . ." his boss began awkwardly, and then he stopped.

"Please just help me, R.J. I know you know people in the Bureau. I know you do. He's been stalking a friend of mine . . . a public figure. She's definitely a target."

R.J.'s voice softened slightly. "How do you know?" he asked.

"They've had contact. I got a wire on her at her last appearance and she gave him her card. He told her he wanted to see her, that he was going to look her up."

R.J. sighed. "Now, Charley," he said. "That's not really stalking, is it?"

"Well, no . . . okay. And it was a couple of months ago, but I personally believe he's coming back. I know he is. I saw this guy in action at the last big music festival, and he was totally checking out the SFPD. I can feel it. And you know my instincts, R.J. You've said yourself—"

"Charley . . ." The older agent interrupted, his voice filled with compassion. "Listen, you may have something or you may not. But that doesn't change the fact you lost your clearance. Finish your work and get your clearance back, and then maybe I can help you."

"But you've still got yours, and this woman needs help. Just take a look at—"

"I can't help you, Charley. I'm sorry."

"R.J. Come on! I'm only on the Seventh Step and this is going to take forever!" There was no reply. "R.J.?"

The line was dead. R.J. had clicked off.

"Hell," muttered Charley. He put the phone away and resolved to go find the missing receipts for the forensic accountant. Or at least call the dude.

That much he could do.

———•◆•———

"Electra? Are you in there?" Frankie knocked on Electra's front door. There had been no response to the doorbell, though a dog had barked inside.

After a moment, Frankie knocked again. "You don't know me, but I'm a friend of Charley's," she called through the door. "I'm Sergeant Kennedy from the SFPD."

Now a curtain parted slightly to Frankie's left. She could see Electra standing in the shadows, peering out at her. Frankie gave a small wave and flashed her badge.

The door opened a moment later, and Electra stood before Frankie, sizing her up. "Frankie Kennedy," she repeated, offering her hand. Electra simply stood there.

"I'm with the SFPD," she continued after a moment, showing her badge one more time. Folding it, she put it back in her pocket. "Charley told me about the evangelical Christian you've been following, and I got an ID on him this morning."

Electra barely glanced at the badge. Instead, she looked at Frankie with disdain. "*Who* are you?"

"A friend of Charley's. He told me about the suspect you've been following. Can I come in?"

Electra didn't budge in the doorframe. "Why do you want to help me?" she asked.

Frankie was taken aback for a moment. "Oh . . . well, Charley told me you've been trying to ID the suspect, and—"

"Officer," Electra interrupted brusquely. "I have private security, so we won't need any help on this."

"I'm sure you do. It's just that I know who this guy is and I believe he is a potential threat to your pers—" Frankie began as the door abruptly shut in her face. *Damn,* she thought. *This woman totally doesn't fuck around.*

Undeterred, Frankie knocked one more time. But then she stopped herself.

Okay, fine, she thought. If Electra wouldn't talk to her as a civilian, maybe she would as a cop. Over the years Frankie had learned that uniforms were remarkably effective in situations like these.

<hr />

Electra watched through the curtains as Frankie turned around and left. *This is all I need,* she thought—*some poser pretending to be a cop who Charley had sent as his mole. Charley really is relentless,* she thought with annoyance. Why couldn't he just get the message? Desperation never, ever wins.

Even if he did, supposedly, have a positive ID on Roscoe.

No, she wasn't going to fall for some would-be "cop" just because she flashed a badge. On the other hand . . . there were thoughts that Electra didn't like to think about.

What if Charley actually did know who Roscoe was and he was truly trying to help her? What if the cop was real and she showed up because she was legitimately concerned? What if Roscoe really was the nut job she thought he might be? What if he was part of a big network of angry evangelicals? What if there was an entire pack of them in San Francisco just waiting to show up in the night and take her down?

Her thoughts just kept escalating. Electra got up to pace.

She glanced at her dog. If someone broke in, he'd probably hide under the bed. And as for security, she'd fired the last guy after he showed up for work stoned. Where the hell could she even find decent security at this point?

Deep in her gut, Electra was afraid. Like cattle at the slaughterhouse, she had that second sense that something was seriously awry. Roscoe intended harm; that much she knew. Whether it was meant for her or someone else wasn't clear. She just knew her mission now was to find Roscoe and somehow defuse him.

Electra sat down once more to her laptop and opened it up. She typed in "Sergeant Frankie Kennedy SFPD" and immediately found her on LinkedIn listed as a patrol sergeant. Then she found her salary, notes from a committee she sat on to hear labor disputes, and quite a bit about her very long career with the police.

Oh.

Electra sat back and considered what to do next. The cop was for real. Which meant the danger was for real.

Shit.

There were times in her life when she just had to cave. Electra knew that. She also knew there were times when she hadn't surrendered, and they'd caused nothing but trouble. Like early on when her marriage crumbled after Randall found the whip in her closet.

She'd lied, of course, saying it was just part of a costume. Just a fun little getup for yet another benefit. This was just the kind of faux-naughty thing the society wives did, so Randall bought it. Or so she thought.

Yet, even then Randall was on to her. Still, Electra refused to admit what was going on. She refused to acknowledge that she was cheating and that she wasn't in love with him anymore. She also refused to admit that deceiving her top-gun lawyer-husband was a very bad idea.

Electra had been willful, and she had been in denial. How easily she had believed that nothing bad would happen, even as she spent more and more time doing these men, these husbands of her friends. Gradually, they became more and more dependent on her sexually and emotionally. Every last one of them needed her within a very short time. So of course it was all going to blow up.

Still, her denial continued. Right up until Electra got that final text from Guy, albeit written in French.

Randall was on it like a bulldog, of course. All he had to do was pick up her phone and start flipping through the texts while she was in the shower. She'd forgotten about Google Translate. She hadn't even thought he might hire a private investigator.

Denial and willfulness. That was the whole game right there. Electra sighed heavily. Here she was, once more, right back in the same place. Nothing learned. Not a thing gained.

The only difference was that this time she truly had no one to turn to.

Electra picked up the phone and looked at her favorites. Peyton, Charley, and her sister in Maryland who couldn't even begin to understand any of this. She tapped Peyton's name, and the phone began to ring.

This wasn't going to go anywhere, of course. Her daughter never answered.

The phone rang four times, and then a fifth. Electra poised her finger to end the call, but then Peyton's voicemail came on. She'd gotten practiced at avoiding her daughter's voicemail over the last few months. She never left a message because there didn't seem to be any point.

"Honey, it's Mom—" Electra began. And then uncontrollably, she began to sob. Just the mere familiarity of hearing a recording of that young, beautiful, vibrant voice was more than she could take.

Horrified, Electra pushed the button to disconnect. No one needed to hear her sobbing into the phone, and certainly not her estranged daughter. Above all else, Electra had to keep it together. This was her challenge now, and she would rise to it.

Furiously wiping her eyes on the back of her trembling hand, she got up and went to the kitchen. *Fuck Charley and the cop and Peyton and all of them. Fuck them all,* she thought furiously.

She would fucking do this alone, come hell or high water.

Grabbing the bottle of vodka in the cupboard, she opened it, put it to her mouth, and drank. The liquor burned a path straight down her throat to her heart. Capping the bottle again, Electra put it back in its cupboard and slowly sat down.

There was nothing left to do but wait.

———————

Randy sat quietly with an unopened Bible in his hands, waiting for inspiration to come, as Arthur lay snoring in the other bed. They were in a hotel just outside of Reno, only hours from their destination.

It felt odd to ask the Lord for instruction on a murder, but honestly he didn't know what else to do. The time would soon be here, and he had to know what to do. Undoubtedly the Lord had a plan for him—just as He had with everything else. There was no doubt about this.

Still, no information was forthcoming.

Randy waited, smoothing his hand across the pebbled black leather of his Bible. He hoped God would not ask him to shoot Electra—he had no gun or even a knife at this point, and he wasn't sure how to go about finding one. Furthermore, the blood would be a problem. He hated the sight of blood.

More likely, Randy thought, *I will wrestle her to the ground and strangle her, or possibly suffocate her with a pillow or a plastic bag.* He'd brought a few grocery bags from Illinois, just in case. He'd heard they didn't allow them in San Francisco.

Daddy would be pleased with this scenario, he thought. Then all those wrestling trophies he'd won would finally be for something. How insistent his father had been that he become a wrestler. And he did it, even though it chafed at his soul. That way they couldn't call him "faggot" anymore—and they didn't, once he started winning things.

Randy sighed and closed his eyes once more, looking for guidance.

He bent his head in prayer.

Show me a sign, Lord, that this is the way you intend for me to eradicate this sinner. I stand ready to do your will, Lord. Direct me now.

Across the room, Arthur snorted and murmured in his sleep. It had been three long days since they'd left Illinois. The sarin sat soundly over on the bureau, and his assistant finally seemed versed in each step of the attack.

All that had to happen now was to receive the Lord's guidance on when to set up his meeting with Electra and how to proceed ahead.

There was less than a week to go.

23

This time, Frankie knocked with the brass doorknocker. She was in full uniform.

There was no reply immediately, but she knew Electra was in there. The woman never went out apparently, because being recognized was a problem. Charley told Frankie this; he seemed to know Electra's every waking move.

"It's Sgt. Kennedy," Frankie called through the door. Still there was no reply. She put her hands on her hips and waited. Frankie wasn't due at the station for another half hour, but she'd suited up early just for this house call.

She rang the buzzer one more time. Above her, a window opened and Electra appeared wrapped in a towel. "Hi, Officer. I'll be down in a minute," she called with a wave. *This is different*, thought Frankie.

Electra appeared a few moments later in a pair of jeans and a sweater, her hair still damp. "Come in," she said as soon as she opened the door. "You caught me in the shower."

Frankie followed her inside. "I'm on my way to work," she told Electra. "I thought I'd just try again."

"Because of my stalker . . ."

"Yeah." Frankie walked toward Electra's silk couch and sat down. She was using her male swagger to appear as big as possible. It was an almost predatory walk, with a slow gait and a bit of hulk to the shoulders. Frankie only put it on in certain situations, like now when she needed to be impressive. She suspected the uniform alone was not going to do it.

Electra sat down on a nearby chair. "So you have an ID on the man who's stalking me . . ." she said.

Frankie nodded. "Yeah. He appears to be an unstable guy. No criminal record, but he's very low profile—almost no trackable ID whatsoever. He's intentionally stayed off the grid."

"So how'd you find him?"

"Through the highway patrol. They picked him up for running a red light. He assaulted an officer, had to be chased and wrestled to a sidewalk before they could take him in."

Electra sat back and listened to this. "Amazing," she said. Then she looked at Frankie intently. "How do you know it's him?"

"A lucky break, basically. I used the picture Charley got of him. Turns out he's got deep religious roots." Reaching into her back pocket, Frankie produced a copy of the arrest record. "This is him, right?"

Electra unfolded the document. There was Roscoe in a mugshot, looking terrified. The caption read, *Randy J. Tytus, Wheaton, IL.*

Electra looked at it for a full moment without responding. "Yeah, that's him," she finally said. "Can I keep this?" Frankie nodded.

Standing up, Electra suddenly turned to Frankie. "Does Charley know you're here?"

"Yeah."

Electra folded her arms and just looked at her. "Seriously? Like you guys thought this was all it would take for me to come around?"

Now Electra strode to the window and parted the curtains slightly. "Oh, for God's sake!" she exclaimed. She spun around to face Frankie. "And I suppose you know Charley is parked outside?"

"What?" Frankie burst. She rolled her eyes. *Oh, sweet Jesus!* She peered through the curtains at Charley, sitting calmly in his car across the street. *Smooth,* she thought grimly.

"Totally sorry about that . . ." Frankie murmured. "Look, Electra. You need some kind of protection. I'm not FBI. I'm just a cop. But I can take down your info and file it, in case something happens. And I could probably alert the folks over at the Bureau about this dude and see if they can do something for you."

She paused and looked Electra in the eye. "I think you need it," Frankie added more gently.

"Whatever . . ." muttered Electra, moving fast toward the door. "I've got it covered, Officer, but thanks for coming by."

Frankie stopped. "Well, actually, Electra, I do have to file a Suspicious Occurrence report. That is my responsibility at this point."

"Must you?" she asked with annoyance.

"Mm-hmm," affirmed Frankie. "It's not a big deal. You don't even have to come in."

"I see," said Electra. This was the last thing she wanted, because then the media would start sniffing around. Somehow they always knew when the police got involved with a celebrity. "We couldn't just sweep it under the rug, could we?" she asked. "Keep it off the record for now?"

Frankie looked at her. "No," she said. "Sorry."

Electra sighed. "Do what you have to do, Officer," she said a bit tartly. Clearly this train was going somewhere fast, whether she liked it or not.

Electra opened the door for Frankie. "Give Charley a message for me," she said.

"What's that?"

"Tell him he can send all the roses he wants, but I'm done."

Frankie stopped in the doorway. "I'll tell him. Hey—you're sure you don't want to come down to the station?" she asked.

Electra shook her head. "No," she concluded firmly. "But go knock yourself out, Officer."

"Fine," said Frankie as she went out. "I will."

What the hell is the big deal with this woman? Frankie thought as she headed down the front steps. As far as she could tell, Electra was a bitch on wheels who didn't mind wasting Frankie's time. Furthermore, she was clueless about her own personal safety.

Frankie caught Charley's eye as she walked by his car. Charley looked up at her like an eager puppy. "Interesting woman," she remarked. "Anyway, your timing is unbelievably bad."

"Uh-oh," Charley said. "Can I give you a lift?"

"Nah. I'll call you later," said Frankie, heading out into the gathering fog.

Frankie needed to walk; she could already see what was unfolding. If they were lucky, Electra would agree to wear a wire, the suspect would surface, and they would hole up in a listening post and get his confession. Charley could be the lead on this, and she could be officially off duty. Or just on duty enough to get support. To cover her ass, she'd file it with the SIT officer. And maybe—just maybe—they could do something here that would make a difference.

If they weren't lucky, Electra was going to go down in a blaze of glory, either dead or attacked.

Of course, there was a third option. The suspect could just disappear and eventually life could go on again. Charley would get over his broken heart, do his paperwork, and get his job back. And she'd still be stuck in the immense stream of shit that was her life for the foreseeable future. Which would probably continue right up to retirement.

Assuming she could keep her job that long.

It was the not knowing that killed Frankie at moments like this. But then that was fate for you, choosing its course and taking no prisoners as usual.

Frankie headed up Fillmore into the mist and tried not to think about it. One way or another something would indeed happen.

———◆◆———

R.J. picked up the phone, hesitated, and then placed the cradle back in the receiver. This was a very bad idea.

Still, something wasn't right.

Charley had sounded a little more desperate than usual when they'd spoken; he'd been pleading and anxious. Charley never got that tinge in his voice unless a threat was real. In fact, R.J. had never known him to get so worked up—ever.

On the other hand, Charley had also never been suspended before.

No, R.J. had to be the bad cop right now. Calling the Bureau was just going to raise a whole lot of questions, and inevitably, Charley's lack of clearance was going to become a big fat rotten egg all over R.J.'s face. After all, the suspect was Charley's lead. So Charley would have to do the briefing, right? There was no way to hide the fact that he'd been suspended.

Things were already dicey enough with those Bureau hotheads who ran the place. As usual, they were looking for more ways to tread on his personal space and discredit the Agency.

R.J. remembered a certain set of contentious emails just six months earlier between him, a snarky woman from the Executive Secretariat, and the deputy associate director of the Bureau. A bad lead provided by Zorik, the agent from hell, had slipped by him and left a trail of slime a mile long. Even though that was a whole lot of hot air about nothing, R.J. still emerged slightly tinged.

But hey, shit happened. Which was why he simply couldn't help Charley out right now as much as he wanted to. All he could do was keep the pressure on Charley until he finally filed his paperwork or did his steps or whatever the hell he was supposed to do. The missing money would turn up, the tax situation would disappear, and life could go on.

R.J. just wished Charley would hurry up. There were wars to start and catastrophes to prevent, and God knew he needed all the help he could get.

Randy pulled the well-worn business card from his pocket and placed it on the nightstand in front of him. It sat next to the telephone and the thin plastic cup of water he'd been drinking from.

It was time to call Electra.

The Tracfone sat on the bed next to Randy like a slowly ticking time bomb. He'd bought it just for the call, and it was his first time using a cell phone of any kind.

Since he didn't use email, he realized he'd need to break his own rules for a change and succumb to technology. But he figured it was just this once. So he made sure to get the disposable kind of mobile phone. Not only was it cheap and temporary, it could be used once and then thrown in the bay. Or dropped from a ten-story window.

Not a soul could ever trace it.

With the instructions spread before him, Randy picked up the phone, flipped it open, and stared at the keypad. It looked like a tiny version of the wired phone he had at home. But then just as suddenly, he slammed the case shut and put it down.

He wasn't ready. He had to prepare.

After all, he'd been thinking of this call for days on end. Randy had imagined just the tone of voice he'd use to sound casual and matter of fact at the same time. As if booking a BDSM session with a dominatrix was the sort of thing he did all the time. He'd also imagined her responses, excited and willing to service him.

Unless, of course, Electra had changed her mind.

Now he started to worry. What if she wasn't actually game to see him anymore? Randy's jaw clenched just thinking about it. Then he'd be in trouble. How on earth was he going to get to her then?

No, he was fairly certain she would see him; she had to. God was arranging this, not him. It would have to work out, because otherwise he wasn't sure how he'd get her alone.

Randy took a deep breath and emboldened, picked up the disposable phone once again. Clicking it open, he held it to his ear and waited for a dial tone. There was none.

Pausing, he looked at the small phone and gave it a shake. Was it *supposed* to be silent? Randy sighed. God, he hated technology with all his might.

Mustering all he had, he decided to plunge in. Randy poked each of the digits of Electra's phone number into the phone with a trembling index finger. Still the phone remained silent.

He looked at it once again. The numbers on the little blue screen glared at him in large type. *Now what?* he thought miserably. Randy peered at the phone's keypad, and his eye lit on a button with a small green phone receiver on it. Poking at it, he prayed.

Like a miracle, the phone began to ring. And then suddenly, there she was.

"Hello?" asked Electra. She'd answered on the second ring. Randy could scarcely believe it. "Hello?" she repeated a bit more urgently.

"Hi," Randy said, clearing his throat. "It's Roscoe . . . We met . . ."

"Roscoe!" she answered. "I know, I know. Hi!"

There was an awkward silence. He was silent, forgetting for a moment what he'd planned to say next.

"How are you?" she purred. *Electra's voice is smoky,* he thought. Just like a good seductress. She sounded enthusiastic, genuinely happy he'd called.

"Great! I had to leave town for a while," he explained. "But I'm back."

"I'm so glad," Electra said. "Are we going to get together?"

Randy's heart was pounding and sweat was starting to pour from his brow. "Yes, let's," he replied with a little squeak.

"Hang on. I'll get my book," she said. Then the line went quiet as she put him on hold for a moment.

Randy tried to steady his now wildly beating heart. He could feel the blood rushing to his head, and he swallowed against the intensity of emotion that was building in his chest.

Here she was. On the phone. Talking to him. *He was going to murder this woman.*

Breathe in—one—two . . . Breathe out—one—two . . .

"Okay!" Electra returned to the phone with gusto. "Gosh . . . April is practical—" she started to say.

"I can't do it until next week," he interrupted. "I'd like to see you May fifth."

There was a beat of silence on the other end of the phone. "Electra?" he asked after a few more seconds.

"You know, Roscoe, you don't get to push the dominatrix around," she said quietly.

"Oh! I'm so sorry," he demurred. *For God's sake!* he suddenly thought with a small blast of rage.

He could hear her pause again. For a moment, he wondered if he should say something . . . but what?

Finally Electra spoke up once more. "Well, you are from out of town," she replied with a little sigh. "So I guess I could make myself available at 8 p.m. on the fifth. The price is $2500 cash, payable as soon as you arrive. Give me an email address and I'll send the details."

"I don't have email," he said. There was another pause.

"Really?" Electra sounded incredulous. "Wow."

"I can give you a P.O. box."

"Okay," she said somewhat dubiously. Randy recited the address of the postal box near the Civic Center he had rented. Electra was silent as she wrote it down. "By the way, how do you spell your last name?" she asked.

Randy remained silent as a surge of panic rattled him. He'd totally forgotten which last name he'd given her. It started with an S—that much he knew. Wasn't it Smith-something? Smithers? Maybe Smithson?

"Is that Stevens with a v or a ph?" she asked finally. Suddenly he had the distinct feeling that Electra knew his name was fake.

Once more Randy's heart started beating wildly. "Oh! Stevens with a v," he replied heartily. "That's what you meant! Yes—it's the English version." Randy had no idea if that actually was the English version of the name; it could be Polish for all he knew. He just knew he had to say something in that moment.

"I really must get off," he said. "Do you have everything you need?"

"Yeah, I think so," she replied evenly.

There was another pause. *Should he say something more?* He wasn't sounding relaxed and debonair at all. No, instead he knew he was sounding neurotic and downright panicky.

"Take care, Roscoe," Electra said. "I'm looking forward to it."

"Me, too," he answered. He heard her hang up.

Examining his phone one more time, he looked for the way to end the call. Gingerly he touched the button with the red phone receiver picture on it and heard the concluding click. Then, lying back, he folded his phone in half and gave a long, shaky sigh.

He really wasn't cut out for this work. But apparently God thought he was, so it was time to man up.

Randy gave another long, weary exhale and considered the new, disturbing possibility that Electra was on to him. But then just as quickly, he dismissed the thought.

She wasn't smart enough. Anyway, she was the heathen

and he was one of the saved. Randy already knew how this was going to go.

It was written, right?

Getting up, he straightened his tie and adjusted his cross. It was time to go out for dinner.

Electra ended the call, put her phone down on her vanity, and just looked at it.

It had happened.

Roscoe had called her.

She buried her head in her hands and covered her face for a moment.

She didn't know whether to exult or to be terrified. Of course, Electra knew this would happen. She'd known it from the first moment she saw him, when she was ineluctably drawn to following Roscoe from booth to booth all over the Folsom Street Fair.

Roscoe was actually Randy J. Tytus, son of the famed evangelical minister, Rudy Tytus, whose 'Kill the Fags' campaign was one of the most polished displays of hate the country had seen in the last fifty years. Electra had just spent the last hour and a half learning all about him. His father was thrust into the limelight just as she had been—an unwitting celebrity simply motivated by the voices in his head.

Her intense focus was only broken by the ringing of the telephone.

Suddenly here was the evangelical's son, asking her to subdue him, blindfold him, tie him up, spank him, whip him, and generally humiliate him. Perhaps he'd want the nipple clamps or the ball gag, too.

There was something so patently absurd about this that she almost wanted to laugh. Which she would have, except for the fact that she was now completely terrified.

Now Electra's decision to be a dominatrix seemed pathetic and shameful. What was she thinking, anyway? She was over fifty, and she had a daughter, for God's sake! Sex workers got murdered all the time, dismembered and stuffed into trash bags that got left in greasy alleyways.

Why in God's name had she even come to San Francisco?

The folly of her entire pursuit was now ringing loudly in her ears. Electra got up and began to pace. She never should have come here. And she never should have listened to Charley.

For a moment, Electra thought about fleeing. She could, of course, just slip away and disappear. She could go to L.A. or the Bahamas or somewhere in Europe. She didn't have to be a dominatrix. Maybe no one would even know her in the Bahamas.

But then what would she do? Sit around all day in sun-filled gardens, sipping Chardonnay, reading, and browsing catalogs like any other woman of her class? Electra sat down on the edge of her bed and fought the black despair that was now rising in her throat. She began to cry. The thought nearly took her breath away.

She didn't want that life. It was exactly what had driven her onto the airplane the day she escaped.

She didn't want that fake, petrified parade of things. She wanted the authentic, genuine, bigger-than-life life that she knew was hers to claim.

Charley understood this perfectly, of course. He, too, had given up a life that had been prescribed for him, one that he didn't want. And unlike her, he'd made a break before he ever grew up. She could almost hear him in her ear, gently encouraging her.

"You don't have to do a damn thing you don't want to do, Electra."

She didn't have to be anyone other than who she was; she knew that. But now what would she do? Now reality, and her first client, had arrived at the very same moment.

Shakily, Electra picked up her phone. It was dawning on her that she could no longer do this alone. Wiping a trembling hand across her face, she punched in Charley's number. She guessed he was sitting outside, parked under the tree across the street, exactly as he had been all day.

He answered on one ring. "Are you there?" he asked.

Instantly, she was washed with a relief so intense, it welled up in her throat, filling her senses, flooding her mind. "I'm here," she said as she began to sob. "I'm here."

"Do you want me to come over?"

"Yes," she practically whispered.

"I'll be right there," he said. Charley hung up.

Lying back on her bed, she realized she'd just given in, to temptation, to vulnerability, and to fear, perhaps. But mostly she'd given in to the powers of being a woman who needed her man in this moment. But not just any man. She needed this one, completely unusual man.

At this moment, Electra no longer cared about anything except wanting Charley by her side, knowing her as he did and feeling her presence as he did.

There was no other choice; Electra realized this now.

Suddenly she understood she had come to San Francisco to meet Charley, to meet Roscoe, and to find her way so brazenly back to herself. A small glow of contentment began in her belly and began to spread through her body as she wiped her tears on the back of her hand.

The doorbell rang.

A moment later, as she opened the door, she was filled with a profound sense of rightness. Charley looked at her and she looked at him, and then they kissed. It was a kiss of promise for what was to be. And of gratitude for what had been.

"I missed you," he said, pulling her closer and stroking her hair.

"Me, too," she sighed. She lowered her face into his chest.

"And all is forgiven?" Charley asked after a moment.

"Yes," Electra said quietly. "Do you forgive me?" she asked, looking into his face. "I acted like an ass."

"I'd say you acted like a woman who didn't want to be screwed with."

"It was idiotic," she murmured into his chest. Pulling back, she looked at him once more. "I love you and I'm sorry," she said.

"Yeah," he replied almost gruffly. "Me, too." She could see tears spring into his eyes. Charley wiped them away casually. He sniffed and smiled, looking down at his feet.

"Yeah, that was crazy. I was way too intense," he remarked. Then he shrugged. "You live and learn."

So Charley, she thought. "Guess what?" she asked, taking his hand.

"He called."

"How did you know?"

"You needed something big to break you down."

Electra was quiet for a moment. "Yeah," she agreed. "Apparently I did. Anyway, I guess I have my first client on May fifth," she added. "My very first as a pro."

Charley smiled and, pulling her tight, kissed her again. "Good," he said. "It's time we got this party started."

24

At this moment, Frankie was helping Electra affix the tiny recording device deep inside her corset and trying to ignore the proximity of her naked breasts. This was definitely not in her usual line of work.

"Ow!" Electra said loudly. "It's sharp!"

"I thought pain was part of the deal," Frankie remarked drily.

Electra looked at her. "I *inflict* the pain," she said.

"Oh. Yeah," Frankie answered. Why wasn't Charley doing this, anyway? He was the one who actually wanted his hands all over this woman. She wondered what was keeping Charley. They should have heard from him by now.

Charley was completing the listening post at a house two doors away. It belonged to the only neighbors Electra had actually met.

Frankie stepped back appraisingly. So far so good; the wire seemed secure. "So how does that feel?" she asked.

Electra wiggled and squirmed a little. "Not bad. How much can I move around?"

"How much do you need to move around?"

"If I have my way with this man, not much," Electra replied.

———— • ◆ •◆ ————

Electra exhaled slowly and looked at Frankie. What was it about Frankie that she found so detestable? And why the hell did she keep questioning her so much?

The encounter with Roscoe was going to be no big deal. She intended to tie him up early, torment him excessively, and not let him go no matter what. But then sometimes intentions went awry in these matters.

Her mind flashed to Luis, the Venezuelan ophthalmologist who turned on her during one of her sessions in New York. Turned out he was far more averse to pain than he thought, and considerably bigger. After she put the nipple clamps on him, he just went nuts. Luis managed to yank the steel manacles out of the walls of the private dungeon she'd rented for the occasion. Then he chained her up instead.

It took Electra hours to talk him down so she could go limping back to her husband, her wrists bloodied and bruised.

That really was the beginning of the end.

But Roscoe was not Luis—not even close. First of all, she knew Roscoe's type—soft, needy, and wounded. And physically they were the same size. There shouldn't be any problem at all.

Hopefully.

Electra tried not to think about the alternatives. There was, of course, the chance that Roscoe would snap and overpower her, that he was a cold-blooded murderer under that pasty evangelical façade. Which hardly seemed likely . . . still . . . If she didn't have the SFPD and Charley listening to everything that went on between them, she'd never have agreed to have Roscoe in her home.

"I should be fine," she told Frankie. "You'll be able to hear everything, right?"

"Yeah," Frankie replied. "We'll have backup ready to come right in."

Frankie stood there silently for a moment, thinking about what she had just said.

The last part was a fib, of course. Frankie had made no headway whatsoever getting anyone in the SFPD to take this threat seriously, mainly because the lead was coming from her. It didn't help that Electra refused to return the many calls from the SIT guys.

"A publicity hound," they called her, because, of course, even Situation Investigation had heard of Electra. They finally closed the case due to lack of response, which did little to help Frankie's cause. She just looked lamer than ever.

So now Frankie was forced to do this job out of uniform while she was technically off duty. Still, once she sent out the request for backup—in or out of uniform—they always showed up.

This time, however, they were going to make her work for it.

Charley would be listening alongside her. He could be counted on to provide some calm, seasoned muscle power if needed. And she had her weapon. *No,* Frankie reasoned, *everything is going to be fine.* If it wasn't—well, it wouldn't be the first time things flubbed in her years on the force. Somehow things always . . . generally . . . worked out.

Yes, there was the destroyed meniscus she got after scrambling over a fence while chasing a suspect in 2003. And then there was the asshole who pinned her to the street and started pummeling her in front of a bunch of tourists who shot the whole thing for YouTube. That was humiliating. But it did get her three months off and a medal of commendation. Those cases were the exception to the rule; Frankie had only been hospitalized twice in twenty-seven years.

As for Electra, she certainly *seemed* tough enough to handle a little duress, didn't she?

"So let's cover the basics, Electra," Frankie began. "What are you going to do if you can't subdue the guy?"

Electra crossed her arms. "Not a problem. I always subdue my clients."

"Maybe, but we don't really know what his agenda is, do we? What if he walks in, flips you on the floor, and pulls a gun?"

"What do you suggest, Sergeant?" Electra asked a bit icily.

"I'm asking you. What are you planning to do?"

Electra sighed heavily and crossed her arms. "I'm going to chain him up and torture him until he orgasms, Frankie—what do you think I'm going to do?" she said dully.

"Do you have a weapon?" Frankie asked.

"No . . . do you?" Electra shot back at her.

Frankie set her jaw. *Electra really is getting to be a royal pain in the ass.* "You know if you'd just talked to the Station Investigation Team this would have been a whole lot easier, Electra. They called you half a dozen times, and you never even picked up."

Electra folded her arms and eyed Frankie coolly. "I chose not to involve the SFPD," she replied.

"Yeah, but you need them now, don't you?" Frankie retorted as

her phone rang. It was Charley. She listened for a moment. "Say something for Charley," she said to Electra. "He's setting levels on the wire."

Good, she thought. They were almost done and she could get the hell out of here. Frankie picked up her backpack and slung it over her shoulder, making her usual check for the heft of her weapon. It was, as ever, still there.

Electra apparently satisfied Charley with her sound test, and he clicked off. It was time for Frankie to go next door to the listening post.

She went to the door just as the doorbell rang. Through the sheer curtain, she could see Charley. He looked excited, like a little boy. Electra was pretty damn lucky to have them both in her corner—even if she didn't know it.

"Frankie," Charley said, giving her arm a squeeze. "It's looking amazing over there. The owner's gone. We'll be all set. Oh, and nice job on the wire. The sound is perfect."

Before Frankie could respond, he looked past her to Electra in her corset and stockings. Charley shook his head and let out a low whistle.

Frankie rolled her eyes. "Stepping out now," she said loudly. "Charley—meet you over there."

"Fine," he said as he made a beeline for Electra. She simply stood there, waiting for him. "Pull the door shut as you go," he told Frankie.

"Good luck," Frankie said, turning to give her a wave. Electra just nodded, not taking her eyes off of Charley.

As the door closed, Charley took Electra in his arms. For the moment, there were no distractions. In this tiny window of time before Roscoe arrived and their scene began, it was just the two of them, finding each other once more. Reuniting in the truest sense of the word.

They looked at each other and there it was again, the fierce magnetic pull that had been there ever since the day they met. Only now, it was seasoned with love. "Are you going to be okay?" he asked gently.

She nodded. "Yeah. I'll be fine . . . better than fine. I'm going to be fantastic."

He smiled and pulled her close. "How do you know?" he whispered as he kissed her hair, her ear, her neck.

"I know," she said simply. "I've been waiting for this—it's my test."

"Test?" Charley's face was buried in her hair, and he was breathing in her scent. "What kind of test?"

"The test of what I'm made of," she said. Electra pulled back and looked at him. "I can't screw this up, Charley. It's the beginning of everything."

"Yeah, I know," he said. He ran his hand through her hair one more time, and his fingertips came to rest on her cheek. "Either way I'm not going anywhere."

She smiled. "Good. Let's hope I'm also still here when it's over."

Charley sighed and, pulling her close, rested his cheek tight against hers. "I promise you this," he said. "I will try with everything I've got to protect you. I'm going to give it my very best—and you know, Electra, that ain't bad."

She smiled at him. As usual, his confidence charmed her.

"I love you," he said simply.

"Me, too," she replied. And now she kissed him.

She tasted slightly of liquor. He paused. "Johnny Walker?" he asked.

"Chivas," she replied. "Steadying my nerves."

Charley smiled. "That's my girl." He gave her one last hug. Then he looked at his watch. "Gotta get out of here," he said. Heading for the door, Charley smiled over his shoulder. "We'll be listening," he said jauntily. "So make it interesting!"

"I'll do my best," she retorted with a laugh. Electra watched him go as the door closed. And then she was alone.

She sat down to wait.

Randy closed his eyes in frustration. "Arthur . . . think," he implored. Then he sent up a feeble prayer.

Oh, God—please help this incredibly inept young man do at least something right in our attack.

"One more time," Randy sighed. "When do you open the suitcase?"

Arthur hesitated for a moment, closing his eyes. Then his eyes snapped wide open. "After I get to the roof and I locate my target down on the street," he said brightly.

"Okay, keep going. What else do you have to do first?"

Arthur was silent.

"God *dammit*," burst Randy. He leaped across the table and put his face up close to Arthur's. "*Think, Arthur . . . for one fucking moment in your life . . . THINK!*" he implored.

Then shuddering as if shaking off a bad memory, Randy retreated to his chair and touched the large wooden cross hanging around his neck. His nerves were worse than ever.

Arthur just sat there mutely. He looked terrified.

"I'm . . . sorry, Arthur. I—" Randy said brokenly. He didn't finish his sentence.

Preparation for tomorrow's early-morning attack was not going well. What had he been thinking, entrusting more than $100,000 worth of sarin to a person who was simply not all there? Arthur was almost certain to screw this up. For a brief moment, Randy considered canceling his session with Electra and doing the drop himself.

Just as quickly, he talked himself out of it.

Murdering Electra was part of the mandate—a critical part. The YouTube video was loaded and timed for release just after the attack. His murder weapon, two plastic bags from Piggly Wiggly with just the right thickness to suffocate someone, were waiting on his dresser. Randy had been forced to think ahead and pack several for his trip, since plastic grocery bags were now illegal in San Francisco.

He figured if he couldn't suffocate Electra with the bag, he could always use it to hang her. The key was to get the job done efficiently. The only tricky part would be getting her into the handcuffs and chains and subduing her first. Randy was starting to wish he had a gun.

But then there was the whole issue of traceability. A weapon was easy to trace, but not a bag from Piggly Wiggly. There were literally millions of them out there.

Randy took a long inhale. "Let's go over this one more time," he said wearily to his assistant. "What do you have to put on once you get to the roof?"

"Latex gloves."

"And do you know where your gloves are?"

"Mmm-hmm," said Arthur. Then he fell silent.

Randy motioned for him to continue.

"Oh. In a box of five hundred next to the TV," Arthur continued compliantly.

"What time do you leave your hotel room?"

"6:15 a.m."

"What time will your alarm go off?"

"5:30 a.m."

"And what will you do for sure before you leave the hotel?"

"Pray," said Arthur. "On my knees. And recite Leviticus 16, verse 3. After I take a shower." *At least that part will go smoothly,* Randy thought grimly.

"Okay, Arthur." He sighed. "We'll see how it goes." Randy closed his eyes wearily. He could feel the fiasco building already.

"I'll be okay, boss," said Arthur hopefully. "I'm going to wear my gloves. I'm going to be really, really careful after I unlock the suitcase so I don't die."

"Huh?" Randy's eyes opened, and he looked at Arthur dumbly for a moment. Then he recovered himself. "Oh! Yes, of course. You'll be fine. If you die, then—"

"Then I'm delivered, sanctified, to the gates of Heaven," beamed Arthur. "That's my favorite part," he confided.

"Right," concluded Randy.

There was nothing more to say.

"Here's the key to the suitcase," Randy said, handing it over to Arthur. "Where are you going to put it?"

"Under my pillow," answered Arthur.

"Okay. Go do it right now." He watched the young man walk across the hotel room, pull back the bedspread, and situate the key in its safe place.

Randy looked at his watch; it was almost seven. He was due at Electra's in an hour. He stood up. "I'm going back to my hotel now."

He had booked into a different hotel from Arthur as a security measure, but now he felt reluctant to leave. "Are you sure you're going to be all right?" he asked one more time.

"Yeah," said Arthur.

Randy looked at him for a moment. Suddenly he felt almost tender toward the young man. "What are you going to do tonight?" he asked.

"Watch *Dancing With the Stars*," he said. "They're at the Magic Kingdom."

"Great," said Randy. "Well . . . okay."

"Yeah," said Arthur.

The two men were silent.

Randy nodded. "Okay," he repeated. He had to get out of here. Still Randy stood there, motionless. Then, stiffly, he leaned over and gave Arthur an awkward hug. "Take care," Randy said.

Arthur smiled at him. "It's going to be fine, boss."

"Right," said Randy dubiously. He walked to the door of Arthur's hotel room and then turned around one more time. "Take care," he said.

Arthur was already busy with the TV remote; *Dancing With the Stars* had snapped on with a blare. "Okay," Arthur said without looking up.

Randy left, closing the door behind him with a soft click.

God's will be done, he thought as he walked down the plush, carpeted hall. It was so hard being the arbiter of justice.

Electra looked at the clock beside her bed. Randy would be here in twenty-two minutes. Opening the chest beside the bed one more time, she made sure all her restraints were within easy reach. Then she sat down to wait.

She'd swapped out her chains for some much heavier ones on a trip to Mr. S. a few days earlier. The boys behind the counter had recognized her, of course. But this time she didn't bother with a disguise for professional reasons. A sweet bearded guy gave her the chains for free. "A token of our appreciation for moving to SF," he said.

Mr. S was the place you went in San Francisco when your strap-on harness broke or your gas mask pinched a bit. They did all manner of leather and restraint repairs. They had chains, too; lots of them. These were in the room just past the eight-foot-tall photograph of an erection.

Electra looked at her watch. Seventeen minutes to go. Maybe he'd be early.

She wasn't one to pray, but suddenly an unfamiliar thought welled up:

God . . . help me get through this alive.

Okay, she thought to herself, *why the hell not?* Leaning forward in her chair, Electra put her head in her hands, closed her eyes, and prayed.

God . . . help me subdue this guy and find out what his deal is. Help me stop him from doing whatever he's planning . . . because I know it's not good.

She sat back and opened her eyes, a little surprised. Just as suddenly, an unexpected wave of optimism washed over her.

Maybe I really will be fine, Electra thought to herself. Standing up, she checked herself one more time in the mirror, and she smiled.

At the very least she looked hot *and* she had great backup. That much she could count on.

———•◦•———

Roscoe patted on a splash of Old Spice and waited for the customary sting. He also waited for that little whiff of confidence that came along with its purported "Re-Fresh Technology."

Yet, none was forthcoming.

But what did he expect? He was about to do several things he'd never done in his entire life. Murder, with or without the chaser of BDSM; it was all new to Randy. After praying and putting on his aftershave and clean briefs, there wasn't much more he could do.

Randy surveyed himself in the mirror. At just past fifty, he was still ever so slightly a catch. At least, he was in his own mind. The son of a famous evangelist and the star of the Wheaton, Illinois pot-luck circuit gave him certain cred with the ladies. He knew that.

Still, here he was, as alone as ever. Randy paused to consider the sad question that murmured across his mind every so often. *Why?* He had been on plenty of dates. There was no question about his valiant attempts, again and again, to find love over the years. Still, no woman ever seemed to stay—or even respond to him, generally. And honestly, he was at a loss to say why.

Randy suspected it had something to do with being so close to the Holy Father. Really, he was more engaged with the Lord than anyone else he knew. Still, in those rare moments when Randy had attempted intercourse with females, something always seemed to go wrong.

There was the torn condom with Lily Parsons; she was never seen again. Then there was his favorite, Esther Scholl, the strawberry blonde poet he dated in college. She'd taken off after he repeatedly failed to have an erection. Something was wrong -- that was for darn sure. Given that it was a sin to have sex before marriage, he wasn't surprised. But maybe his sexual shortcomings were about more than the wrath of God.

It had been years since he'd even considered sex. He'd engaged Electra so he could murder her, yes. But Randy also figured if this was his last night on Earth, he'd like to experience some decent sex as well. It was a last hurrah of sorts.

For better or for worse, San Francisco had awakened his libido. Not that this was a good thing, given the bizarre direction his libido seemed to be heading these days. A little heterosexual heat would at least turn him back in the right direction before he ascended.

Really, at this point, what did it matter, anyway?

Randy fully suspected that he would receive at least a life sentence in prison for this little escapade. That was if he survived. Ideally, of course, he would die and be welcomed into the Kingdom of Heaven, where angels and archangels would sing his praises and Daddy would be the first to greet him.

And Daddy would, of course, be terribly proud.

That would be glorious. In fact, it was what he was going for. It was the full reason he'd made the YouTube video. If Randy was going down, it had better be in a blaze of glory with his reasons explained to the world at large. Just the way the jihadists did it.

On the other hand, there could be handcuffs and SWAT teams and police in bulletproof vests looking for the mild-mannered killer with the bag from Piggly Wiggly.

In a dark sort of way, it was all pretty exciting.

Randy surveyed himself one more time in the mirror. He was wearing his nicest short-sleeved shirt—a patriotic red, white, and blue plaid. Honestly, Randy had no idea what to wear to a BDSM session or to a murder. This was his best shot.

He glanced at his watch. Twenty-four minutes to go. He really needed to be on his way. Falling to his knees, he prayed one last time for guidance, for strength, and for forgiveness.

Please guide me, Lord, in delivering this one to your flock, for she has strayed so far away. Help me find in her release the sanctity of your holy word. I follow your word, Lord, and stand ready as your foot soldier in our war on the heathens of this world. World without end . . . For ever and ever. Amen.

Standing up slowly, Randy wiped a tear from his eye and slipped his hotel card key into his shirt pocket. Then, checking the two Piggly Wiggly bags for holes one more time, he folded them neatly and slipped them into his back pocket.

He was ready to go.

25

Things seemed very quiet over at Electra's. Aside from listening to her pee several minutes ago, Charley could detect little or no movement. The suspect was due to arrive in less than seven minutes.

Charley patted his brow with a folded linen handkerchief. He was more nervous than he expected. Not that he would let Frankie know.

"Is it hot in here or is it just me?" he asked.

"You're too young for hot flashes," Frankie noted wryly.

"Do I make lesbian jokes around you?" he shot back.

"So you're going to get a dick before menopause, aren't you?" she asked. "I mean . . . if it was me, I'd totally be doing that. That's got to be the ultimate defense."

Charley just looked at her. "Are we seriously discussing this right now?"

She smiled and shrugged. "Just a thought," she replied.

They listened to Electra walking. Then, all of the sudden, the doorbell rang. Immediately, the mood shifted to one of concentration. "You ready?" he asked, and Frankie nodded.

Charley smiled. It felt good that they were in this together.

———•◦•———

The doorbell rang.

Electra paused in her hallway. Randy Tytus was now less than ten feet away from her, albeit on the other side of the door. And he was four minutes early.

She sat down on the chair. A moment later, he buzzed again. Through the curtain she could see his vague outline, and she knew he could see her. Still, she did not answer.

At seven minutes past the hour, Electra finally rose and opened the door. Randy was sitting on her stoop, his back to her.

"I said be on time, not early," she remarked tartly. "That's going to cost you, Roscoe"

———•◦•———

Randy jumped up, startled by the opening of the door. He turned around and looked Electra. She was taller than he remembered, wearing jeans and a black cotton shirt unbuttoned well into the shadow of her cleavage. A bit of lace appeared at the opening. Her hair fell loosely around her shoulders, and her mouth looked a bit drawn. She also wore a pair of black spike heels.

He stood up and slowly ambled up the stairs. "Hi," he said uncertainly.

Electra opened the door wordlessly, and then she shut it behind him. "We talked about the price," she said.

"Oh . . . yes." Randy pulled out a wad of hundred dollar bills and carefully counted out twenty-five of them. "Two thousand and five hundred," he said finally, handing the cash to her.

They looked at each other. In that moment, Randy felt himself weaken slightly. He could take her down; he could wrestle her to the floor if he had to. Of course he could—he knew he could. She would resist, of course, but he could do it.

Still, why rush things?

Randy's hands had begun to sweat.

Electra looked at him. "What are you waiting for, Roscoe?" she asked.

"Am I . . . supposed to do something?"

Electra folded her arms. "I don't know, Roscoe. Are you?" she asked.

Now he was confused. He thought dominatrices were supposed to take charge, to be bossy and demanding. Weren't they?

Randy still stood there uncertainly.

"Take off your clothes," she ordered over her shoulder as she disappeared into the kitchen just beyond them. Randy could hear the sound of ice being dropped into a glass. Maybe she was getting them a drink.

He was still standing in the hallway. "Here?" he asked. "You want me to take off my clothes right here?" There was no answer.

"Electra?" he asked, his voice hanging in midair. Surely there was a bedroom somewhere for him to change in. Or at least a bathroom.

Electra did not answer. Slowly Randy unbuttoned his shirt. Still she did not emerge from the kitchen. For lack of anything better to do, he took his shirt off. Then he caught sight of himself in the hallway mirror.

God, he looked pasty. And fat.

"Electra?" he called again weakly. There was no answer. Now Randy walked to the door of the kitchen. In an instant, she was on him. "Did I tell you to come in here?" she snapped. "No, I did not. What did I tell you to do?"

He took a step back and swallowed. "You told me to take my clothes off," he replied in a small voice.

She looked at him. "You haven't done that yet, have you?"

Randy was barely breathing now. "No," he said. For a guy who was supposed to commit a murder, he was failing miserably right now.

"No, what?"

"Huh?"

"No, *Mistress*," she commanded.

"Yes . . . I mean, no, Mistress," he murmured as a chill slithered down into his groin. Already his libido was rising. *What does this mean?* he wondered. Randy was too distracted to pray.

Electra took a step toward him and a long drink of the cocktail in her hand. The drink was only for her, apparently. She put it down on the table. It appeared to be scotch on the rocks, not that Randy knew much about these things.

"Take off your pants," she said.

"I just thought—"

"Take them off. Right now," Electra demanded.

"But I thought—"

"*Forget what you thought,*" she snapped. "Oh, for God's sake!" she said as she began reaching for his crotch. "Am I going to have to do this myself?"

Intuitively, Randy reached to cover his groin as the first handcuff clicked neatly into place. "What?" he burst. He jerked backward, but Electra was faster. Darting forward, she grabbed his other wrist and snapped the second handcuff around it as he jerked his arm up. A pair of police handcuffs now confined Randy's wrists.

Randy just looked at them dumbly. Then he looked at her. "What are you doing?" he muttered.

Electra laughed. "What did you think this was, Roscoe? Pretend?"

Grabbing the small, neat comb-over on the top of his head—the one Randy had fussed over for several minutes to hide his bald spot—Electra pulled him in tight to her face. Randy suddenly felt very small. She peered down at him; she was at least two inches taller in her heels.

"Ow," he said.

"That's not the right response, now is it, Roscoe?" she asked, her grip on his hair tightening.

"No?" he asked. Fear fluttered up from his belly.

Electra rolled her eyes. "No, *what?*" she hissed.

Randy swallowed. "No . . . Mistress," he murmured. *Why did he say that?* Already he was hooked.

Her intention, or perhaps her attention, was so pure, so powerful, he realized in that moment he just wanted more of it. "No, Mistress," he said again more fervently.

"Let's get clear about something, Roscoe. You don't get a choice when you come in here. I am in control of you. Do you understand?"

Suddenly Randy felt like throwing up. This was all too much for him. His entire head was beginning to ache from her grip on his hair.

"Yes, Mistress," he said, eying her. Her face was closer to his than ever.

"I need to—" he began.

"You need to stay right here," she said quietly. "I'm not letting you go until I'm good and ready, Roscoe."

Randy closed his eyes against the swell of his nausea, and it settled slightly. "Yes, Mistress," he replied.

————— ·•· —————

Charley pulled off one headphone and turned toward Frankie. "Holy shit . . . did you hear that?"

She nodded. She hated to admit it but Electra was good, better than she'd anticipated. Frankie had hesitated to give Electra her extra handcuffs. But she had two pairs in her backpack, so what the hell?

Charley clamped his headphones back on, rapt. There was no distracting him. "What a woman," he murmured under his breath.

Frankie stole a glance at him and rolled her eyes. *Men!*

————— ·•· —————

Randy turned his head slightly to the right. He didn't bother to tell Electra that he had a chronic stiff neck or lower back pain. Somehow it seemed inappropriate. This wasn't like an aerobics class where the instructor wanted to know all about your injuries before class began.

No, he'd willingly lie down on Electra's bed and let her chain his handcuffed hands to the headboard. He didn't even balk when forced to lie facedown.

At least he wasn't naked, but he suspected that was coming. For the moment, she'd left the room.

Randy could hear Electra moving around in the apartment. He thought maybe she was getting something. Like a whip. Another wave of fear moved through his body when he thought about this. Did he honestly want to be whipped?

Yes, oddly.

Randy's heart quickened at the thought, and his penis stirred inside his shorts. He could feel himself becoming aroused just thinking about it. *Who knew?* he thought to himself. *How could this even be possible?*

But it was. And more than just possible, it was real. Randy began to surrender to the unfamiliar stirrings in his body as he anticipated what she might do to him. God and his unholy religion were the furthest things from his mind in that moment.

"Electra?" he called out to her, raising his head from the mattress. But there was no reply.

Instead, he heard the front door shut.

Electra had apparently just gone out.

Now what was he supposed to do?

Where the hell has Electra gone?

It was hard to tell exactly what she was doing. Charley looked over at Frankie, and she shrugged. It sounded like Electra was getting into a car.

Apparently it was her car. They listened to her turn on the car engine enough to open the windows. Then she clicked the ignition off again. It appeared that she was just sitting there.

"What's she doing?" Frankie asked, but Charley couldn't answer. Honestly, he had no idea. For all he knew, she was about to drive to the opposite side of the city, and for God knows how long. In that moment, he just wanted to talk to her.

There were no more sounds from the car.

After a while, Charley sighed. This was a turn he hadn't expected.

———— • ◆ • ————

Electra sat quietly, studying the back of the Volvo parked in front of her. "Wage Peace" read the sticker on the back window. She wasn't sure exactly how long she intended to sit here. She just knew that it was going to take a while for Roscoe to break down completely.

Electra was going with her gut on this, because that was all she knew how to do. She sighed and settled herself against the headrest. Then she looked at her watch. *This could take a while,* she thought.

Not for one minute did it occur to her to tell Charley and Frankie what she was doing. In fact, she'd forgotten she was even wearing a wire.

As usual, Electra was flying solo. But then, she usually did.

———— • ◆ • ————

"Jesus," said Charley, taking off his headphones. "You think we should go check on the suspect? It's been at least an hour." As far as they could tell, Roscoe was still chained up on her bed. They doubted he'd be waiting patiently.

"Oh, just go bursting in with our badges or what, Charley?" Now Frankie took off her headphones, as well. "At least we've got the bug in the bedroom. I mean, he's quiet enough. Right now, at least. " She sighed and looked at him. "What the fuck is this woman doing, anyway?"

He shrugged. "I have no idea, Frankie. I guess we just have to wait." Charley ran his fingers through his hair distractedly. "If only we could talk to her," he said.

Frankie sighed and put back on her headphones. It was just another night on the SFPD.

Now Charley looked concerned. "Do you think I should worry?" he asked.

"No, I don't think you should worry!" Frankie burst with exasperation. "If anything, we should go get a pizza. But we're not, are we? We're going to sit here and wait."

Shaking his head, Charley got up and began to pace. Frankie was right. It was going to be a very long night.

———•—•———

Randy raised his head and looked at the bedside clock. It was 11:43. Where in God's name did Electra go? And when did she go? It seemed like she'd been gone for hours.

A new feeling of desperation began to overtake him. Of course, she didn't say exactly what would happen during their session. In fact, she said very little about it. By now he'd imagined that he would have had at least one orgasm. Then he'd just murder her, go find the rent car, and clear out of town. Canada would be his next stop, if he wasn't stopped at the border.

Electra hadn't noticed the two neatly folded Piggly Wiggly bags in his pants pocket. But perhaps she would when she came back. If she unzipped his trousers. Nakedly, he would stand there, wearing nothing more than black socks, as she placed each article of clothing on the chair by the bed. His murder weapon would now be all the way across the room, and he presumably would still be in handcuffs.

For one brief moment, Randy pondered the murder that was supposed to take place. Then he thought about what had already happened.

Electra had led him back to the bedroom. She was almost tender as they walked together, gently guiding him along by his handcuffs. "This is where I sleep, Randy. I'm letting you use my bed because now you are starting to behave yourself," she had said.

Her voice in that moment had been kind and almost soothing. It had reminded him of his mother: his mother giving him a bath, sponging his back when he was six years old. And then later, when he was closer to adolescence, his mother stroking his head and his brow when he was sick. They were powerful memories. So powerful that in that moment, he would have followed Electra anywhere in spite of himself. Somehow he was completely in this woman's thrall.

Randy pressed his brow into the mattress and tried to relax. Much as he hated to admit it, he was enjoying this. A prayer for salvation was the last thing on his mind. At any rate, he might die tomorrow, so then what good would all that praying do?

He wondered how much longer this would go on.

For a while, he hoped.

———

Arthur lay staring at the ceiling. It was 11:43 p.m. He knew because he'd been glancing at the clock off and on for nearly the last three hours, ever since *Dancing With the Stars* ended.

He was simply too nervous to sleep. Now he was obsessing about the car. They'd gotten the rent car to pick up the sarin, and for some reason, Randy didn't want to return it quite yet.

But what if Randy died during the attack? Or what if he did? Who was going to return the rent car then?

What if they both ended up going to the Kingdom of Heaven? Wouldn't there be a really big problem with the rent car? And it was illegally parked in a tow-away zone, no less.

Arthur rolled over and clamped his eyes shut. He had to try to get some sleep.

But what if it had already been towed?

He'd never rented a car before, but this much he knew: it had to be returned when you were done with it. Sitting up, he snapped on the light, put on his pants, and picked up the rent car keys on the bureau.

Then another thought stopped him. It was the middle of the night. The rental car agency would be closed.

Arthur put the keys back down, slowly took off his pants, and got back into bed. He would return the car as soon as the sun came up. The rental agency opened at 6:30 a.m.

Then he would do the sarin drop. It wouldn't be quite as early as Randy wanted, but that would be okay. It had to be.

At least the rent car would be returned. That, Arthur knew, was really, really important. Randy would be proud he'd thought of it.

Closing his eyes, Arthur gave a long sigh and tried to settle down. Then he rolled over and tucked himself into a tight ball, awaiting sleep.

Everything would be all right.

———————

Electra turned the kitchen doorknob as silently as she could. She'd spent the better part of the last forty-five minutes quietly creeping, step by careful step, around the far side of her house. Her intention was to sneak back into the house to keep an eye on Randy. Still he could not know she was there. Not yet, at least.

Charley and Frankie also had no idea where she was, she suspected. But that was all right—she could handle this. On the other side of the house, her subject gave a low moan. He sounded helpless, utterly defeated. *Good*, she thought.

In that moment, it was critical that she feed the illusion that she was gone. Indefinitely. A good dom never would walk out and leave a client chained to the bed, of course. That was entirely against the rules of BDSM, such as they were. But this was no ordinary session, and Roscoe was no ordinary client.

So for now, Electra was simply playing with him, whether Randy realized it or not. Yet the same time, she was also being redeemed. She noticed this as she made her way through the darkness of her yard. The painstakingly slow, step-by-step certainty with which she moved had been refreshing. The mindfulness of it gave her plenty of time to think.

As Electra looked back over the previous year, something occurred to her. There was no reason to regret a single goddamn thing she had done. When she blew her marriage to smithereens, she had simply been trying to find her way. Could she have done this better? Differently?

Perhaps not.

Now, as she crept silently through her darkened kitchen, Electra could feel that her power was back. Not only that— clearly, it had never left.

She stepped on a floorboard near the refrigerator, and it gave a small squeak. *Hell.* Then she heard Roscoe stir in the bedroom. Electra froze in place.

"Is someone there?" Randy called from the bedroom. "Electra?"

For a moment she didn't breathe. Still, she remained calm; she knew what to do. Electra had always known what to do in the tormented game of cat and mouse she played with this man. Just as she had known what to do when she destroyed her marriage.

In some deep, unseen place in her heart, she needed to be released. And she needed to do it loudly and badly. Electra even needed to become known for her secret vice—a vice that filled her soul the way art fed the artist.

Her mind moved back to Randy, who was still moaning in the bedroom. He called her name one more time, and then he began to weep. Randy had been chained up for a few hours now . . . long enough to play with his sense of reality.

By now she suspected he was starting to break down; he would be ready fairly soon, she reasoned.

On the other hand, it was entirely possible that Randy had somehow freed himself from the handcuffs. It was also possible he knew she was there, and that he was faking his torment.

Sooner or later, of course, he knew she would return. Randy could be waiting to kill her right now, knife poised from his hiding place next to the bedroom door.

Electra glanced uneasily over at the knife block beside her stove and did a quick tally of its contents. The knives were all there, except for one of the large chef's knives. She peered into the sink to see if she'd left it there, but the sink was empty. Had she even used that knife that day?

Then she dismissed the thought. She would simply go outside and look through the bedroom window. Then she could see what he was up to.

Slowly, Electra turned. She began to make her way toward the back door, step by silent step.

This was just starting to get interesting.

26

Charley was beginning to pace.

"Hey—could you just sit down?" Frankie asked plaintively. "Christ, I should have brought Scrabble."

"Sorry," he said, taking his chair once again. "You think she's okay?"

"Oh, sweet Jesus, Charley! Yes, I think she's okay for the fifteenth time. She's not even there, for one thing."

They could hear Randy's shuddering sobs. He'd been crying intermittently for a painfully long time. The bug under the bedside alarm clock recorded all of it.

They'd listened to him call Electra's name again and again. They'd heard him grunting and heaving and cursing softly, trying to contort himself into different positions to free himself. And they'd listened to him cursing more and more loudly, screaming until he was hoarse. They'd heard Randy scream for help again and again, but nobody came.

Finally, they listened to him pray. But not even prayer could help Randy tonight.

Charley shook his head. "It's been almost two hours,

Frankie. Do you suppose something happened to her?"

Frankie didn't answer as silence filled the room again. Suddenly, Electra's channel lit up. Charley leaped on the volume knob, turning it up as static gave way to a conversation.

A moment later, they heard her footsteps walking on what sounded like pavement. Frankie and Charley looked at each other, listening. It wasn't clear where she was walking.

A moment later, they heard a soft scraping sound, like garbage cans being pushed aside.

"Good girl," said Charley. "She's looking in the bedroom window."

"Hnnh," said Frankie noncommittally.

Clearly Electra was going to do what she was going to do, whether they liked it or not.

—————◆—————

Electra pushed the front door open. Moments earlier she'd finally made it to the bedroom window and peered in. Randy was still there, lying facedown on the bed, exactly as she had left him.

"I'm back! Have you been a good boy, Roscoe?" she called from the foyer.

She heard him let out a moan. "Electra?" he cried hoarsely.

After a moment, she stepped into the bedroom doorway and surveyed her client. The bed around his face and upper body was soaking wet. Randy looked up at her. His eyes were red and swollen from crying.

"Here," she said, offering him a cup of water. He took a sip.

"Where did you go?" he asked. "Why did you leave? My arms are numb, my shoulders hurt. And my neck is killing me. Take these off of me now."

"Oh, Roscoe, I understand. But we haven't gotten to the fun part yet," she said, feeling his arms for circulation. *So far so good*, she thought. ."You wouldn't want to quit now, would you? We have so much more to explore."

Randy said nothing. He just looked at her.

"You know there are a lot of people who would give anything to be right where you are right now," she continued. "People who would pay me far more than just $2500, Roscoe."

"But why did you leave?" he asked after a moment.

"Because you needed me to," she said. "You needed to know who was in charge, honey. And you needed to melt a little."

"Oh," he said in a small voice. "Can I have more water?"

She fed him a bit more of the water in her cup.

Now she sat on the bed beside him and very gently began to stroke his back. "Why have you been crying, baby?" she asked. "What's the matter?"

He lowered his head to the bed and did not answer. She continued to run her hand across his back.

"We all have skeletons in the closet, Roscoe. Even you. And it's okay," she said after several moments.

"I don't have any skeletons in the closet," he protested tightly. "Take these off of me."

It was her touch that undid him, more than anything.

Her hand just kept moving evenly across his naked back, reassuring and warm, and he found himself clinging to it. This was what had been missing with all of those women he'd been unable to seduce.

"It's okay," Randy heard her say. "It's okay . . ."

"I don't! I—" He stopped. What she was doing to him felt incredibly good. He lay there, feeling her stroke his back again and again. Now Randy was confused.

"Can't you just uncuff me?" he asked feebly.

"Not yet," she soothed in a voice like melted honey.

"Dammit," he cursed. "I just—" His ire was missing now, gone into the void that had opened up in his psyche as he lay there for hours, weeping. Randy felt weak.

"How are you?" she asked tenderly. If only her voice wasn't so sweet and her touch so consoling. She really did remind him somehow of his mother.

"How do you think I am? I'm . . ." His voice trailed off. Again he was silenced by her touch. How he'd missed being touched all these years. How he'd missed love, in whatever form it showed up in. Suddenly he felt a pang of connection with Electra—an odd intimacy he'd never experienced before. It had something to do with being subdued.

Randy swallowed hard. "I missed you," he admitted into the mattress. "I was afraid you wouldn't come back."

"But I'm here, honey," she said. "You just needed to know who was in charge."

"You are," he said hoarsely after a moment. "You are in charge, Mistress."

"Yes," she said with a smile. "I'm glad you understand."

"My arms are so numb," he said again. "I can't even feel them. And my wrists, Mistress—the handcuffs hurt."

"Mmm-hmm," she said. Together, they looked at the handcuffs on his wrists. He had pulled and chafed against them until his skin was bruised. "Oh, look at that," she said in a consoling voice. "Yeah, they are uncomfortable, aren't they?"

Still Electra made no move toward taking them off.

"It would be lazy and irresponsible for me to let you go, Roscoe," she explained after a moment. "This is what you paid me for."

Now she lowered herself on the bed and lay down beside him. She began to stroke his cheek and his neck. He felt himself fasten on to her in this new, tender thrall they were developing.

"Come on, Roscoe. You'll be okay," she said, laying a soft kiss on his shoulder. Once more, he began to weep.

"What is it?" she asked, her hand on his back. "What's the matter, sweetheart?" Still he did not answer. He just wept.

"I know you," she said after a moment. Electra looked into his face. "I knew it the moment I met you. We have karma, Roscoe. Do you know what karma is?"

"No," he whispered.

"It means we have destiny together. That it was inevitable in this one short life that we meet, and that we are forever changed because of that meeting. Perhaps that is why you are crying," she suggested.

His weeping moved to sobbing as shudders began to shake his body.

"I don't want this," he said. "I don't want to know you."

"But you have no choice, Roscoe. It's God's will."

"This is *not* God's will! Please release me," he begged now. "*Please.* I'll do anything you want."

"I am afraid I can't, sweetheart," she said gently. "You are mine now, Roscoe. It is time for us to share our karma."

"But I don't want this karma or whatever the heck it is—I'm a Christian! I don't believe in karma. I do not sin. I've never sinned. I've never had a sinful thought in my life!" he burst.

She smiled at him. "Ever?" she asked. "Really, Roscoe? How is that humanly possible?"

His sobbing overtook him now in great heaving waves.

Randy strained at the handcuffs as his body shook beside her. Still she held him and caressed him.

"I don't care!" he wailed. "I don't care about you or my father or the church or any of it. I hate you! And I hate God! I hate God!" he burst. Then he said it again in a voice strangled with desperation. *"I fucking hate God!"*

Electra kissed his cheek and caressed his hair one more time. "Shhhhh," she consoled. "It's all good, Roscoe."

"Fuck you!" he burst. "It's not all good. None of it is good. Nothing I was made to do was ever *good!*"

"Oh honey, I'm sorry . . ." she consoled, wrapping her arm around his heaving body. Again and again now, Electra kissed his arm and his shoulder tenderly. "Whatever you were made to do . . . it's all okay now," she soothed.

"It's not okay!" he burst. "None of it was okay, then or now! I hated them and I hated myself!"

Stroking his arm, Electra looked at him tenderly. "Who did you hate?"

Randy pressed his face into the wet mattress below him. His voice was muffled. "The boys," he said.

"Which boys?" she asked gently.

"The mean boys," he said into the mattress.

"The boys at school?" she asked.

"Yes," he replied. "They wanted to . . ." Randy's voice trailed away.

"To what?"

He shuddered, unable to answer.

"It's okay, baby," she cooed into his ear. "You can tell me."

Randy opened his eyes and looked at her, his eyes red and swollen. "They said I was a faggot, and they would fuck me with a baseball bat."

Electra nodded.

"My father couldn't stand that. So we set them up. It was his idea," he whispered.

"Set them up how?" she whispered back.

"In the chemistry lab. We broke in one night and made it look like they'd been in there cooking meth." Randy fell silent for a moment. "I left Robert's baseball cap. Robert Weissman. I stole it from his book bag the day before.

"I didn't want to, but Daddy made me," he admitted after a moment. "He said this was how I could be a real man."

The two of them lay there silently for a moment, until Randy continued.

"I've never told anyone this before," he said.

They looked at each other.

"Go on," she said.

"They got kicked out of school. One of them never went back, Robert. He died, dragging his father's car. But no one has ever known the truth." Now he began to weep again. "No one ever knew that we killed him. We killed him with anger. That was a sin, Electra," he cried hoarsely. "Daddy wanted me to be popular like they were. So we had to destroy them."

Randy lay silently, his face pressed into the mattress. He continued after a moment. "That's envy—it's one of the Seven Deadly Sins, Electra. I did that," he said sadly. "I sinned. And my father made me do it."

Now he turned and looked at her. "I'm no better than anyone else," he said. "I'm just another sinner." His weeping intensified. "And my father . . ." Randy sobbed, barely able to speak the words. "He was . . . a sinner, too."

Electra looked at him. Their faces were only inches apart. "I know," she said quietly. "We're all sinners, Roscoe. And not one of us is better than another."

Randy just looked at her. He didn't know what to think.

27

Arthur slipped behind the wheel of the rent car and put the key into the ignition. The valise full of sarin sat beside him on the passenger seat. He looked at his watch—6:35 a.m. He had plenty of time to return the rent car and then get to his post by 7:30.

The race wasn't starting until then, so he figured that was time enough.

It had taken a while to reach the car where he'd left it, all the way over on the other side of Market, at the edge of the Mission. But Arthur didn't mind the walk. He was just relieved the car was still there. It was cool and grey out as the sun began to burn away the fog—a pleasant morning altogether. Here and there he spotted costumed runners moving toward the Bay to Breakers starting line down near Spear and Howard.

He pulled out of his parking space. The car rental agency was back at Van Ness on the other side of Market. Up ahead he could see more costumed participants streaming up from the BART station nearby. He drove the three blocks up to Market as more and more runners appeared on the street.

Arthur pulled up to a stoplight, and as he did something occurred to him. There were suddenly a lot of people walking by—an unusual number. Maybe this was because of the race? The light changed, but no one moved. Around him drivers beeped impatiently.

He looked over at the car next two him. Two people in giant bird costumes sat in the backseat. The driver was painted silver. Rolling down his window, the silver man leaned his head out to see what was wrong. Then he got out of his car. Arthur noticed the painted man was wearing nothing more than a silver thong.

"Shit," Arthur heard him say as he got back in his car dejectedly. Nothing was moving.

The Bay to Breakers crush had already begun. It was now Arthur and 160,000 other people, all trying to get somewhere in San Francisco at the same time.

This was not good. How was he going to get the car returned in time?

Arthur sat back and contemplated what to do. Might as well wait in the traffic, he figured with a yawn as he inched forward.

God's will would still get done, even if it wasn't exactly on time.

———•◦•———

Randy was on some kind of unholy roll. He had been lying in Electra's arms for close to an hour now.

He swallowed. "And my thoughts, Electra. I also have impure thoughts," he continued.

"What kind of impure thoughts?" she asked.

"Of . . ." He hesitated. Then Randy closed his eyes. One moment ticked by, and then another.

"Tell me, baby," she said, smoothing his hair.

"Of men," he finally admitted.

Electra just nodded. "That's okay, Randy."

His eyes snapped open and he looked at her. "Quit saying that! It's not okay! It's never been okay. *I am not gay.*"

"Maybe you're not," she answered evenly, "but maybe you are."

"I'm not gay," he cried, and then his voice rose to a scream. "I AM NOT GAY!"

Electra just pulled him closer. "Shhhh . . ." she said consolingly.

"I'm not!" he insisted, his voice ratcheting up in pitch. "I can't be! It's a mortal abomination."

"I know, I know," she soothed.

Randy fell silent again for several moments. Then finally he spoke. "How would I know if I was?" he asked.

Pulling back, she smiled at him. "You try it," she said. Randy looked baffled. "That's the best way to find out," she continued. "It's just like BDSM—you have to try it to know you like it."

Randy sighed. "I can't be gay," he despaired. "It would kill my daddy."

"He's dead, honey," she said softly, rubbing his neck. Randy broke down now and began to sob even more loudly. Heaving sobs wracked his body.

"I know," he cried, his voice shaking. "I know. *He's dead.*"

Sitting up, Electra reached overhead and released the chain that bound Randy's handcuffed hands to the headboard.

"Thank you," he said, turning toward her.

"Yeah, it's time to unchain you," she murmured for the benefit of the wire. "I'll take off your handcuffs in a little while. Come here." Electra took Randy in her arms. He lay his head on her shoulder and began to cry more softly.

"That was all in the past, Randy," she said gently. "You're okay now. Everything's going to be fine."

Randy said nothing. He just cried for several more moments. Suddenly he raised his head and looked at the clock. It was light out. The sun had been up for hours and it was well past 7 a.m. "Oh, my God," he said with a jolt. Randy sat up. "You need to take these off of me right now," he insisted urgently.

Electra sat up on one elbow. "What?" she asked.

"The sun is already up. I . . . have to get home to pray."

Electra laughed out loud. "No, Randy. That's not going to work here. Sorry."

He turned to her, stymied. "I need you to let me go now. I've been here all night long!"

"You may think it's over, Randy, but I don't. We have more work to do."

"Work?" he said weakly.

Electra grabbed the handcuffs and pulled them up tight. With the other hand, she reached for his groin. "Turn over," she commanded, gripping his testicles tightly.

"No!" he protested, trying to wiggle across the vast expanse of her bed.

A look of white hot panic now passed across Randy's face. *"I have to get out of here,"* he insisted.

"You don't have to go anywhere. Not while I'm in charge."

She gave his balls a harder squeeze, and Randy shrieked, allowing her to subdue him completely. Compliantly, he turned over, face once more to the mattress. "You don't understand," he wailed miserably.

"You're not done here, Randy," she said as she straddled him with her full weight. Reaching up, she reattached his handcuffs to the headboard.

"Electra, *please*," he pleaded helplessly. "There's something I have to take care of."

Randy gyrated and twisted away from her with the little strength he had left, but finally he collapsed underneath her. She wasn't about to let him go.

Kneeling over him, she grabbed his balls more tightly.

"Ow!" he screamed. Momentarily he was immobilized.

"Don't fuck with me, Randy," she said, giving him another squeeze. "You know who's in charge. And you know how much you want it."

"OW!" he screamed. "I don't want it—I never wanted it! I just . . ."

Now she put a knee into the middle of his back. "What?" she asked pleasantly. "You wanted to murder me?"

Randy fell silent. He was breathing hard. He didn't answer.

"Apparently I'm not the only one," she bluffed. "You're darker than I am, Randy. Why don't you just admit it? That's why you have to go kill the rest of the sinners, too, don't you?"

"I don't know what you're talking about," he said unevenly.

"Murder is a sin, too, Randy. Isn't that one of the Ten Commandments? 'Thou Shall Not Murder?" Electra continued breezily. "You don't get to kill people just because they're different."

Randy's brain scrambled and spun. *How on earth does she know?*

"I wasn't going to murder anyone . . ." he began quietly. "I was just going to—"

"Drop a casual bomb? Or a chemical weapon, maybe?"

How the hell does she know this? "I don't know what you're talking about," he repeated uneasily.

"Don't lie to me, Randy," she bluffed. "I know all about it.

I know about your arrest and how you tried to flee the police. Too bad they didn't catch you. I've made a real study of you, my friend. Even off the grid. You're bad news for us deviants, aren't you?"

Randy swallowed hard. The situation was rapidly deteriorating. "Please . . . you're wrong," he repeated with what little voice he had left. *How did she find out?*

"I can't even begin to consider letting you go, Randy. That would be a grave disservice to all those innocent people you want to kill—and also to you. Because I know you, my friend, and I know you don't want to repeat the past. You killed Robert Weissman. Isn't that enough?"

"I didn't kill Robert Weissman," he protested.

"You said it yourself, Randy. Just a little while ago."

"It was my father's idea!"

"Oh really? Who set up the fake meth lab?"

Randy just closed his eyes as if he could will himself a thousand miles away. *Of course she knows the truth.* This woman scared him thoroughly. Randy's heart was beating hard, and he found it hard to breathe. He was having a panic attack.

"I can't breathe!" he gasped.

"Come on, Randy," she coaxed, ignoring him. "Tell me."

"What?" he squeaked, still gasping for air.

"Where the Bay to Breakers attack is planned," she bluffed. "I know that's what you're doing."

"It's—" he began. Then he stopped himself. "What Bay to Breakers attack?" he rasped feebly. So feebly, in fact, that Electra burst out laughing.

"Are you for real, Randy? Fucking tell the truth. The charade is over. You are planning to kill hundreds of people at Bay to Breakers." Electra was bluffing in the only way she knew how—out front and good and loud.

"I—" he began, and then he stopped himself. "I'm sorry . . ." he finally murmured into the mattress.

"What did you say?" she asked for the benefit of the recording.

"I'm sorry," he said more clearly.

"What are you sorry for?" she demanded. Randy began to cry. She sat on him even more heavily. "Ow!" he sobbed.

"We've got all day, Randy. I'm not going anywhere."

Raising his head, he looked at the clock. "Oh, Jesus," he moaned miserably. By now Arthur had the sarin in hand and was advancing on the target.

In that moment, the idiocy of what he had begun had become glaringly apparent. He didn't want to kill anyone. He really didn't. *What have I been thinking?*

"Okay, okay! You're right," he burst. "Get off of my back and I'll tell you."

"No way," said Electra. She continued to straddle him, and now she grabbed his hair in her hand. "Where is the attack?"

"At the Hayes Street Hill . . ." he gasped into the mattress. "580 Hayes Street. Off the rooftop around 7:45 a.m., before the race starts."

"580 Hayes Street at 7:45 a.m.," she repeated for the benefit of Charley and Frankie. "What kind of attack is it? Where is your weapon?"

"My assistant has it. It's a metal suitcase filled with sarin vials. He's going to throw them off the roof into the crowd one by one."

"Sarin vials from the roof—clever. What's his name?" she asked, pulling his hair a little more tightly.

"Arthur," he gasped. "Ow!"

"You should be ashamed of yourself, Randy," she said thoughtfully. "Innocent runners do not deserve to die."

Randy had begun to sob now. "I need to call Arthur. Let me call him—I need to stop him," he begged.

"No calls, Randy."

"No—I want to stop him. Please let me stop him."

"Forget it."

"I have to call him—people are going to die," he pleaded.

"You're not going anywhere, Randy," announced Electra, "and you're not calling anyone. If a few people die, then no biggie, right? Life is cheap," she concluded.

Just then, Frankie burst through the front door. Gun drawn, she came into the bedroom followed by two other officers in uniform. "SFPD. Freeze."

"Oh my God," wailed Randy.

"She's the victim," Frankie said hurriedly, pointing out Electra to the two backup officers. "She'll give you the full story." Electra could hear Frankie talking into her cell phone. *"I need additional units for an outside officer, 6'1" blond male, chasing a suspect at 580 Hayes. We need hazmat on a possible chemical weapon threat. Sarin."*

"Take my unit," an officer said to Frankie, tossing her the keys.

The other now had a gun on Randy and had begun reading him his rights. Electra retreated to the corner of the bedroom.

"You have the right to remain silent when questioned. Anything you say or do may be used against you in a court of law . . ." droned the cop to Randy.

"What should I do?" Electra called after Frankie as she hurried back out to the street.

"Stay here," Frankie yelled back. "Marty will take care of you."

Electra nodded.

"And Electra—" Frankie called out. *"Nice* work."

"Thanks," she replied.

Retreating to the bathroom, Electra closed the door and looked at herself, still wearing her baggy clothing. Her hair was windswept from the beach, but her eyes were clear and bright and alive, perhaps for the first time in years. Electra looked at herself and smiled.

She was back.

Oh yes, *she was back.*

28

"Arthur, pick up. You need to pick up right now. Stop the attack—we're not going to do it. Answer me!" Randy pleaded into the cell phone an SFPD officer now held to his mouth.

"He's not answering," he told them. The officers exchanged looks. "I'm trying!" blubbered Randy, once more in tears.

"We're dialing it again," one of them said.

Arthur was taking no calls. He never answered his cell phone while operating a moving vehicle. That was a law. He glanced at the phone that lay ringing on the seat next to him and looked away.

Who knew how long he'd be in traffic? He'd moved exactly three blocks in close to forty-five minutes. Still Arthur wasn't far from where he was supposed to be. Or so he thought.

He pulled out his map of San Francisco and unfolded it.

The map was sprawled across his lap and the steering wheel as he continued to inch forward. All he had to do was park the car and walk four blocks to the west on Buchanan and he'd reach his site.

It was closer than he realized.

Arthur sighed. Parking was always so very hard in San Francisco. And today . . . well, where could he possibly park in this huge crowd?

But then a brilliant idea popped into his head. He'd pull up to a red zone, leave the emergency flashers on, and park. After all, this was basically an emergency, wasn't it?

Arthur swerved over to a red zone nearby, ignoring the placards advising *No Parking During Bay to Breakers*. Snapping on the car's flashers, he grabbed the metal suitcase of sarin and began walking briskly up Buchanan Street.

After a moment, he reappeared, locked the car, and then set out again. He'd heard San Francisco had a problem with car break-ins.

———— ·•·•· ————

Arthur felt like a character on *The Man from U.N.C.L.E.* as he walked toward his target with his suitcase of sarin.

He reached the building at Hayes and Gough just a little past the appointed hour. First he stood there, waiting for someone to come out, but no one did. Finally Arthur contemplated the row of apartment buzzers, names attached, and he followed Randy's instructions, pushing one button and then another.

No one answered.

He waited another moment. Then he checked his watch. He could hear Randy's voice in his head. *If no one answers, press all the buzzers.*

Quickly, his hand moved down the column of buzzers, pushing each in turn. It felt like a wild, reckless thing to do, but then so did everything else he was doing this morning.

Almost immediately, someone buzzed in his entry as other voices crackled across the static of the intercom. Arthur entered and headed for the stairs.

———•—•———

Charley ran as fast as he possibly could. He raced the mile and a half up the course toward the top of Hayes Street Hill as crowds of groggy early-morning partiers gathered to watch the race. People milled around dressed in all manner of regalia, from nude to fully costumed.

Some stopped to watch him, an unexpected runner in street clothes far ahead of the front runners. In fact, the race hadn't even started yet.

Charley glanced at his watch. Two minutes clicked by, and then three. Did he still have a five-minute mile in him?

Now spectators began to scream for Charley as he tore along the race course, giving it everything he had. For a moment, it reminded him of his quarterback days back with the Blue Jays when they were high school divisional champs.

Somewhere behind him, he could hear sirens. Charley hastened his pace. No police car was going to break through this logjam of humanity. He hoped they had their bikes.

The apartment building that Electra had described into the wire was just ahead. Hayes Street Hill was widely known as the best place to see the full breadth of the moving cocktail party that was the Bay to Breakers running race. As usual, the sidewalk was packed.

Little did they know that every last one of them could be

dead in just a matter of moments. That is, unless Charley made it to the rooftop first.

Charley reached the buzzers of the building and began pressing every button without stopping to catch his breath. Within seconds, two apartments had buzzed him in.

That's how it is on a party weekend in the city, he thought happily as he tore inside.

Chaos made everything easy.

———•◦•———

The wind was cold on top of 580 Hayes. Arthur peered over the side of the building and observed the crowd below. In his hand was the first of the sarin vials. It felt weightless and delicate. The liquid was crystal clear.

Getting the suitcase had been a struggle because he was nervous, but finally he unlocked it. Things that locked were not generally his forte.

Now came the moment when he could just stand there at the edge of the rooftop, sarin in hand, and contemplate his act of greatness.

Below him swarmed an unsuspecting crowd of partiers and other well-wishers. Across the street, balconies were loaded with twenty-somethings, drinks in hand. Nearby someone was blasting a song on a pair of oversized speakers about dancing, its bass reverberating.

Arthur watched two naked gay men stroll by hand in hand, carrying a rainbow umbrella. They wore nothing but red high tops.

They would become his first targets.

All he had to do was drop one small vial, and they would die. There would be death and destruction everywhere. The thought filled Arthur with a deep sense of satisfaction, especially because Randy wanted him to do it. He wanted to please Randy almost as much as he wanted to please God. That was for sure.

Closing his eyes, Arthur began the Lord's Prayer as he prepared to release the first vial of sarin from his fingertips. But then a sobering thought stopped him cold.

He wasn't wearing the latex gloves.

Arthur sighed and opened his eyes. He'd promised to wear the latex gloves. He had to do this right for Randy.

Arthur replaced the vial, tucking it back into the open suitcase before him. Then he reached into his back pocket for the gloves. With horror, he realized then that he'd forgotten them.

The latex gloves were still in their box by the television in his hotel room.

Now what was he going to do?

Thank frigging God they sent Marty, thought Frankie as she barreled up the street after Charley. *Today I got lucky.*

Marty was a sergeant who didn't have time for the bull-shit. He was just an honest, car-pushing regular. She could trust him to handle everything fast and clean.

Marty will be decent to Electra, too, she thought. At this moment, Electra had risen substantially in Frankie's eyes. Even if she did have to listen to Charley swoon when Electra pinned the guy.

But even Frankie had to admit it. That woman gave some pretty damn good wire. Her reputation for toughness was well deserved.

Frankie jumped out of Marty's patrol car and raced on foot along Divisadero toward Hayes. Up ahead, she could see the apartment house on the corner the suspect had ID'd.

She hit the first buzzer and then the second. "SFPD. Open up!" she barked into the intercom repeatedly. Windows began opening above her as residents looked out.

Frankie got buzzed in immediately and began to take the stairs two at a time. Backup was arriving at any moment, along with the hazmat guys from the fire department.

By the time they lumbered in in their big white suits, things would be in total slow-mo.

Frankie knew she had to get there first.

"Hey, Arthur! What are you doing here?" Charley cried as he made it through the door of the roof.

Ahead of him stood Randy's frightened assistant. The suitcase of sarin was open on the ground before him, and he was contemplating it uncertainly.

He looked up at Charley in alarm. "Who are you?"

"You don't remember me? I'm Charley MacElroy," he said, extending his hand for a shake. "We just met yesterday—come on!"

Arthur looked confused. "No?" he said slowly.

"Seriously? We were talking about . . . you know . . . the usual stuff . . ." Charley edged closer to the suitcase as he approached Arthur. All the vials appeared to still be in their tidy velvet slots.

"What do you have there, Arthur?" he asked amiably.

Arthur leaned over and shut the suitcase with a snap. Then he picked it up protectively in his arms. "It's nothing," he said.

"Killer day up here, isn't it? Look at that blue sky! I just came up here to see the race," Charley rambled on as he edged closer to Arthur. "How about you?"

He was calculating what it would require to take him down and remove the sarin from his arms without dropping the case or cracking the vials.

"So when are you heading back to Wheaton?" Charley asked, giving Arthur's arm a friendly pat. "You're from Wheaton, Illinois, right?" He moved a step toward Arthur, who in turn edged closer to the edge of the rooftop.

"Winfield, actually," Arthur answered slowly. "But I live in Wheaton now. Are you sure we met?"

A few floors below them, Charley could hear revelers drinking their mimosas on one of the balconies. The faint strains of a disco tune, "Keep on Dancing," drifted up from below.

"Sure we met. You don't remember?" Charley bluffed.

He could hear the front-runners now rapidly approaching as the crowd's cheers grew louder. The street and sidewalk had to be completely filled with people now. Everyone and their brother was down there right now, from runners to the major media.

Charley put his hands in his pockets, affecting a casual air. "Yeah, nice day to be up here," he remarked.

"Yeah," said Arthur uncertainly.

Together the two men looked over the edge at the crowd milling below. A tutti-frutti display of colors and textures dotted the street. People dressed as clowns, fairy princesses, revolutionary Redcoats, Adam and Eve, bananas, tropical birds, and everything in between lined the sidewalks. And that was just the spectators.

"Look," said Charley, pointing down Hayes. Two runners who appeared to be Kenyans were racing fast in their direction.

Behind them, a straggling line of elite runners appeared, followed by a moving wall of color and sound that was the rest of the 68,000 runners.

"Wow!" said Charley. "That is a LOT of people."

"Yeah," nodded Arthur dumbly. For a moment, Charley hesitated, unsure quite what to do next. Out of the corner of his eye, he surveyed Arthur coolly.

Arthur was rapt, watching the approaching mass of humanity. It was as if he had never seen anything like it before. In fact, he probably hadn't.

Gently, Arthur put down his suitcase, mesmerized. In an instant, Charley was on him. Hurling himself at Arthur, he knocked him backward away from the valise of sarin. Arthur screamed in surprise and pushed Charley away with all of his strength.

He was stronger than Charley expected, and for a moment, they rolled over and then once again. Finally Charley managed to get Arthur into a wrestling hold, landing on top of him with most of his weight. As he did, his foot struck the suitcase.

The sarin toppled over with a soft thud. Turning around, Charley eyed the suitcase nervously. It appeared to still be in tact. Meanwhile, beneath him, Arthur wriggled this way and that, straining to get away from him while reaching an arm toward the suitcase.

Arthur began twisting his body back and forth, trying to dislodge Charley's hold on him. Pinning him even more tightly with one knee, Charley threw his full weight against him. Still he could feel Arthur's grip on his arms tightening.

For all he knew, Arthur could have been a high school ˙ling champ.

ˑly, Arthur rose up in a surge and threw his weight ˈˑv. He managed to flip Charley on his side. The two men rolled over once, and then twice again. This time, Arthur kicked the valise toward the wall, where it landed with a smack.

Shit, thought Charley as he climbed up onto Arthur one more time. This time, he managed to land on Arthur's back and press his face into the roof. He needed Frankie and the backup now. Eying the newly dented valise, Charley tried to see if the suitcase was leaking, but he couldn't get close enough.

Which is probably a good thing, he thought. *At least they aren't in a confined space.*

He looked down at the still-wriggling man underneath him. "You're not dropping the sarin, Arthur," he announced. "It's not going to happen."

Arthur looked at Charley sideways, his cheek still slammed into the roof. "God's will be done," he muttered.

"Exactly," agreed Charley.

Just at that moment, he could hear Frankie's footsteps bounding up the staircase below. She burst through the open hatch, followed by another officer. Both of them had their guns drawn. "SFPD. Freeze," she said. "This one's the outside officer," she explained, referring to Charley. "He's CIA."

"Here's your man," said Charley, holding down Arthur as the other officer snapped on the handcuffs. Charley stood up and dusted off his hands as the officer began to read Arthur his rights. Arthur looked completely bewildered.

Now a handful of firefighters emerged through the door dressed in full hazmat gear and began to circle the dented suitcase of sarin. Evidently the vials were still in tact. Charley and Frankie slipped past them as they headed for the exit.

"That was different," remarked Charley as they passed the vast array of emergency workers now filling the stairwell.

"Took a lot to take him down, huh?"

Charley just shook his head. "I had my eye on the suitcase the whole time."

"Well, you're still here, so apparently none of it leaked," reasoned Frankie.

"I've got to hand it to you, Frankie. Agency work is definitely easier than this."

Frankie gave a little smile and a raise of her eyebrows. "It's all relative," she remarked. "I'm just glad we got those douchebags."

"Score one for Team Q," said Charley, pulling out his phone. "Now it's time to call my woman." At the very least, maybe they could finally manage a little time alone.

"I think you'll find her at the station," Frankie offered. "How about a lift?"

"I'll pass," he said. "Let me know when the station's clear of media, and I'll come in if you need me." He smiled at his friend. "Time to put the cover back on."

"I get it," she said with a grin. "And hey. Thanks, Charley. This is going to make a big difference. "

"For you and me both," he countered. "I'm the one who should be thanking you."

Walking on, Frankie climbed into her patrol car and drove off, heading for the station, as Charley slipped into the crowd. Around him, people cheered, music blared, and thousands of runners sped by.

San Francisco was its usual undulating carnival of weed, liquor, and revelry in that moment, as clueless and casual as ever.

And so the race went on, unblinking, as runners ran, undisturbed, toward the sea.

"I thought I'd have the crab," Electra began, menu in hand. "I've never actually had Dungeness crab, you know."

"Seriously? It's one of the main reasons to live here," said Charley.

At that moment, they were sitting in Cliff House. It was a monumental old place that clung to the cliffs above the Pacific. The patent leather surface of the Pacific undulated just below it.

The two relaxed into time and space, as if finally they had a moment to breathe. The sunset had begun to glow in the vastness beyond them.

Charley raised his glass of Chardonnay. "To you," he said.

Electra smiled and looked down. Then, raising her glass, she countered with a toast of her own. "To us," she said simply.

They were officially an "us" now. Since the attack, the two had flowed easily between his bed and hers. Every day, she said, was a surprise in love. For it wasn't only Electra who had to learn new tricks in bed.

Her own interest in kink was taking Charley places he'd simply never been before. Much to his amazement, he liked it.

A lot.

"To Frankie," Charley countered, raising his glass once more.

"Absolutely," she agreed. "To Frankie in Maui." They drank to Frankie and smiled at each other once again.

Frankie was now on her first vacation in seven years. Not only that, she had received a DGO Gold Medal of Valor, the department award for being an especially good cop. Given the large number of lives that were saved, Frankie's cred had just gone way up with the chief of police. She now had an appointment on the books with the chief to share her insights on the graft ring. There was even talk of a promotion.

Electra looked out once again at the Pacific. "I love this place." She sighed happily.

"Cliff House is ancient," Charley remarked. "When it was first built in the 1850s, people used to ride all day on horseback to get here from the city."

She looked at him. "I mean here in California. The Bay Area." Electra turned her gaze happily to the sea. "I came here looking for something, and I really didn't know what it was. Turns out it was me, Charley. The true me." Shyly, she smiled at him. "I might have been looking for you, too," she added.

Charley took her hand and drew closer. "R.J. was so right about you," he said. "You're going to make one hell of a spy."

"Yeah, except for my noisy cover."

"It's been done," he said. "Look at Mata Hari."

"Didn't she get executed?"

"Okay, bad example," he demurred. Together they watched the sky continue to put on its show. The setting sun sent up new vivid streaks of green and peach. It was a silent symphony of fire, playing just for them.

"Electra, you have access other agents only dream of," he said. "You're going to help a lot of people. Anyway, we'll be working together."

"In Paris," she said.

"You'll love the oysters," he remarked.

"Maybe. But mostly I'm just going to love you."

Charley smiled, finding himself wordless in that moment. He was flooded with gratitude, for his life had suddenly become everything he'd wished for. Even without a penis.

For not only had Charley found a new and uncommon love, he had been exonerated with the Agency as well.

He paid his taxes and did his Step work, and the entire accounting issue magically disappeared. It really wasn't known who stole the money or why Charley got blamed for it. All that mattered was that Charley had been sufficiently chastened and now relied on a financial app and a coach to keep his money in order.

The plum assignments were back, and the suspension had been put behind him. "A learning experience," R.J. called it.

"Here's to life, with all of its surprises," he proposed.

Their wine glasses clinked softly. Then they dissolved into a kiss as the sun slipped silently behind the sea.

This is it, he thought contentedly.

It simply didn't get much better than this.

Before you go...

What's Next For Charley & Electra?

Transformed: Paris – Book 2

Charley is in Paris to stop a Neo Nazi dirty bomb plot, and Electra comes along to improve her French. But soon she finds a group of sinister expats. Then she promptly disappears. Charley is frantic to find her – and the dirty bombs – hidden in the City of Light.

Transformed: POTUS – Book 3

The first post-Trump President is a POTUS who can't keep his pants on and loves to hang in Vegas. Undercover agent Charley MacElroy is called in to vet his possible flings just as a bad actor tries to infiltrate – and POTUS loses the nuclear codes. Then Charley's dominatrix fiancée, Electra, shows up ... Is she the one who will take this naughty President in hand? A hilarious, wild ride through Vegas!

"Offbeat, romantic, and engaging..." Kirkus

About the Authors

Suzanne Falter

Suzanne Falter is an author, speaker and blogger who has published both fiction and non-fiction. Her first novel, was *Doin' the Box Step* (Random House.) Her non-fiction titles include *How Much Joy Can You Stand?* and *Living Your Joy* (both Ballantine) and more recently, *Surrendering to Joy*. Suzanne's online writing and videos can be found on Facebook, Google +, YouTube, Pinterest and on her blog at www.suzannefalter.com. Suzanne lives with her partner in the San Francisco Bay Area.

Jack Harvey

Following retirement from a successful career on Wall Street in corporate finance and venture capital, Jack Harvey has turned his attention to fiction and the increasingly popular area of gender dynamics. In his first novel, *Transformed*, he is partnering with his cousin, author Suzanne Falter. Jack and his wife have two grown daughters and live in Manhattan and Connecticut.

Acknowledgements

The authors wish to thank the following people for being so very supportive of our efforts, both in the creation and the publication of this book. You are deeply appreciated.

Zander Keig
Dr. Robert Akeret
Kitty Harvey
PSM
Susan Katz
Filip Galetic
Isabel M. Carden
Darcee Lewis Sellers
Jon Leland
Sky Esser
Courtney Umphress
Maureen Cutajar
Ray Shappell
RDG
and
Andrew Solomon for his seminal book,
Far From the Tree

Transformed: San Francisco
The Guide for Readers and Book Clubs

Questions for Interested Readers to Talk About

1. What character were you most drawn to, and why?
2. Who would you most want to have lunch with?
3. Which scene set in San Francisco would you most like to visit?
4. Which scene would you run screaming from?
5. What do you think of Charley as a man? Was there anything unexpected or surprising about him?
6. What advice would you have for Charley when he was feeling so lost and alone toward the end of the book?
7. What advice would you give Electra about her relationship with her daughter?
8. Does Charley understand women better than the ordinary straight guy might?
9. Did reading about Electra's journey shift or affect your opinion of BDSM?
10. Did reading about Charley affect your understanding of or feelings about transgendered people?
11. Why have figures like Caitlyn Jenner and Chaz Bono created so much popular buzz at this particular time?
12. Are you connected to people who you know are transgendered in your work or personal life?
13. Why do you think BDSM has ignited popular interest, as proven by the success of *Fifty Shades of Gray*?
14. Should Charley have bottom surgery?

Some Books that Inspired the Authors

Far From the Tree: Parents, Children and the Search for Identity
by Andrew Solomon
An examination of the experience of parenting children who are different. "Solomon documents triumphs of love over prejudice in every chapter."

The Ultimate Guide to Kink: BDSM, Role Play and the Erotic Edge by Tristan Taormino
The first major guide to BDSM in a generation. It's filled with provocative essays that teach anyone the basics.

Cool Gray City of Love: 49 Views of San Francisco by Gary Kamiya
Forty-nine essays by someone who walked every inch of the city, and explored every corner. A neat blend of in-depth history and contemporary snapshot.

Hung Jury: Testimonials of Genital Surgery by Transsexual Men by Trystan T. Cotton
The first comprehensive book on the subject, and ground breaking at the time of publication. Each testimony is raw, unadulterated and important.

Manning Up: Transsexual Men on Finding Brotherhood, Family, and Themselves by Mitch Kellaway & Zander Keig
Twenty-seven transmen discuss their roles as dads, brothers, boyfriends, husbands and more. A thorough and unique take on what it means to be a man.

Patrick Leigh Fermor: An Adventure by Artemis Cooper
The character of Charley was inspired by this dashing, well-heeled World War II/Fifties era spy who charmed his way across Europe and the world. Fermor's ability to talk to anyone about anything helped the allies win the war . . . and that was just for starters.

Stairway Walks in San Francisco: The Joy of Urban Exploring by Ada Bakalinsky & Mary Burk
San Francisco is a city of staircases—and this guide takes you up all of them. Comprehensive and fun!

Places in San Francisco that Inspired the Authors

Center for Sex & Culture
www.sexandculture.org

The Folsom Street Fair
www.folsomstreetfair.com

Hardly Strictly
www.hardlystrictlybluegrass.com

The Citadel
www.sfcitadel.org

Crissy Field
www.presidio.gov/explore/Pages/crissy-field.aspx

Zappos Bay to Breakers
www.zapposbaytobreakers.com

Cliff House
www.cliffhouse.com/home/index.html

Mission Beach Café
www.missionbeachcafesf.com

Samovar Tea Lounge
The Castro
www.samovartea.com

Advance Praise for
Transformed: San Francisco

"Falter and Harvey write with a hard-boiled verve that captures their colorful characters with humor and precision ... a breath of fresh air—and marginalized experience—that revitalizes many of the old tropes."
— **Kirkus Reviews**

"A fun romp through San Francisco, the book is a novelty of sex, gender issues, sexual orientation, hate, love, and mystery ... While this book should be in the library of every GLBTQ person, it's a delightful read for everyone."
— **The US Review of Books**

"*Transformed: San Francisco* is a delightfully entertaining mystery full of quirky, complicated and personable characters, full of the verve and enthusiasm of San Francisco culture."
— **IndieReader**

"*Transformed: San Francisco* follows characters through some of their most challenging times, exploring their fears, their hopes, and, ultimately, their triumphs. With brisk pacing and engrossing character arcs, the novel is both exciting and touching.."
— **Foreward Reviews**

"... its' characters are quirky, different, and steeped in San Francisco culture ....This reviewer is a City native, and observes that San Francisco's cultural nuances could not have been better captured!"
— **Midwest Review of Books**

"Both funny and disturbing, thrilling and romantic .. Charley is brilliantly portrayed, capturing the fears and the doubts of a man still on the edge of his final transition. ... The cover blurb calls this a "funny thriller", but I would expand that somewhat to call it a "funny thriller with a lot of heart."
   — **Bending the Bookshelf**

74618245R00168

Made in the USA
Middletown, DE
28 May 2018